Delilah's

John Maley

First published by

303a The Pentagon Centre
36 Washington Street
Glasgow
G3 8AZ

Tel: 0141 204 1109
Fax: 0141 221 5363

E-mail: info@nwp.sol.co.uk
www.11-9.co.uk

Scottish
Arts Council
LOTTERY FUNDED

11:9 is funded by the Scottish Arts Council National Lottery Fund

ISBN 1 903238 54 4

Typeset in Utopia
11:9 series text design by Mark Blackadder

Printed in Finland by WS Bookwell

Acknowledgements

The author would like to thank Andrew Lindsay, Gerry Loose, Willy Maley, Dave Manderson, Donny O'Rourke, Liz Small, Hamish Whyte.

The author acknowledges receipt of a Scottish Arts Council Writer's Bursary in 1999.

Rory's Kitchen Drawer, Papa and Mama and *Bridging The Atlantic* previously appeared in *New Writing Scotland. Jeannie and Joanie* and *Going Back* first appeared in *Nerve. Keep The Claws* first appeared in *Nomad.*

Contents

Glasgow is Full of Invisible Lovers

Glasgow is full of invisible lovers. They don't hold hands in the street or walk arm-in-arm in the park. They don't kiss in public places. These invisible Glasgow lovers could pass for friends or strangers. Their unions aren't blessed. They fade into family backgrounds, feign eccentricity, their lips and fates sealed by countless small dangers. Glasgow's invisible lovers are jealous of their reputations, want to keep their jobs.

Some of them vanish without trace, unable to bear their own reflections. Some of them materialise in each other's beds, where they have great or guilty sex. Some of them disappear for years, then reappear in a marriage of convenience or a public convenience, dropping their trousers and their guard. Some of them stop caring what happens to them; some of them stop speaking to their mothers. Some of them enjoy making mischief while invisible. Some invisible lovers fall so deeply in love they don't give a fuck what the world thinks. Some invisible lovers are so glad when they find each other they feel like they're walking on the moon. Some of them feel they could breathe more easily and be more at home on the moon. Some of Glasgow's invisible lovers go to a place called Delilah's, sweet, ugly, glorious Delilah's, where they can meet like-minds and mouths and escape from the madness of being invisible. Glasgow is full of invisible lovers who don't want to be invisible any more.

Joanie added his final touches of lipstick and pouted into his dressingtable mirror. He felt sick after a night of debauchery. Something had rattled his cage, he wasn't sure what, and he had ended up getting pissed and getting a stupid idea in his head that he must find love. He'd ended up with a giant brute of a man escorting him home. Joanie suspected the cad had spiked his drink, the tenth one had tasted a bit funny. He remembered they had a wrestling match in his bedroom before he hit his amorous assailant over the head with a slingback to prevent himself being spiked. The man had toppled like a skittle and Joanie had gasped 'See you in court' before fainting onto the bed. Two hours later he awoke to find the ogre on bended knee asking for his hand in marriage. Joanie had graciously accepted the proposal, backing a hunch that this would get rid of his beau quicker. Even so, Joanie had to half-push, half-drag the guy down the hall and out the front door, all the while his new fiancé pecking at him like a giant bird and murmuring terms of endearment.

Even a good vomit hadn't made Joanie feel any better. It had been awhile since he'd had a blow-out like this one and he hoped there hadn't been too many witnesses. He still wasn't sure what had got into him. Sometimes it was just the stress of work creeping up on you; sometimes it was loneliness springing at you like a mugger from an alley.

Joanie took a few deep breaths and adjusted his wig. He decided a guy was entitled to let his pants down once in a while. The only trouble was, today he couldn't sleep it off. The brewery chain that had recently bought Delilah's had some young rep coming up from London on what they called a 'fact-finding mission'. Joanie had a rendezvous at two with the guy. They were meeting at Delilah's which at that stage didn't open till five on a Sunday. This was one of the things that were going to change.

Joanie sighed and wrote Never Again on the mirror with his lipstick. Then he phoned a taxi.

By five to two Joanie was rattling his keys at the doors of Delilah's. He switched off the alarm, put on the lights and gave the premises a brisk inspection. Everything looked neat. The cleaners had done a great job. He knew he could trust Jeannie, the regular, to keep the place shipshape. Joanie flicked through the till receipts, the accounts, gave the bar another quick wipe, then sat on a stool waiting for the rep to arrive. He wondered what the brewery's plans were. They could close the joint, sell it on, turn it straight, turn it into something else, a restaurant or a gym. Joanie had decided not to worry. Delilah's made good money. He'd counted many a pink pound in and out of those tills.

Eventually the bell rang and Joanie adjusted his wig, cleared his throat and hurried to the door. He opened it on Toby, who looked like a wee tailor's dummy in a three-piece grey suit. They introduced themselves and Toby sat in a booth while Joanie got them a couple of Cokes. Then Joanie sat down opposite, and they smiled at each other. Toby had a black leather briefcase in his lap. He noticed Joanie looking at it and shoved it under the table. They chatted about the weather and Toby's journey from London (he'd flown). When they'd finished their Cokes Joanie showed Toby around the place. They inspected the long bar, the booths, the backroom, the loos, the staffroom/cloakroom, Toby never saying a word or asking any questions – just making an 'mm' sound. When they found themselves back at the bar he finally said 'Fine'. Joanie made them coffees and they perched in a booth again.

'Tell me about a typical week in Delilah's,' said Toby. Joanie felt his headache coming back.

'I don't know whether there is a typical week,' began Joanie, 'but here goes. We have karaoke a couple of nights a week – currently a Sunday and a Wednesday. Friday and Saturday are pre-club nights so we usually blast out the music. Mondays we've been having the odd quiz. Thursdays we sometimes have entertainment – a singer or a comic. Jist now and then. The joint is jumping because the people that come in here want to have a ball or two. Come tonight.'

Toby gave Joanie a sceptical look. 'I hate karaoke,' he said.

'Check the accounts,' shrugged Joanie. 'Business is booming.'

Toby looked as sick as Joanie felt.

'What about you John?' he asked.

'Joanie.'

'Joanie. What's with the get-up?'

'The get-up?' asked Joanie.

'The drag business. The cock-in-a-frock number,' said Toby.

'What about it?' asked Joanie, defensively.

'Isn't it a bit Blackpool 1970s?' asked Toby.

'You're not old enough to have been born in the 1970s,' replied Joanie.

'I'm just saying it's a bit old hat,' said Toby.

'I've turned this place around,' retorted Joanie. 'As for ma appearance, glamour is always in fashion.'

Toby smiled, softened a little. Joanie decided he wasn't going to let him away with anything. In between pointless fumbles in his briefcase Toby told Joanie something about the brewery's operations which spanned the length and breadth of the UK and encompassed gay and straight venues including two strip clubs.

'I can't understand how you get the business up here,' said Toby. 'I mean *are* there any queers in Glasgow?'

'Seeing is believing,' said Joanie.

'When I think of this town,' continued Toby, 'I think of junkies, alcoholics, terrible accents and people who want to rearrange your face just for the hell of it.'

'You're thinking of Hollywood,' said Joanie. 'Glasgow's got a wee bit more class than that.' He felt like rearranging Toby's face. The boy had a lot of nerve.

Toby changed the subject, as if he was picking up how much he'd pissed Joanie off. He asked Joanie if there had been any problems with drugs in Delilah's. One of the London bars had recently got busted.

'I only know what I see,' said Joanie. 'If people are doing drugs they're doing them discreetly. We sell a lot of booze in here.'

Toby nodded, satisfied with the answer. He asked Joanie for a pint. Joanie got him a beer and a mineral water for himself. He thought it was unprofessional for Toby to drink on duty but reckoned a few pints might loosen the pompous little prick up a bit. Toby asked Joanie for the accounts and Joanie brought them over to the table. Toby took out a laptop from his briefcase and punched some details into the machine. Joanie didn't know whether to laugh or cry. He wished he could go back to bed.

'We get so many fly-by-night staff in here,' remarked Joanie. 'I'm the only person holding this joint thegither.'

Toby was too engrossed in his laptop to respond.

'We've had students, actors, singers, jugglers – looking for a lumber or a few extra quid to pay their way through college or keep up the mortgage payments. Some are good, some are hopeless, but none of them last. Shitty hours and shitty pay don't help.'

Toby made an 'mm' sound and closed his laptop. He put it back in his briefcase, which he tucked under the table. He drained his glass and asked for another pint. Joanie obliged, but wondered when he was going to get rid of the wee runt so he could get psyched up for work.

The two of them sat in the booth, Joanie on the wagon and Toby slowly falling off it. Toby looked like a wee boy trying to be a grown-up. He made Joanie think of the Divine classic *You Think You're A Man (But You're Only A Boy)*. Several pints later he even treated Joanie to the low-down on his love life. He didn't actually have one, only snide things to say about the scene.

'One night stands and time wasters and prick teasers and drag queens,' said Toby. 'I'm fed up with all that crap. I'm looking for love.'

Joanie smiled ruefully.

'Never look for love,' he said, with quiet authority. 'I went lookin' for love last night and ended up with spunk in ma best wig and ma reputation in tatters. Now I'm engaged to a maniac. He'll probably sue me for breach of promise.'

'That's what I hate about you,' replied Toby, petulantly. 'You're all so cynical.'

'Cynical? Haud yer horses, hen. You've jist sat and trashed

everybody and his fucking mother!'

Toby burped and slurped at his pint like a big baby.

'All I'm saying,' he said, in a conciliatory tone, 'all I'm saying is we shouldn't have a ghetto. Why should we have separate pubs? Why can't we all booze in the same boozer?'

Joanie shrugged.

'I'd like tae see everyone getting along as wan big happy family wan day,' he reasoned. 'But until that day comes I think Anne Frank's going tae need her attic. Anyway you get all different types of pubs. Show bars, disco bars, Irish bars, Country and Western bars, vodka bars, lap dancing bars, wine bars, snooker bars. Why not a fabulous fairy bar?'

'I don't believe in fairies,' said Toby.

'Look in the mirror, sweetheart,' said Joanie.

Toby surprised him with a smile and asked for another drink, then went upstairs to the loo while Joanie poured the pint. Joanie sat in the booth with another coffee and waited for Toby to come back and attack his drink.

'I don't want tae play mother or anything,' said Joanie. 'But are you okay? I mean yer not driving or anything?'

Toby shook his head like a wee boy denying mischief.

'I'm staying overnight at the Hilton,' said Toby. 'I'll get a cab. D'you mind?'

'It's up tae you. But don't ye want tae come and see the place in action?' asked Joanie.

Toby sighed.

'I'm going to get pissed and go to the hotel and crash out. This is the only way I can sleep in hotels.'

He picked up his pint and gulped. Joanie was used to watching people get pissed. It was his job. He thought it was funny how it affected different people in different ways. People got horny, morbid, violent, high, bitchy, or sparkled like diamonds and found a *joie de vivre* they never thought they had. Night after night he saw them in Delilah's: Dr Jekyll turning into Ms Hyde, prudes turning into sluts, mice into lions, roaring at their own dirty jokes. Most touching of all was the way strangers turned into friends and lovers. But he also saw people turning into alcoholics. Joanie always tried to let people know when they had enough. But he was running a bar and booze was the name of the game. He knew he was never going to get on the AA's Christmas card list. Toby finished his drink.

'Pint please,' he said, smiling. Joanie fetched the pint.

Toby began to rattle on about his background as if he was being interviewed. His parents split when he was ten, then his mother remarried. His step-dad was a publican and his mother helped tend the bar.

'They were like Den and Angie in *Eastenders* … Except they fought more,' said Toby.

'Didn't it put ye off the business?' asked Joanie.

'I'm going to Uni,' said Toby. 'I'm going to be an accountant.'

Joanie could see it. He looked the part. The quicker he got out of the brewery business the better. The more pissed Toby became the more talkative he was. He pestered Joanie about what made his ideal man.

'A pulse and a penis,' quipped Joanie. Toby went on to describe his ideal man. All Joanie could picture from his description was some blandly beautiful magazine model.

'Mm,' he said, and watched Toby demolish the beer.

After another toilet stop it was evident that the beer had gone to his bittersweet little head. Joanie looked at his watch. It was half four.

'We open up in half an hour. Are ye sticking around?' he asked.

Toby shook his head and started fumbling in his pockets for his mobile phone. Joanie had to help him get out the phone and he called the taxi. Toby picked up his briefcase and Joanie ushered him to the doors of Delilah's. When the taxi arrived they walked to it together. Toby looked at Joanie with sad, bloodshot eyes.

'Do you like being gay?' he asked, in a voice that suggested nobody ever could.

'Love it,' said Joanie and bundled Toby into the cab.

Going Back

George liked trains. His earliest memories of trains were happy family seaside trip scenarios. Saltcoats. Ardrossan. Ayr. He hadn't been back to Glasgow for years. People said you could see the difference in the landscape as you passed from England to Scotland. George couldn't. But it didn't matter this time as it was winter and dark by the time they crossed the border. He liked the sound of the train. He liked the scalding hot tea in a plastic cup. He'd drunk four cups and was up and down to the toilet like a yo-yo. He'd eaten some sandwiches earlier on but still felt a bit hungry. He'd bought a caramel biscuit with his last cup of tea and could feel toffee stuck in a cavity in a back tooth.

The wages of sin.

He was going back.

George's mother sat at the kitchen table filling George in on all the family news. Auntie Rose had died. Cancer. A cousin was in Barlinnie for bank robbery. Most important of all, George's sister Leanne had just had a baby. She was engaged to a soldier who wanted her to come to Germany and live with him. George was forced to look at some photos of the happy couple. The boyfriend looked like a bullet-headed bastard but George's mother had assured him he was A DEAD NICE GUY. His mother had changed. She looked older. And finer. Fragile, as if she had lost a lot of her strength. During the three days George stayed she fluctuated between hyper-hostess and being tired and irritable.

George had left Glasgow ten years before and had known he was HIV positive for the last five. His visits back to Glasgow had been sporadic at best but this was the longest he had left it. He phoned now and again, and wrote less so, but he hadn't shown his face for more than two years. He liked the expression: showing your face. Like you were really showing something, a part of yourself. Maybe that was why he hadn't come to Glasgow for so long. Afraid of showing his face.

Glasgow seemed to have changed. It wasn't the buildings or new shops or shopping centres. It was something imperceptible. Or maybe it was just a strangeness George felt in a place he called home, but could no longer connect with. He had severed most of his ties with Glasgow. He partly regretted this, not feeling he belonged anywhere now. Not in his mother's house at any rate. But his mother and sister adapted to his presence. It was like some kind of hollow compromise. Three days of small talk and lazy nostalgia. It was like coming back as a ghost: he had a weird sense of being disembodied, of not really being there.

They did things together. Old things. Glasgow things. They went to the Barras and looked around the market stalls. His mother bought a manky old coat that hung like a tent on her and stank of cat pish. George tried to dissuade her but she was adamant the coat would save her life this winter. So George offered to buy her a new coat, but his mother refused, seeking instead to perpetuate the bogus myth of her as some kind of bargain-hunter extraordinaire.

She bought fish suppers from the local chippie and they made a grand ceremony of eating them, hunched over the kitchen table and declaring every bite of the burnt chips and bony fish 'delicious'. His sister Leanne plastered nearly a whole bottle of tomato sauce over her supper to 'bring oot the flavour'. The meal was washed down with weak tea and more old memories.

But George didn't want to be cynical about this. He loved his mother and sister and he loved hearing their voices, the lingo – it was so refreshing. His accent was a mess, years of trying to be understood in London. The funny thing is, nobody ever did understand him in London or any fuckin where. He loved, too, the family photos. There were a couple of albums, but the real gems were to be found in an old shoebox. There was a hilarious picture of him at fifteen holding a Bullworker that was supposed to give him a Samson-like physique. He had a funny look on his face. He remembered something Allen Ginsberg wrote about 'that haunted look all young fags have'. Was that it? Haunted?

There were nice photos of his father. But they made George think about death and so they were shuffled under newer photos of Leanne and his mother and various pals and relatives. George's favourite was a picture of his mother wearing a psychedelic dress and sporting a Harpo Marx perm. It captured her essence – ridiculous, ebullient and lovely. At times like that he thought of his mother not as his mother but as an old flame.

On the Saturday afternoon, as they wandered about town, there was a difficult conversation about George's fictitious girlfriend. He had had a string of fictitious girlfriends over the years. It was easy and lazy and stupid but there was a vicarious pleasure in inventing a relationship that would pacify his mother. It saddened George that all the real love, blood, sweat and tears were hidden in favour of banal tales of going steady with a nurse from Newcastle. (There had been a nurse from Newcastle – a big hairy guy who had begged to be spanked. This, however, was not the nurse under discussion.) George didn't feel too bad about lying to his mother – family life was founded on delusion anyway. But he felt he had performed badly with this latest romantic deceit and that maybe his mother was, after all, wise to him all along.

It was good to see Leanne again. The baby was cute and was, according to the consensus of those in the know about these things, 'a good baby'. Leanne was pretty laid-back about motherhood and had somehow managed to skip the family neurosis gene. There was always a distance between him and Leanne that had been determined by the ten-year age gap between them. George felt more like her mother than her brother.

On Saturday night he felt compelled to get away from the house after a bout of paranoia following his nurse-from-Newcastle number. He headed into town after making up some story about looking up an old pal. George made for a pub he had formerly known as La Maison. On arriving there he saw it had changed into a place called Delilah's. It was still a queer shop, though. It was much more mixed than the kind of taverns of testosterone he had been used to in the old days. But he liked women's company.

George wasn't cruising. But he had this need to be in a gay environment. That was all it was. Just to have that sense of ease, of belonging. There was a drag queen called Joanie behind the bar who seemed pretty friendly. George had a couple of drinks and immersed himself in his own thoughts – family reminiscences, morbid thoughts about his own future, images of dead lovers. He was left in peace for a while to reflect and watch and listen. But an enormous tranny, who was obviously on the lookout for a new and possibly gullible face, suddenly parachuted into his lap. He panted and purred and blinked giant false eyelashes at George, rubbing his crotch with a big sweaty hand. George hated himself for getting a boner. The transvestite put his scarlet lips to George's ear and whispered, 'My body is a secret, urgent to be told.' A fleeting look then passed between them. A kind of understanding. Or maybe this was just some line from a trashy porno video where two muscular male models mechanically fuck each other on some crappy beach to a warped muzak soundtrack. The *femme fatale* gave him a warm, welcoming smile and shimmied off to plump his fat arse on somebody else's unsuspecting lap, like some giant pussycat. George made his escape.

My body is a secret, urgent to be told.

George sat on the couch and watched his mother sleeping in a chair. Like he had once sat and watched a lover sleeping. His mother was a quiet sleeper, unlike his father, who roared like a bull elephant when he slept. His mother had once asked George if he'd heard of a cure for snoring. Suffocate the bastard, he had replied (the voice of teenage rebellion). George thought he saw a bogey hanging out of his mother's nose but a closer, more focused inspection discovered it to be hair. They were a hairy-nosed family. George clipped his own nose hair with nail scissors. He had once slept with a man who had shaved his pubic hair off. The guy said it heightened sensitivity.

George looked at his mother sleeping and felt a desperate

compulsion to wake her up and declare his love, to tell her he loved her, that maybe he would die before her, that he was sorry he had become a stranger but that his exile was not self-imposed. But he decided not to disturb her or be a drama queen or provoke any extreme emotions. He hadn't cried in ages and felt if he started now he'd never stop until he choked himself. He let her sleep; his mother, his lover, his old flame.

On the train back to London he munched sandwiches his mother had made for him that morning. He had stood and watched her prepare them just as he had stood as a boy and watched her make 'the pieces' for his father for his work. He had nearly cried then and had to look away. Now, he thought of Leanne and her baby sitting on the couch like Madonna and child. He thought of his mother's sleeping face. He decided he would buy her a coat and send it to her. He began to cry. He cried for himself and for his mother and for all the unacknowledged pain and unspeakable love that welled up inside him, urgent to be told.

Bridging the Atlantic

Tam sat at the bar and watched Joanie wiggle his arse, pour endless pints, and blink his big false eyelashes. Joanie had fallen in love.

'He's a Yank,' Joanie had beamed at Tam. 'Six foot two, eyes of blue. His name's Lance. He's a computer software man. I'm interested in his hardware.'

Tam sipped his pint and nodded approvingly. He only sipped his pint because he had been so drunk the night before. It was nice to watch Joanie now, suddenly, transformed by love. Well, if that's what he wanted to call it, who the fuck was Tam or anybody else to disagree?

Tam had tasted love, American style, too. He'd been in Bennets one night when he was cruised by a big beefy guy called Johnny. Think William Shatner and half the size again. Johnny was a trolley dolly doing Boston to Glasgow runs. It had been one of those ten-to-three nights. Ten-to-three and no man. Then of course the dance of the desperadoes started. Johnny appeared out of nowhere. By three o'clock they were in a taxi, heading for the Morgan hotel, Johnny's big right hand down the front of Tam's trousers. Sometimes you gave a fuck what the taxi driver thought and sometimes you didn't.

The hotel foyer had seemed floodlit and Tam suddenly felt shy as he followed Johnny like a lost puppy-dog past the bar area and into the lift. It being late, it was just the two of them. Johnny turned to look at Tam with adoring eyes.

'You're so handsome.'

Tam liked the complimentary approach. He glanced up and down the length of Johnny's body and felt pleased with himself.

In the hotel room they took off their shoes, had a dry hump on the bed, then raided the mini-bar. There was no beer, so Tam drank some gin and tonic. As he mulled over his drink he looked at Johnny stretched out on the bed. Johnny's tee shirt had slid up revealing a big hairy belly, and two things came to Tam then. First, so much for trolley dollies being skinny male models and second, there was no rapport. They had nothing to communicate to each other.

'Jerk me off.'

Tam sat astride Johnny and wanked him. Johnny closed his eyes and smiled contentedly. He might as well have been doing it himself. After he'd come Johnny wiped his belly with some tissues and pulled at Tam's zip.

'I'd like to return the compliment.'

During the night Tam woke and lay beside Johnny in the darkness. He listened to Johnny's breathing. He couldn't see his face. He could see the back of his head, his fine sandy brown hair, his broad, bare back. Tam leaned forward to brush his lips tenderly against Johnny's back.

Walter Weinstein had been Tam's other American. He was older. Forty, maybe. Tam had been aware of Walter for some time. His face had kept cropping up throughout the night. Firstly, in Delilah's, through the smoke and the stench, he'd seen him smile. Then in Club X, Walter loitered in the shadows, smiling again. Smiling at Tam.

He had his own company. Something in travel. He gave Tam his card. On it was the name of the company and 'Walter Weinstein, Company Director'. The sceptic in Tam thought anybody could have a card printed. 'Tam McCormack, President of the World'. But he had no reason not to believe Walter. They got a taxi to the Wagner. Tam would have walked.

Walter sat on the edge of the bed drinking a soda and lime. He wanted to talk. He talked about how beautiful Scotland was. How he travelled for business and pleasure. He talked about Ohio, where he lived and worked, and how he lived alone. He used to live with a guy as house buddies but 'got pissed with it'. Walter said it's hard to live with another adult you're not having sex with. Tam felt so tired he lay down on top of the bed. It was then that Walter began to take off his clothes, slowly and unselfconsciously. Tam yanked at his own clothes. This wasn't going to be a shagging party. The tone of the evening had been set.

Once they were both under the covers, Walter turned off the bedside lamp. Everything seemed magnified; the sound of Walter swallowing, the creaks of the bed, the smell of Walter's aftershave – whatever it was. Walter put his arms around Tam. He held him so tight, Tam thought his ribs would crack. He was still in Walter's arms. This was all that was needed, this closeness.

In the morning the sun shone into the room. Walter made small talk and coffee and they sat on the unmade bed. Walter looked older and sadder in the morning. Tam was usually depressed anyway after a one-night stand. It used to be guilt a long time ago but now it was just the alcohol and wondering how the fuck to get home. Then again, Walter had further to go home than he did. After a while they fell quiet. Tam thought about hotel rooms and how they seemed to have been especially designed for casual sex. He thought it was a good idea. Neutral territory. Neither was at home here.

They each had a shower, but Tam could still smell the stale cigarette smoke that had stuck to the Brylcreem on his hair. His eyes were bloodshot and his hair was defying gravity. As he dried himself he thought he could hear Walter whistle in the room.

Dressed, Walter and Tam stood a foot apart at the window. Walter had opened the curtains and they both looked out at the city below. They never said a word. They just stood there, looking out at Glasgow, bathed in strong winter sunlight. It was as if they were both trying to remember who they were, where they were.

Papa and Mama

Everybody loved Papa Spenser. He was a fine figure of a man. But he was a fool: he drank too much, chased chickens and threw his money around. He had silver hair, cut short and neat, and a warm, weathered face. Some guys swore they could see all the colours of the ocean in his deep blue eyes. He always seemed to wear the right thing: when he wore a suit it hung on him beautifully, elegantly. When he dressed casually he looked like he'd just stepped off a yacht somewhere, cool and collected. Some older guys thought they could knock twenty years off their age by wearing Lycra shorts, living half their lives on a sunbed, chewing gum and pretending they could dance. Not Spenser. He seemed to have come to terms with the ageing process effortlessly. A weakness of Spenser's, however, was the demon drink. He wasn't the only steamer in Delilah's by any stretch of the imagination. But somebody as dignified as Spenser had further to fall from grace.

He was an estate agent, a senior partner in a prestigious Edinburgh firm. People said he preferred the Glasgow scene because he found it less pretentious. He was certainly rarely out of Delilah's. He often came in alone but for a period of around a year he had brought a lady friend with him. She was maybe late thirties and called herself Miranda. Nobody liked Miranda. She was rude, bossy and worst of all used to get pissed and sit on Papa Spenser's lap – a coveted spot if ever there was one. She wore so much gold it would have taken a mining expedition to rob her.

There were various tales about Miranda. One of them was that she was a Glasgow madam who built up her business from a spooky bedsit shop to a string of penthouse flats where the good and the great got their rocks off. Other people said she was legit – and had her own accountancy firm. Many Delilah's regulars resented her presence on the arm of the stunning Spenser. Guys who had formerly fluttered around Papa Spenser now felt intimidated. Any conversation was now three-way, Miranda constantly butting in. Even when she was quiet, which was a rarity, her gaze was ruthless. No one escaped her scrutiny. Prior to the addition of Miranda to his company, Spenser had always been approachable. He still was, but it was hard to flutter about and fawn over the sweet silver-haired Papa Spenser when everything had to be done under the rather large and snooty nose of Miranda.

'If he'd only get shot of that big-beaked fag hag,' complained one of Spenser's unrequited loves, 'I might stand a chance. I mean who is she? His mentally defective sister?'

'I think she's a scary big dyke,' said a love rival. It was generally agreed that this wasn't the case – that Miranda was straight and that there was maybe a business connection between her and Spenser. Bobbie, a punky lesbian in her late thirties, fancied Miranda. She even claimed to have finger-fucked her in the ladies loo. But as Bobbie had also claimed similar carnal delights with, amongst others, Jodie Foster and Madonna, her conquest of Miranda was consigned to the realms of pussy pulp fiction.

Although Miranda gave the initial appearance of vivacity, it soon became apparent to anybody with an ounce of sense that she had all the social skills of a rabid dog. One of her nasty habits was to slap whoever she was talking to and guffaw loudly. This was almost forgivable if she'd just been told a hilarious joke, but she did it no matter what was said to her. You could have told Miranda your only child had just croaked and she'd skelp you and howl with laughter. One evening she made the mistake of hitting Joanie.

It had been an especially rowdy night in Delilah's. A karaoke competition with the major prize of a week's holiday for two in Gran Canaria (and, swore the compere, all the cock you could possibly suck) had been held. The place was mobbed and the sense of hysteria pervasive. In the thick of it were Miranda and Spenser. Every now and then Miranda would unfurl herself from Papa and go on her rounds, slapping and howling all the way. On one occasion she knocked a pint tumbler off the bar. Joanie stepped round with a brush and dustpan to sweep up the debris. The problem was Miranda. It didn't dawn on her to either move or attempt to assist Joanie. She simply stood amongst the remains of the pint glass giggling. This irritated Joanie.

'Move yer ass tae I clean up the glass!' he yelled.

Miranda fixed Joanie with a look of astonishment, slapped him hard across the face, and shrieked with laughter. Joanie wasn't taking this lying down. He slapped Miranda back and in a matter of seconds the catfight to end all catfights broke out. It began in the main bar with a wrestling match that looked like two blind drunks trying to do a waltz and ended in the ladies' loo with Miranda trying to flush Joanie's head down the toilet.

Now I'll tell you why Spenser came to be known as Papa. Spenser had a young boyfriend for a while, a young Italian waiter who looked sixteen but claimed to be thirty-one. He had brown eyes the size of small planets and hair darker than the night. He affected a thick Italian accent but it transpired he was born in Govan and had never been to Italy, land of his parents. It was he who christened Spenser 'Papa'. He'd look lovingly at Spenser, drape his arms over his shoulders and sigh 'Papa.' It caught on and soon everybody was calling Spenser 'Papa.' Even when the Italian boy had cut loose (a police inspector had offered him a plum position as a houseboy) the name Papa had stuck. Papa Spenser was nowhere to be seen during the Krystle versus Alexis catfight in Delilah's.

Bobbie said he was in the men's room giving a rent boy a wank but her story was never confirmed. Despite his lack of involvement in the slapstick fight between his lady friend and Joanie, Papa Spenser was barred by the management, along with Miranda. For a while nothing was seen of Papa. There was a rumour that he'd sold his business and moved to London and opened his own bar. Bobbie said that she had it on good authority that he had married Miranda and was regularly giving it to her up the arse.

Quashing both these rumours, Papa Spenser came into Delilah's one night with a new lady friend, Edith. Papa presented Joanie with a small bouquet of flowers by way of apology, and, visibly moved, Joanie said that as the catfight really had fuck all to do with him, Papa wasn't banned after all. Edith was fifty and didn't care who knew. Everybody took to her right away. Bobbie, who initially commented rather acidly 'Papa's got a brand new fag hag,' soon ensconced herself into her company, saying she felt Edith had a 'matronly glamour'.

Edith was a neurosurgeon at a hospital on the South Side. Everybody was impressed. Bobbie said she bet she had a good bedside manner, and it was only a matter of time before she dragged out another tired old finger-fucking fantasy. Edith didn't know much about her predecessor, but the whole of Delilah's soon dished the dirt. Edith warmed to Joanie and she often stood chatting to him at the bar, leaving the coast clear for Papa Spenser's many admirers to put their various proposals to him.

One night Edith and Joanie spoke about the catfight. Joanie explained that he was deeply ashamed that he had stooped to violence, which was something he absolutely abhorred, but 'that woman,' as he called Miranda, had been provocative in the extreme. Joanie also divulged to Edith that his daddy had beaten him when he was a boy and he had vowed never to let anyone hit him again. Edith had heard Joanie had given a good account of himself in the bar-room brawl, but Joanie shook his head. He said his face was nearly down the bend of the lavatory pan and his whole life had flashed before him when Miranda pushed the flush button for the third time.

Joanie and Edith became great friends. Joanie was glad something good had come out of the catfight. He even gave Edith her pet name. As she was Spenser's new sidekick there was only one thing to call Edith. Mama.

Advantage Navratilova

Ruth watched Laura jostle at the bar of Delilah's with a curious combination of love and loathing. Love because she was Laura, her lover – beautiful, slim, sexy, babe of babes – Laura. Loathing because she was Laura, snobby, yuppie, selfish, pompous Laura, who made her feel smaller than bacteria.

It was a Wednesday night in Delilah's and Ruth and Laura had just been at the badminton courts across the road from Laura's work. It was a regular thing with them, badminton on a Wednesday night. Their relationship was rigorously structured and timetabled by Laura, who would sit woodenly on the living-room settee with her nostrils flaring violently if Ruth so much as suggested a change of plan. But Laura's appalling selfishness was partly what made her so damned attractive. Brats were so used to being lavished with love and affection by their inadequate, fucked-up, parents that you couldn't help being drawn into the same psychotic patterns with them. Me want this. Me want that. Me want it now. Me totally fucking selfish.

Ruth watched Laura jostling away, trying to get served and growing more agitated by the second. Ruth fantasised momentarily about spanking Laura's bare arse; just taking Laura over her knee one night and spanking her. Almost as soon as it came into her head, Ruth dismissed this fantasy – first, because it was too much of a turn-on to contemplate and second, because she felt guilty for even thinking of doing such a pervy thing with Laura, who was such a vanilla dyke.

Laura finally got served. She turned to head back to their table when she was cut off at the pass. A seven-foot-tall stick insect with a huge frizzy red mane of hair waylaid her and started to chat her up. Ruth saw Laura dart her an anxious glance, then begin to simper smugly at the redhead. Ruth knew the score. Laura would flirt with this matchstick on fire, this Towering Inferno, then sally over to the table full of herself, clutching a scribbled telephone number in a pathetic attempt to make Ruth jealous. It usually worked. Ruth was a stone overweight and had a boxer's nose. She wore great clothes and looked terrific but Laura was the pretty one, the skinny calendar girl with baby blue eyes.

But this time Laura didn't come over to the table. She stood with a glass in each hand as the ginger giant wrapped herself around Laura like an enormous python. Now and again Laura would glance over, anxious but excited, to check how green and sick with jealousy Ruth's face was becoming. Ruth played nonchalant. She knew Laura's game, knew that Laura was in a huff because she had whipped her arse at badminton. Laura was not a good loser.

It had been a dream night for Ruth. She hated badminton and usually was outmanoeuvred by the lissom Laura on the badminton court. The whole concept of competition was repulsive to her. She also knew that Laura was one sore loser. Once, not long after they had met, Ruth had beaten Laura at Monopoly. Laura had burst into tears and sobbed in the locked bathroom for an hour. But tonight Ruth had pulled off her kid gloves and taken no prisoners. She had pranced like a gazelle around that badminton court. She had leapt like Margot Fonteyn. She had summoned the strength and stamina of Navratilova to beat Laura into submission. At one point Laura had even slumped across the net, her bottom lip trembling, and feigned an asthma attack. Ruth had suggested they abandon the game but Laura had then come back with a vengeance, making scary and totally unsexy grunts every time she whacked the shuttlecock. Ruth rose to the challenge. She could see the sickening spoilt-brat tears spring up in Laura's eyes as she smashed the shuttlecock over the net and past Laura's head like a fucking bullet, claiming victory at last.

Laura could account for her shock defeat all too readily. A freak asthma attack. Her new training shoes. A pounding headache. Ruth just smiled regally and savoured the moment. So now it was time for Laura's revenge: to swan around Delilah's and flutter her big eyelashes at any passing dyke. But Laura was a vanilla-dyke, crybaby, crap-bag, scaredy-cat who didn't actually have the nerve to get off with somebody else. She just liked having her ego massaged and looking slyly at Ruth, as if to say, 'You just watch it, sweetheart.'

Ruth saw tonight's victory as being about more than just badminton. The whole thing was kind of symbolic. The power Laura had over her was gone. The spell was broken. For Ruth the thing that tied her to Laura was a strong sexual attraction. And loneliness. And the feeling that, fuck it, this time she was actually going to try to have a relationship. But it was a relationship in name alone. There was no relating going on. They were poles apart. Ruth was a socialist and hated money-grabbing materialism; Laura would suck cock if it came wrapped in a five-pound note. Ruth loved dancing; Laura refused to ever dance with her, and on the one memorable occasion when Ruth had coaxed her onto the dance floor, Laura had stamped up and down like a constipated child in a tantrum. Ruth had tried to make allowances for her, apologies for her rudeness, excuses for her selfishness, but in the end it was about respect. Ruth just didn't respect Laura anymore. Worse, Ruth was losing respect for herself: she was turning into one of those indulgent mothers who take a perverse pride in their brat's behaviour.

Laura stood on her tiptoes and peeked over the redhead's shoulder, searching Ruth's face for signs of distress. But Ruth smoked a cigarette and beamed with satisfaction. Laura turned her attention back to the redhead. It was a war of attrition. Laura would expect her to come over and 'rescue' her and they could swan back to the table together. Laura would then make some snide remark like 'You know, if I wasn't already hitched …' and then huff and puff all night, giving other girls the eye.

It was about more than badminton all right. It was about honesty and self-respect. Ruth thought of the feeble excuses she had tormented herself with in order to justify staying with Laura. *She'll change. I'll change her. Nobody's perfect. So she has confidence, is that really so terrible?* But here was a woman who had criticised her diction; her weight, her friends, her beliefs, and who also played petty little power games.

Ruth looked at Laura now, standing with the redhead, and tried to summon up a big sexy emotion – jealousy, anger, passion. She felt only amusement. Maybe even pity. It had been a spell; some kind of enchantment.

A pal of Ruth's had advised her to hang in there. Relationships didn't come ready-made; they had to be worked at. They were good together; everybody could see that. But they weren't good together. They were both becoming increasingly miserable and insecure. They would end up like Joan Crawford and Bette Davis in that spooky old movie if she didn't bail out now.

'Hi, I'm Janice. Would you like a bottle of beer? I hate drinking alone.'

Janice sat down opposite Ruth and put the bottle under her nose. Her boxer's nose.

'I'm sort of waiting for someone.'

'That's cool. But a girl like you shouldn't have to wait on anyone.'

Ruth blushed and took a swig from the bottle of beer, cracking her front teeth in the process.

'Don't be nervous. I'm just being sociable. I don't know anyone here.'

Ruth looked at Janice. She had long dark brown hair and deep brown eyes. She had big red lips that seemed to grow bigger and more kissable by the second.

'I'm waiting on my girlfriend.'

'You don't mind if I sit here meantime?'

'No. And thanks for the beer.'

They got talking.

It turned out Janice had just split up from someone and so was back out on her lonesome-ownsome once more. Her ex had been a fiercely possessive Klingon who had isolated Janice from her friends. So now she had made her escape, she was footloose, fancy-free and lonely as fuck.

'So you're in a relationship?'

Ruth looked at Laura, who by this stage was pinned to a wall and was being virtually dry humped by the rapacious redhead.

'I'm on the way out of one.'

Janice smiled broadly and brought a bottle of beer to her luscious lips.

Luck be a lady tonight.

Jeannie and Joanie

Jeannie finished wiping off the toilet seat then pressed the flush button on top of the cistern. She barely noticed the graffiti on the WC doors now. At first she would giggle and shake her head. Now, well, they couldn't shock her. You needed a sense of humour in this job. She had been cleaning Delilah's pub for two years. She did nine to eleven five mornings a week. They had a girl who came in the other two mornings; Jeannie had never met her. She used to work with another cleaner but lately the manager had decided it was a one-woman job. It was a big place to get through. Over the last two years a succession of young girls had been employed alongside Jeannie, but none of them had stuck it.

The fact that Delilah's was a gay bar didn't bother her. It was no cleaner and no dirtier than any other place she had worked. It was handy to get to, being in the town centre. She needed the money. She had met some of the staff and they were nice. Jeannie especially liked Joanie, the bar manager.

She took off her rubber gloves and walked into the ladies. She knew it was silly to walk out of the gents and into the ladies just to wash her hands, but somehow she never felt right about using the facilities in a men's toilet. As she walked downstairs she could hear Joanie coming in. There was the rattle of the keys, the noise of the door opening, Joanie's footsteps. Joanie whistled, too. Jeannie smiled as she turned at the bottom of the stairs and came around into the bar area.

'Mornin' Joanie.'

'Mornin' Jeannie. Have ye time for a cuppa this mornin'?'

Jeannie nodded. Every morning Joanie would offer her a cup of tea. Sometimes she would just want to get home she'd feel so tired. Other times, like this morning, she wanted to take up the offer. She had got to know Joanie and liked him, enjoyed their chats. She sat on a chair at the bar and watched Joanie make the tea. He was dressed in jeans and a tee shirt and wore trainers. He looked like an ordinary young man. Jeannie knew that Joanie was gay and dressed up as a woman. She had seen photographs. There was one behind the bar. Joanie was wearing a sparkly gold dress and a big honey blonde wig. You had to look closely to make out it was really Joanie under the make-up. Of course, Joanie wasn't his real name. It was John. He used to say to Jeannie she should come in one night and actually see the people she was cleaning up after. Jeannie would offer various excuses. She couldn't afford it. Joanie would say drinks on the house. She was too old for this sorta place. Joanie would say age is no' an issue in here. She had to watch her granddaughter. Joanie would say get a baby sitter. It was no use. Jeannie wasn't interested, that was obvious to Joanie. But Jeannie *was* curious. Alongside the photo of Joanie behind the bar were other photos of Delilah's regulars. Young lassies and boys with their arms around each other, laughing.

'Teatime, doll.'

Joanie put the cups of tea down in front of them. Jeannie sat on the other side of the bar, across from Joanie.

'Mind if I smoke?'

Jeannie shook her head. Joanie lit up and sat with an elbow resting on the bar. He looked pensive. He'd had a rough week of it. He looked at Jeannie. She looked knackered. Joanie wondered what age she was. He guessed late forties. Sometimes she looked a good bit younger but today she looked worldweary. Done in. Joanie knew that cleaning was a hard job. His mammy had been a cleaner on and off for years. He remembered getting up for school some mornings when his mammy was just getting in from early morning shifts. He would be going out the door to school as she was coming in.

'You look done in, hen.'

'Ta very much.'

Joanie patted Jeannie's hand.

'It's a sair fecht innit?'

Jeannie smiled.

'It's ma grandwean's birthday. She's six the day.'

'Aw the nice. Are ye havin' a wee party?'

Jeannie shook her head and took a sip of tea.

'She had a few pals roun' yesterday fae school. We're jist havin' a few family roun'. An' the neighbours weans.'

'Sounds damn near a party tae me.'

'Aye, that's her six noo. Cannae believe it.'

'Who's watchin' her this mornin'?'

'Her great Auntie Agnes.'

Joanie puffed at his fag. Jeannie opened her cellophane wrapped biscuit.

'How's yer love life this weather?'

Jeannie knew that Joanie had been seeing an American businessman. He had told her he was in love. She'd seen a photo of the guy. He looked very handsome. Joanie faltered. He put a hand up to his face.

'That's a bit of a sore point.'

'Oh. I'm sorry, love.'

'He's gone an' chucked me. Pissed off back to the States.'

Jeannie could see that Joanie was close to tears.

'I suppose he had tae go back home eventually. But I had big plans for me and this guy. I never even got a chance to say goodbye.'

Joanie wiped away a tear. 'I'm always fallin' in love wi' people I don't know.'

Jeannie felt a bit embarrassed. She was unnerved by the strength of feeling in Joanie's voice. Joanie had a hanky out by now.

'I'm sorry, Jeannie. I knew it was just a holiday romance for him. I was kiddin' maself on.'

Joanie talked then of his lost love, of how they'd first met. Lance had come into Delilah's one Saturday night and hung around at the bar. He'd taken a fancy to Joanie right away. It certainly seemed that way. He was over in Glasgow representing a computer software company. Joanie made it a rule never to get involved with punters, but Lance was different. He was passing trade. He was handsome personified. Joanie liked everything about him. Even his name. A pal had said, 'Lance – isn't that somethin' you do to a boil?' But Joanie would brook no criticism of Lance. He decided to take a chance on romance with Lance.

They had dated. They'd go for dinner. Go to the cinema. Drink in wine bars. Lance was easy company. He told Joanie that he had been married back in the States and that his wife had died in a light plane accident. She was having an affair with a millionaire playboy who was a keen pilot. The eerie part of the story was he said Joanie reminded him of his wife. Lance had told his wife the score about him and they had led separate lives. But they were best of friends and her death had been a terrible blow. Since then he'd thrown himself into his work and decided to live life to the full. So here he was, in a city many miles from his home in Texas, dating a drag queen. The nice part about Lance was he didn't pretend Joanie was a woman. Not like those guys who were so far in the closet, so deep in denial, the only way they could sleep with another man was by pretending they were with a woman. No, when Lance and Joanie got down to the bare essentials, it was as two throbbing, sensual, naked men yielding to the night. That's how Joanie liked to look at it anyway. Dragging up wasn't a sex thing. He knew it was kinky but it was just a showbiz thing. He didn't always dress up on dates. So it was always a surprise with Lance. He didn't know what to expect when Joanie showed up.

Joanie crunched a biscuit and paused for a moment, reflecting on his nights of passion with the Texan.

'Go on,' urged Jeannie, eagerly.

What spooked Joanie was the dead wife patter. He wanted to be loved for himself, not for a passing resemblance to a deceased spouse. He decided not to drag up anymore for Lance and just be John the whole time. It was then things started to go wrong. Lance began to insist that Joanie dress up for him. He even began to buy clothes for Joanie to wear. It was like that Hitchcock movie. Joanie wanted real love, not some kinky morbid fantasy. He told Lance so.

'I love *you*, honey,' Lance said, softly. Then he handed Joanie an aquamarine dress with matching scarf and shoes. It was what Lance's wife had been wearing the night she fell to earth with a bloody bump. Blue dress, blue scarf, blue shoes.

'Did you wear them?' Jeannie asked.

'Of course I did,' replied Joanie, 'I was a fool in love.'

Lance had been in Glasgow three months and had said he would be staying another three. But the morning after the blue dress episode Joanie woke alone in his bed. Lance had split. He'd left a note saying he'd always have a special place in his heart for Joanie, but to see him again would only bring back painful memories of his dear dead wife. Joanie bowed his head in sorrow and reflection.

There was an awkward silence. Jeannie reached for her bag. She found her brown leather purse and took out a small photograph of her granddaughter, Jade. She handed the snap tentatively to Joanie.

'This is ma wee grandwean. Jade. Int she lovely?'

Joanie looked at the photo. It was an image of a wee freckly-faced five-year-old lassie. She smiled broadly and her eyes were screwed up tight.

'Aw the nice. She's a wee darlin'. Does she take after her mammy or her daddy?'

'Oh her daddy. She's her daddy's girl.'

Joanie knew that Jade's daddy was dead. He knew that Jeannie looked after Jade and had done for three years. He didn't really know how Jade's daddy had died or where her mother was. There was something about the way Jeannie spoke about it that made him too cautious to ask. It all came out this particular morning.

Jeannie began to speak of it now. Her eyes were fixed on the photo of Jade.

'It was drugs. Aye. Drugs that killed ma boy.'

She told of how her son had been a drug addict since he was seventeen. Jeannie and her man had tried everything to get him off it. His da had begged him, gave him money, battered him, locked him in, disowned him, but nothing had worked. He was loyal only to the drugs. He had taken up with a lassie, Jade's mammy, and they had hoped he'd change and settle down. But that wasn't the end of it. The lassie was a junkie too. She had even stolen from Jeannie's house to feed her habit. They had both served time for thieving and when they got out went straight back to the drugs.

Then the lassie had got pregnant. She said was coming off the drugs. Jeannie's boy had said the same. Now they were going to have a wean they didn't just have themselves to think about. The lassie's sister had told Jeannie they were both still using but when Jeannie confronted them they denied it. They had got a council flat, on the seventeenth floor of a multi-storey block. The council had said they'd give them a lower down house when the baby was born.

The lassie gave birth to Jade in the November. She was under five pounds and a poor wee thing. The doctors had said she was born an addict too. Jeannie didn't believe that. The lassie was adamant she'd never taken drugs during the pregnancy. It would've killed the wean if she had.

Jade was kept in hospital for four weeks before she was allowed home. Both her ma and daddy went on methadone programmes for a while. One night social workers had brought the baby to Jeannie's house. Her ma had overdosed and Jeannie's son was up at the hospital by her bedside. He gave Jeannie's name to the social workers. Jeannie said, of course she would look after the baby. Her man had gone to their son's house with the social workers to collect some of the baby's things – the place was a tip.

After the social workers had finally gone, Jeannie watched over Jade as she slept. She shook with fear at the thought of the social workers being involved. She was terrified they would take Jade away and they'd never see her again. Her man had said they should keep her, him and Jeannie; their son was a junkie and his house wasn't fit for pigs.

But they gave the wean back to her parents. They had said they were going straight. They cleaned up the house. Again, for a few months, things had seemed okay. Jeannie and her man did what they could to help. They baby-sat. They helped out financially, leaving themselves short. Then, one morning, when Jade was only just over a year old, they had the police at the door. Jade's daddy had died of an overdose.

For the next few weeks Jade and her ma had stayed with

Jeannie. The lassie said she was going to get clean and look after Jade. Jeannie said those weeks were hell and it was only the thought of the wean that kept her going. A few weeks after the funeral the lassie did a disappearing act. She turned up a month later to see Jade. Then she'd be off again. This was the pattern with her. Jeannie was worried she'd take Jade with her one of these times. Eventually they had heard Jade's mammy was in prison. It was something to do with the drugs. She'd be inside for a few years. The social workers had helped them get interim custody of Jade. Jeannie and her man had talked of adopting Jade, if that was possible. It all depended upon what happened when her ma got out of prison. They didn't want to cut the wean off completely from her mother. Jeannie had even travelled to Cornton Vale to see her but she didn't have much to say for herself.

Jeannie sat with the photo in her hand. Joanie lit another cigarette. That was the story. The wean was as good as an orphan. Slowly, tears began to trickle down Jeannie's face. Joanie held her hands in his.

'She's got you, darlin',' he said reassuringly, 'and you're worth yer weight in gold.'

He gave Jeannie a hanky and she wiped her face and blew her nose. She kept apologising. Joanie asked her what she had got Jade for her birthday. She had got her a doll, and a doll's pram, and a Teletubby. Jade was mental for the Teletubbies.

'They dae ma heid in,' said Joanie.

He insisted on making another cup of tea for them. While he made the tea Jeannie went up to the toilet to sort her face. She left the photo of Jade lying on the bar. Joanie picked it up and looked at it again. It felt different from looking at it the first time, now that he knew the whole story. He looked at the photo. It'd bring a tear to a glass eye. He wrapped the photo in a ten-pound note he took from the pocket of his jeans and put it in Jeannie's purse that lay beside her empty cup. He poured the tea. Jeannie was up in the toilet for a while. He thought maybe she was crying some more. He was going to go up and check on her and then thought the better of it.

Jeannie came back. She had obviously been doing a power of crying.

'I hope you wurnae makin' a mess up there. You've jist cleaned the bloody place.'

They both laughed. Jeannie sat down and brought her tea to her lips. She noticed the photo was missing and panicked.

'It's okay. It's in yer purse. I put it in yer purse.'

Jeannie fumbled in her purse for the photo. She found the tenner.

'Just tae get somethin' nice for the lassie.'

Jeannie put the money on the bar.

'I can't take that. You cannae afford that, son.'

Joanie was determined.

'Keep it. And buy wee Jade somethin' nice.'

Jeannie thanked him and put the money back in her purse. She finished her tea and then said she'd better be going. She thanked Joanie again and then left. Joanie cleaned the cups. He looked at the clock. It was eleven thirty and a long day in Delilah's stretched out in front of him, like an ugly boyfriend at bedtime. He thought of the stories we tell ourselves and each other, to break our hearts and mend them.

'Where are they?'

Rodney looked as if he was just about to explode with rage. His face had taken on a strange, imperious quality. He stood motionless at the bedroom door and glared at Matt, who was lying across the bed, trying to recover from a late night's clubbing.

'Where are what?'

Matt was too tired to argue. He knew what was missing.

'My fucking Diana stamps that's what!'

Rodney seemed to be trembling and Matt realised that some kind of appeasement was required. He knew he should never have used the Diana stamps. Circumstances had conspired against him. He had decided to write some letters that were owed to people – his mother, for one. She had refused to speak to Matt since he had told her – 'announced', as she put it – that he was gay and was moving in with Rodney. They hadn't spoken in a year but Matt had it on good authority that she was beginning to get used to the idea of having a homo son. His sister was on the case. He had written his mother a chatty letter saying how things were going with him and Roddy, making it all sound as matter-of-fact and devil-may-care as possible. He dwelt mostly on his new job working in the university library. Moderation was the letter's primary virtue but he had closed with a tantalising 'Speak to you soon' which, he considered, might have been a bit presumptuous. So that was the letter to his mother.

The next person he needed to write to was his friend Suzy. She had moved through to Edinburgh to live with a woman twice her age. Suzy was twenty-seven and her girlfriend was fifty-four. When Suzy had first told Matt about her she had built up to this matter slowly.

'She's older than me,' she had said, shyly.

'How much older?' asked Matt.

'Several decades,' Suzy replied, enigmatically.

Matt had immediately imagined a tufty beard and continence pads. But he had subsequently met Suzy's woman, who turned out to be a warm, vibrant, sassy, sexy virago.

'Her hair is silver,' said Suzy, decidedly, 'but her heart is gold.'

Matt had been through to see them a lot when they first moved to Edinburgh. He was single at the time and Suzy was his confidant. He could tell her about his one-night stands, his unrequited loves, his loneliness, and she would nod benignly and say all the right things. No one was more delighted than Suzy when Matt met Rodney.

'Now I won't see you for dust,' she had said, as she dropped him off for the train at Waverley. Matt was determined to keep in touch with Suzy. She was, after all, his best pal. They phoned often but they wrote too. They enjoyed receiving letters from each other. Nothing beat receiving a warm, funny letter from a friend.

Matt also had to write to a CD club who had been demanding money with menaces from him. He had been a member of CD Sonic for a year and bought around thirty CDs from them by mail order, which was probably twenty more than he could afford. He had decided to cancel his subscription after the year but they kept hounding him, claiming he owed them money. He wrote them a firm letter saying that his subscription was now annulled and that he had paid them all the money (he had bank statements to prove this) and that any further correspondence from them would be treated as harassment. Matt hoped this would do the trick. All of these letters he had written in one sitting, punctuated by cups of coffee. He drank too much of the stuff.

The fourth letter wasn't a letter at all. It was a birthday card to his pal George, who lived in London. George wasn't really Matt's pal. He was a guy Matt had fallen in love with. George had strung him along for a while then made it clear there was no way they were going to get it together. Matt knew he shouldn't have anything more to do with George but they sent each other Christmas and birthday cards. Matt couldn't help keeping in touch with him.

Having written four letters the question was now how to get

them posted. Matt knew from experience that if he didn't post letters right away, they lay in drawers or were carried around in his jacket pockets until they were too crumpled and torn to post. He knew he couldn't leave these letters lying around. He had to post them right there and then.

First Matt looked in his wallet, as he normally kept stamps in there. He had been relieved to find a little stamp book inside. When he opened it there were no stamps. He couldn't work out how he'd have kept just the empty cardboard, unless some of the stamps had fallen out. He checked in amongst the notes but there was no sign of a stamp. Matt decided then to go to the drawer where they kept bills, passports, and stationery. He worked his way through everything and still could not find a stamp. He then thought about going to the newsagents to buy some. He dropped the idea in favour of looking in Rodney's jackets. Rodney was at the theatre with a friend. Matt opened the wardrobe door and started dipping into Rodney's pockets. He found a packet of Clorets, two cinema tickets, four hankies, five theatre tickets, about fifteen pounds and, at last, four stamps. A strip of four first-class stamps. Matt took them over to the kitchen table where he had been writing the letters. He looked at the stamps that he held in his right hand. They were Diana commemorative stamps. Each stamp was a different head-and-shoulders shot of the late Princess. A purple border framed all four. In the left-hand corner was the number 26 denoting the price of the stamp. In the right-hand corner was a small silhouette of the Queen, in purple. At the bottom of the stamps, in white on the purple border, were the numerals 1961-1997.

The first picture was a really elegant one. Diana was wearing an off-the-shoulder black dress and a pearl choker with what looked like a black brooch-like centrepiece. Her hair was as short as he had ever seen it. Her eyes and lips looked heavily made up. Although she was smiling, Matt thought she looked a little aloof. The second image was more homely. Her hair was bigger and fuller. She was wearing pearl earrings (only one was visible). She had a blue dress with lapels trimmed with white. Diana looked more natural and at ease in this shot. The third stamp had a regal image of Diana wearing a crown. She had pearl drop earrings (*quelle surprise*); a very ornate looking crew neck dress with what looked like paisley pattern stitched with pearls. Again, she looked more heavily made up in this photo, and a little older. There were bags under her beautiful eyes. The final picture looked like it had been taken outdoors. Whilst the previous images looked very much studio bound, the final image looked like it was a natural shot. The background looked like grass and trees, although it was out of focus so you couldn't really tell. Diana was looking to her right, her head lowered slightly. She was wearing a hound's-tooth jacket with padded shoulders. Or it might have been a dress. Matt guessed it was part of a suit. She looked essentially herself in this photo, sort of shy and charming and sweet. Her eyes were carefully delineated by eye pencil. This was his favourite, Matt decided. He had been surprised to find the stamps, as he was aware of some kind of controversy over whether the stamps were to appear at all.

Matt tore off one of the stamps, licked it, and stuck it on the envelope addressed to his mother. Then he hesitated for a minute. What would Rodney say about him using his stamps? Matt dismissed the thought. He could always buy more stamps. He tore off the second stamp and stuck it on the envelope addressed to CD Sonic. The one with the crown he stuck on the letter to Suzy. The final one, his favourite, he stuck on the envelope addressed to George. He kissed that envelope. Then he went and got his jacket and keys and grabbed the letters. There was a post box just around the corner of the street.

Matt had gone out later that night with his pal Benny and got pissed in Delilah's. While they were there they had overheard some guys talking about Diana. One of them said he was running in the Flora margarine marathon, with all proceeds going to the Diana, Princess of Wales Memorial Fund. This guy said that he would never get over her death, which, he added, was no fucking accident. No, he said, an order had gone out that Diana must be silenced forever. And that order, he added ominously, came from the top. Another guy said that the night after Diana's death, his

Auntie Fanny had woken up to find the spectral form of Diana standing at the foot of her bed, loving arms outstretched. She had written down her story and sent it to a man who was compiling a book, *Diana: Ghost of Love*, all about spooky visions of Diana. The third guy in the group said that he had come to terms with Diana's passing, but that he would never get over the death of Dodi, with whom he'd fallen in love since first seeing his photo in *Hello!* magazine. Matt turned to Benny and shook his head. He thought the whole thing was way over the top.

Not that Matt had been completely unmoved by the death of the Queen of People's Hearts. He'd been as shocked as anybody and thought it was a downer. He found it depressing that someone so rich, attractive and ever present, was suddenly gone. Matt had lost his father the year before and the whole Diana tragedy had brought back all the pain. He remembered that week after her death. Rodney was inconsolable. In fact, he was a pathetic drama queen. Matt felt he couldn't bear the saturation coverage and vowed not to watch the funeral. He was plagued by feelings of mortality.

'If you truly love me,' Rodney had whimpered through a hanky, 'you'll be there for me.' He was referring to the televised funeral. Matt had backed down and agreed to watch the funeral with Rodney. He ended up sobbing on the carpet at the sheer fucking tragic majesty of it all.

Matt looked up at Rodney's pained face. He knew he was in trouble. Big trouble.

'I used them.'

'You what?'

Rodney fixed Matt with a cold, haughty look. Matt got up and sat on the bed. He couldn't look at Rodney.

'I used your stamps. I'll buy ye new ones okay?'

Rodney went to speak and was lost for words momentarily. He stuck his hands in the air.

'You'll buy me new ones? And what if you can't buy me new ones? What if they're sold out?'

Matt looked at his bare feet.

'I'll get some okay?'

'Why did you have to use the whole four?'

'Because I had four letters to post.'

'Smart arse. You could've at least left me a note. It would've been common courtesy.'

Matt looked up at Rodney now and had to smile.

'And I don't know what's so fuckin' funny!'

'I'll get you some new stamps on Monday okay?'

Rodney gave an indignant, exasperated sigh and walked out of the room. Matt could hear him banging about in the kitchen. Then he came back into the bedroom.

'What were all these letters you were writing anyway? Are you doing a correspondence course? Found yerself a coupla pen pals?'

'Rodney, you're making a mountain out of a molehill.'

Rodney turned away again, then around again. He put his hand up to his face and shook his head.

'Those weren't any old fuckin' stamps, Matt. They're called commemorative stamps. They're meant to commemorate Diana. They're – they're mementoes.'

Matt thought they had done all this. Diana had been dead nearly six months now. He thought all the hysteria had died away. He wondered if there was something else wrong with Rodney and he was using the stamps to create some kind of row to let off a bit of steam. Matt had begun to hate the whole business of icons. Rodney stood rigid for a moment.

'It's the lack of respect, the disrespect,' he said, tearfully.

Matt looked sadly at Rodney.

'If I could bring her back,' he said softly, 'I would.'

Matt got fifty minutes for lunch but that Monday it took him one hour and twenty minutes to get the replacement stamps. He had to go to three different post offices and get a taxi back to work. The boss gave him a verbal warning for being half an hour late. But he had got the stamps. They were folded in his shirt pocket. The pocket had a button and Matt made sure it was fastened. Periodically, in stolen moments, he would check the stamps were still there, take them out and look at them. He had also bought a card with a pussycat on the front. Inside was the word 'Sorry'.

On the way home Matt sat in the back seat on the top deck of the bus. He took out the stamps. It was the same sequence. Matt wondered if these were the only four, or perhaps four in a series. He looked at them carefully, the elegant one with the black dress and pearl choker, the one with the pale blue dress and bigger hair, the HRH one, and Matt's favourite, Diana looking down and to her right. Matt wondered who she was looking at, smiling at, oblivious of death. He looked up at the people on the bus, oblivious too, it seemed, of the certainty of their own deaths. He carefully folded the stamps and returned them to his shirt pocket. He put his left hand up to the pocket and held it there. He felt his heart beating.

That night he and Rodney had dinner together. Rodney always insisted they ate together at the table if they were both at home. After dinner they opened a bottle of red wine. Matt gave Rodney the card with the four Diana stamps inside. Rodney swallowed nervously as he opened the card. He looked down at the card and gave a small, sweet sigh.

'I'm sorry,' said Matt. Rodney smiled. Matt looked at Rodney's big blue eyes blinking back tears through a thick blond fringe and could've sworn it wasn't Rodney who sat opposite him at all, but the sweet and radiant Diana herself.

Judy

One rainy Saturday afternoon a bunch of queens were having coffee in a booth in Delilah's. As Joanie scuttled back and forth with various cappuccinos, espressos, doughnuts and fairy cakes, he found himself being drawn into their conversation. There were four queens: a gargantuan peroxide blond clutching a handbag, two bearded ladies with lumberjack shirts who were obviously a couple, and a wee skinny guy with thick-lens specs.

'Why do queers love Judy Garland? I mean whit is it about Judy?'

The big blond bowed his head in thought.

'It's her *joie de vivre*. Her fuckin' *joie de vivre*.'

The lumberjacks nodded politely.

'It's the whole torch song thing. All that tragedy and defiance in her voice.'

The specky guy scratched his chin.

'For so many guys Judy was that significant other. Let's face it. She was the one who knew. And a million star-struck queens knew.'

'Knew whit?'

The blond peered over his coffee cup.

'That if we could just get over that fuckin' rainbow, skies really could be blue. Dreams really could come true.'

One of the lumberjacks 'hmm mmed' in agreement.

'I used to go out with this bloke in his forties who used to style himself on Judy. He'd put on giant false eyelashes and sing *Over The Rainbow* to me.'

His boyfriend pursed his lips in disapproval. The blond rambled away as he rummaged in his handbag.

'She wis camp as fuck. All that torch song diva stuff. Wee Judy givin' it big licks and breakin' everybody's heart intae the bargain. Did you ever see that auld TV special she did wi' Sammy Davis

Junior and Dean Martin? *The Man That Got Away!'*

Joanie butted in as he collected the coffee cups and emptied the ashtray.

'Judy had style. Pure style. But it wisnae put-on style. She had sincerity.'

He went back to the bar to get another fairy cake and make more cappuccinos. He had a habit of butting into customers' conversations, private or not.

The specky guy lit a cigarette and took a deep drag.

'Judy.'

He let the word drift like smoke. There was a pensive pause.

'Judy. She sang her sweet little socks off. She rolled with the punches. She loved and lost. But it was in Judy's voice that she spoke tae us fairies. The cadences. The cadences of her voice. The expressiveness.'

The blond eyed his big pan in a compact mirror.

'I first saw *The Wizard of Oz* when I wis seven. My mammy had a pair of hideous red high heels. I put them on and clicked the heels. My da belted me wan.'

A lumberjack bubbled with enthusiasm now.

'She wis so talented. I mean she came from that time in Hollywood when you had to be able to do everything. Sing, dance, act, the bloody lot. And she could.'

'Showbiz personified.'

'Judy was showbiz. Absolutely.'

'Even at her pilled-up, boozed-up, fucked-up worst, she was the best.'

Joanie arrived with cappuccinos and fairy cake.

'Her real name was Frances Gumm. Fanny Gumm. Disnae have the same ring does it?'

Joanie returned to his duties.

The bespectacled intellectual removed his glasses and began cleaning them methodically.

'*The Man That Got Away. Somewhere Over The Rainbow.* Songs of longing and loss. Songs about being on the outside looking in. What was that one she sang to a photograph of Clark Gable – or was it Cary Grant ..? They're writing songs of love, but not for me. Get it? Longing and loss. Exclusion and otherness. Judy – Judy stands at that border crossing between acceptance and rejection, exclusion and inclusion – because after all guys, we're all clicking our ruby slippers and trying to get there.'

The blond Goliath licked his lips after demolishing another fairy cake.

'Where? Get where?'

One of the lumberjacks wrung his hands, exasperated.

'Over the rainbow, of course!'

'It's the emotion. We don't get to express emotion. And here's this torch singer bursting with emotion.'

The lumberjacks held hands.

'All those grand emotions. Which is why, of course, queens adore opera.'

The blond grimaced as he picked fairy cake from a cavity.

'I hate opera.'

Joanie wiped the table in the next booth.

'Then of course there's Liza.'

The group eyed each other suspiciously.

The thoughtful thick-lens took up the gauntlet thrown down by Joanie.

'A chip off the old block. No doubt about it.'

There was a snort of indignation from the blond bombshell.

'That freeloader.'

The lumberjacks sprang to Liza's defence.

'Didn't you see *Cabaret*, petal?'

'You don't win a fuckin' Oscar for nothin'.'

'So she just inherited aw this talent?'

'Watch the movie!'

'Longing and loss. That wistful, plaintive, poignant gaze over the rainbow. Maybe this time, I'll be lucky. Deny it at your peril.'

'Lisa Minnelli!'

'*Liza!*'

'Liza or Lisa, the lassie's no fit tae lick Judy's ruby slippers.'

The egghead blinked behind his thick-lens specs and smiled wryly.

'Liza. High-kicking, lung-bursting, show-stopping, fag-hagging Liza. To deny Liza is to deny thyself!'

The lumberjacks gathered their shopping bags, nodding now and then as the egghead meditated on the magic of Minnelli, the glory of Garland.

'Maybe this time, they'll write a song of love for us. Maybe this time, that man won't get away. Maybe, if we could just get over that rainbow. Liza and Judy. Judy and Liza. One note from Judy, one kick from Liza, and closet doors all over the world burst wide open. That scene in *Cabaret*, Liza and Michael, Duchess of York. She knows the score. Liza knows he's queer. A chip off the old block. That fabulous scene, she's had an abortion, and her beautiful big Betty Boop eyes are blinking back tears. No, my darling, the torch was passed from Judy to Liza and burnt brighter than ever.'

Seeing the lumberjacks fidgeting, Joanie arrived with the bill. As the group divvied it up, Joanie threw in another gauntlet.

'I tell you what, guys, that Bette Midler, the best in the fuckin' business.'

The blond rolled his big blue eyes.

'Oh don't you start, Joanie doll. We'll be here aw fuckin' day!'

Morag stood at the edge of the crowd in the backroom at Delilah's and watched Carol stride the stage, belting out *Three Times A Lady*. There was a lump in Morag's throat. Maybe it was a hysterical Adam's apple. Carol had always said Morag was the butch one. She felt a pain in her sinuses as tears threatened to spill from her eyes. She stifled a sob and took a deep breath. It was over between her and Carol.

Carol was Catwoman. She loved cats with a passion. She owned two – a black cat called Naomi and a tabby called Cindy. Her whole flat was covered in catty things. Cat tea towels, cat dishes, cat tablemats, cat pictures, cat ornaments, cat rugs. It was Cat City. Morag hated cats.

The cat sat on the mat. Morag recalled a mad primary schoolteacher who had, on her first day at school, made her chant all day, 'The cat sat on the mat'. Even then she had hated cats. She didn't come from a family of animal-lovers (or people-lovers for that matter). Dogs she could understand. Dogs knew their names. They answered to them. They brought you the newspaper, your slippers. They were loyal. They were useful. They were guardians. But cats just sat around all day licking their arses. And what was all this about trays of cat pee and shit lying around in people's houses? Dogs at least crapped outside and pissed against lampposts. What was so cute and cuddly about a box of piss and shit? But Carol would truck no criticism of cats.

'Dogs bite people,' she informed Morag.

'Cats sit on babies' faces.'

Carol said that was an old wives' tale. Morag found that phrase sexist but there was just no reasoning with Carol. Women's rights, queer rights, they meant nothing compared to animal rights. In the end it was Carol's love of the feline species that drove them apart.

The first major row between Morag and Carol was when Morag

caught Naomi licking her dinner plate. They had just enjoyed a romantic candlelit dinner, and Morag had torn herself away from the table to answer a call of nature. As she sat on the lavvy pan she thought of how perfect the evening had been. The gorgeous idea came to her that the night was not over yet. Her heart raced. But she would never forget that moment when she turned left off the hall and back into the kitchen. Naomi, the devilish black cat, was up on the table and licking her plate with a frightening nonchalance. Morag summoned a scream but could only gasp in horror. Worse still, she looked at Carol, but there was an expression of smug pride on her face. Morag lunged forward and pushed Naomi off the table. Carol exploded.

'Don't you dare hit that cat! Don't you dare!'

She got up off her chair and gathered Naomi up in her arms, kissing and petting her.

'She's only an animal. Anyway, you'd finished your dinner.'

Morag was embarrassed and confused.

'I just don't think animals should eat off people's plates.'

'But that means she likes you.'

Carol looked at Morag like an irate adult trying to explain some basic truth of life to a naughty four-year-old. Naomi, that stinking black ball of fur, miaowed pathetically.

'She forgives you.'

Carol peppered Naomi with kisses.

That night Morag and Carol made love for the first time. Carol was so beautiful and tender in bed, everything seemed to fit. There was a congruence, Morag decided. Physically, at any rate, they seemed to be right together. But there was a nagging doubt at the back of her mind. The incident with the cat had been petty and sickening. So Carol had two cats. That was something she'd just have to get used to.

The next morning Cindy and Naomi lay on the bed with them. Naomi rested on Morag's feet like a bag of potatoes. The lazy bastard was obviously trying to break her ankles. Cindy crawled over Carol, licking and nuzzling her. Morag couldn't disguise the contempt she felt for the cats. Carol eyed her suspiciously. Cindy buried her ugly, pointed face in Carol's hair and Carol purred with satisfaction.

It was then that Morag's fantasies of felinicide began. She would put rat poison in their cat food and stand back like Bette Davis in *The Little Foxes* whilst the cats staggered around the kitchen, gasping and choking. She would train a dog, a pit bull terrier, to rip them to pieces. She would grab them by the tails and bash their brainless little heads off the wall. Despite the enormous satisfaction Morag derived from these sick fantasies, she always felt guilty for indulging in them. After all, they were only animals. The root of the problem was Carol, who had projected all these feelings, emotions, personality traits, onto two dumb animals whose only purpose in life seemed to be to eat, shit, scratch, piss, purr and miaow. But Carol could tell their every emotion and thought, for crying out loud, by a wag of a tail, a certain pitch of miaow, a lick, a yawn and a stretch. Her interpretations of their every noise and movement were increasingly inventive, not to say bizarre. When Cindy licked Morag's hand with her rough, repulsive, tongue, did that really mean it was time for bed? When Naomi dug her claws into Morag's velvet skirt and pulled, did that really mean 'welcome back Morag, have you had a nice day?'

Things got so bad Morag diagnosed Johnny Morrisitis. It was straight out of *Animal Magic*. Chris was a delirious dyke version of Dr Doolittle – she had long meandering conversations with two sleepy, indifferent moggies.

'Cats have no personality.'

'Yes they do, Morag. Every one is different. Each cat is as unique as a human fingerprint.'

'You feed them. Of course they'll stare at you and follow you around.'

'I bonded with those cats immediately.'

'Maybe they were hungry.'

Persuasion was useless. Carol was simply a Cat Person. They could do no wrong. Morag had watched aghast as Carol lovingly wiped up cat vomit from the kitchen floor or smiled shyly as she slowly (too fucking slowly) cleaned out the litter tray.

Naomi and Cindy were housecats. Housecats, mused Morag, were cats who were too lazy to drag their hairy over-fed hindquarters outside to crap or pee.

'Cats are of low intelligence.'

'They're as smart as you or I.'

Carol would always translate for Naomi or Cindy. She wants you to stroke her. She wants you to turn the TV over. She's seen a ghost (because cats are psychic). The only thing 'she' really wanted, felt Morag, was a swift kick up the little pink bumhole.

Everything else in the relationship seemed to be fine. Coaxed for a moment away from cat-speak, Carol could actually hold a conversation. Out on dates they had some great times together. Fun times. But even then, now and again, Carol would glance anxiously at her watch or chew her bottom lip, worried about how her precious cats were coping without her.

Morag knew that sooner or later the cats would come between them. That moment came all too soon. Morag had drunk nearly a whole bottle of wine one night and decided to phone for a Chinese carryout. In a weird repetition of their first meal together, Morag had abandoned her sweet and sour chicken for a powder room stop. On her return, she discovered both Naomi and Cindy up to their whiskers in the Chinese cuisine. In a drunken fury Morag metamorphosed into Bruce Lee and a flying kick with her right foot sent Naomi, Cindy and the sweet and sour chicken, boiled rice and prawn crackers, cascading around the room. The food landed on the walls and mantelpiece of Carol's lounge. The startled cats ran round the room three times before landing with a yowl in Carol's lap. A deathly silence ensued, a silence Carol finally broke.

'Morag, I think we need to talk.'

They talked.

Carol did most of the talking. She didn't like the way Morag treated Naomi and Cindy. If she had any respect for her at all, she had to accept that those cats were the most important thing in her life. They loved her, unconditionally. They were the most affectionate and giving creatures. They had always been there for her. They picked up her moods better than any woman ever had or will. They were Naomi and Cindy. Her beautiful cats. She could not tolerate them being abused or assaulted before her very eyes. Morag had to consider her position very carefully now. Either she, too, had to pledge her heart to Naomi and Cindy or Carol would have to ask her to go.

All this was delivered in a patronising monotone. Morag didn't know whether to laugh, cry or throw up. Her position was untenable.

'I think I'd better go.'

Back in her own flat Morag threw herself onto the bed and watched the room dissolve in tears. Perhaps she had been unnecessarily mean and cruel to the pussies. Perhaps she had been jealous of the easy, natural affection between Carol, Naomi and Cindy. Surely Carol was right, you had to respect the things dear to your lover. And those cats were so precious to Carol. Had Morag foolishly let her aversion to cats spoil a special, loving relationship? Gradually her thoughts hardened, crystallised. Those cats had been allowed to stink out Carol's flat, puke and slobber over everything, scratch the wallpaper, tear the curtains and scavenge off her plate. Carol had spoken more to those cats than she ever had to Morag – she had shown them more affection, attention and respect. Morag steeled herself against regret. She had a strong urge to go over to Carol's and throw herself at her mercy. But there was only one pussy she had enjoyed stroking in that flat, and it was not called Naomi or Cindy. It was a package deal: love me, love my pets. It was over.

Now, as Morag stood in Delilah's two months later and watched Carol sing the Commodores hit, she could begin to put things in perspective. Just as Carol had projected various thoughts and feelings onto those cretinous cats, so she had projected emotions onto Carol that Carol herself did not own. In retrospect, Morag could see that Carol didn't really love her at all. She loved simply herself, and those insufferable moggies. Carol had curled up in her lap for warmth, nothing more. Morag felt a tear trickle down her cheek as the crowd in Delilah's applauded Carol's vocal performance. Morag wished that she had never met her. She wished death-by-fur ball on those stupid, stinky cats. As she pushed her way through the bar, a young karaoke queen started bawling out 'What's New Pussycat?' Morag fled into a taxi.

That night Morag dreamt Naomi and Cindy had crapped on her bedroom floor and Carol was holding her by the hair and forcing her face down onto the cat-poo. Rubbing her nose in it.

Straight-acting, Self-hating

Pat hated Delilah's. He hated anything connected to homosexuality. He knew he wasn't like them, the sad fucks who lisped and leapt around Delilah's like fairies on speed. As for dykes – there was no such thing, only ugly birds who couldn't get a man. He wasn't quite sure how he had come to be counted amongst their number. Some monstrous accident of fate had marked him like Cain with a murderous desire to lie with his own sex. But he had fought it, oh, how he had fought it. He had stood in the changing room at his gym club and fought it, his terror acting like deadly gravity on his semi hard-on. He had fought for breath like a drowning man. He had dated and courted women, and claimed to love them and lain between their thighs and done his duty, though he longed so intensely for a man he thought his balls would burst. Still he fought.

Yet here he was on a blind date. He had, after months of soul-searching, placed a contact ad in *Get Out*, a trendy listings magazine that was not identifiably gay. Pat had deliberated carefully over the composition of his ad. He was satisfied with the final result and hoped he would attract suitable candidates to compete for his heart. 'Attractive, intelligent, straight-acting, thirty-something, gay man seeks long-term relationship with handsome, discreet man. Photo and detailed letter. No fats or fems.'

The response was disappointing. A couple of the dials looked as if they were awaiting their invitations to the Ugly Bug Ball. Photo booths made everybody ugly but these were something else. One letter had stood out though. Or maybe it was the photo, which made Rick stand out. A young, sexy, muscular guy. A university graduate working for some kind of training agency. Pat responded immediately, pouring out his heart to the handsome stranger. He anticipated the date they had made with a combination of lust, excitement, hysteria, guilt and shame. The worrying aspect for him was the proposed venue of the date: Delilah's. Delilah's revolted Pat. He had dragged himself, drunk and despairing, into the hellhole a few times, and was nauseated by the gaudy, brazen queerness of the place. But Rick, his date, had insisted.

Pat accepted there were advantages in meeting at Delilah's – he knew where it was and no one really knew him there. There would be anonymity. The idea of being discovered, of being uncovered, made him shake violently.

Pat had prepared well for the date. He had bought new underwear. He had washed his bed linen and spring-cleaned the flat. He had gargled with mouthwash and flossed his teeth. He had had his hair cut and polished his shoes, and agonised over what to wear, what to say. He had plotted conversations. He had fantasised about the sex. The sex with Rick. Another man. For a week he had wondered and wanked about this man. Now was the moment. The moment he had waited for all his life. The moment had come.

'Hi doll!'

The greeting was yelled from behind Pat. The two words revealed a multitude of sins, bleated in a shrill, camp voice that made bile rise in Pat's throat. Fairy. Screamer. The sooner Rick arrived and they could get out of here the better.

'Hiya doll!'

Pat turned and saw Rick standing there at the side of his booth. He looked even better in the flesh. He was wearing a light blue shirt and a pair of Levis. He beamed broadly at Pat.

'Thought you'd stood me up there, doll.'

Rick flounced forward and squeezed in beside Pat.

'Were you waiting long, pet?'

Pat couldn't believe his ears. He couldn't believe that this horrendously poofy voice belonged to handsome, hunky Rick. It was as if an evil queen was using Rick's beautiful body like a ventriloquist's dummy. It could not be true.

'Cat got your tongue, love? Lucky old cat.'

Pat stammered.

'– I – I'm nervous.'

'You need a stiff one, doll. But I'll get you a drink first. What're you drinking? Lager? I'll be right back.'

Rick tiptoed up to the bar. Pat surveyed his surroundings looking for an escape route. There was a bottleneck at the exit. The nosiest customers would stand there, constantly complaining of cold draughts, but eager to see who was coming and going and who would stay. Pat closed his eyes and sighed. Was there a man amongst them? He decided he would sweat it out for a few pints. If he ever needed a drink, then it surely was now.

Rick came back with a coo-ee and squeezed in beside Pat. He put the two pints of lager in front of them and purred softly.

'So here we are, doll.'

'Here we are.'

It was hopeless. Pat knew they had nothing to say to each other. He'd been in this position before – with a woman. They had sat on her sofa sipping coffee. In silence. Eventually she rose majestically and put on the TV. Later that evening they had brought the date to a harrowing conclusion by having a mannered, laboured, dry-hump on the sofa, both of them faking any feeling. A dangerous thought cruised in the bushes of Pat's tortured mind. Yes, Rick was a poofter, but he still looked fantastic. Handsome as fuck. Firm, muscular body. Was a shag out of the question? Pat mulled this over. He could never possibly be seen out with Rick or introduce him to friends or workmates. As soon as he opened his mouth a neon sign declaring FAIRY would appear above his glorious head. He would drag Pat down with him, guilt by association.

'I'm glad you showed up, lover-boy. If you hadn't I was gonnae throw myself off the Kingston Bridge.'

'I'm a man of my word.'

'Words are fine and dandy. But actions speak louder.'

Rick rubbed Pat's thigh with a warm, purposeful hand. Pat laughed nervously, blushing. Rick removed his hand and winked at him.

'Don't worry, love. I'm no gonnae bite you. Just suck you.'

Pat found himself on the defensive.

'I'm not really into one-night stands.'

Rick blinked his big brown eyes.

'A puppy's for life, doll, not just for Christmas.'

They drank their lager. The music was more poppy then usual in Delilah's. Not the hideous robotic techno that Pat hated with a vengeance. He felt aroused by the presence of Rick beside him and tried to fight it. It was a man he was looking for, not a mutant. He looked shyly at Rick, whose eyes were elsewhere. Pat's face was wounded with disgust. He tried to smile and failed miserably. Rick was mouthing the words to some poofy disco song and nodding his head from left to right, like a ten-year-old girl trapped in a twenty-five-year old man's body. Pat craned his neck towards the exit. No way out. Rick turned to him suddenly, as though snapping out of a trance.

'D'you like karaoke, baby love?'

Pat mumbled and shook his head. He hated it.

'I do a fantastic version of *My Guy*. They're getting the karaoke on later. I'll sing it for you, pet'

He sung a few bars right in Pat's mortified face.

'I'll save the best for last.'

Another dirty wink.

Rick asked him about his work. Pat had invented a fictitious job in a fictitious workplace. He reckoned if things turned out okay he could always come clean to the right guy, and if it was the wrong guy, lies covered his tracks when he escaped. Pat struggled to answer Rick with more than one syllable. All the while he was having nightmares about a chance encounter sometime in the future with Rick, when he was with family or friends or workmates. Pat wasn't sure if he could live with this possibility. He decided he would have to leave town. Rick, of course, was an open book.

'Everybody and his granny knows about me.'

How could they have possibly guessed, thought Pat. Rick went on about how everybody knew he was gay, he didn't give a fuck, and if they had a problem with it then that was their problem. Closets were for hanging your coat, not yourself. Rick's mother had met all his boyfriends and up until recently had exercised a final veto on his choices. Now Rick felt he was old enough and pretty enough to make his own mistakes. Occasionally he gave Pat's thigh a stroke. Pat found these strokes unbearable and felt he would come if Rick touched him again.

'I see you've got yerself a husband at last. Is there a man in this pub you've no shagged?'

It was Joanie, butting in as usual, and teasing Rick, who laughed like a hyena, and slapped the air with his free hand, his other hand now placed firmly between Pat's aching thighs. It was then Pat made a break for it. He was desperate for a pee, and possibly a wank. He stammered something and squeezed by Rick, who pinched his bum.

'Missin' you already, doll.'

Pat fought his way upstairs to the safety of a cubicle. He sighed and pulled down his zip. It was then he realised he would have to wait a bit. He had a rock-hard cock to contend with. He stood before the lavatory pan and read the dirty and hilarious graffiti on the wall. But he did not, could not laugh.

He thought of Rick, Rick's body, and his sweet brown eyes. Physically, he was everything Pat adored in a man. He was broad and dark and handsome. Pat had seen that he was also hirsute, a veritable rug of a hairy chest was bursting over his loosened shirt. Yet he could not think of Rick. His horrendous, camp voice and demeanour. He was a ridiculous queen. Pat resisted further thought of Rick and gradually he was softening, and able to pee. But when he finished, he could not move. He shook his dick, put it away, zipped up, pulled the plug, and stood in the cubicle, unsure whether to stay or go. Could he get drunk and bury his sad and desperate face in Rick's hairy chest? Or should he run out of the pub, the stinking fairy grotto of a shirtlifting dive, into the night and home to the merciless loneliness of his bachelor pad? He hated Rick and he hated himself.

Suddenly he heard a burst of song from behind the cubicle

door. It was Rick giving a heartfelt rendition of *My Guy*. He finished abruptly and gave the cubicle door a brisk rap.

'How's yer arse for love bites?'

Pat opened the cubicle door, dragged Rick inside, snibbed the door, and kissed him passionately on the mouth. It was to be the first of a million kisses.

Papa and the Golden Shower

Papa took off his clothes and lay down naked in the cool dry bath. He closed his eyes and sighed. He opened them again and looked at his pick-up, a serious young guy who couldn't be more than twenty-five. The guy unzipped his jeans, pulled out his prick, and peed on Papa. The pee was yellow in colour and as it splashed and dappled Papa's bare skin he could smell it and feel its soothing warmth.

He wasn't sure how long he was out for but guessed it couldn't have been more than ten minutes. He sat up in the bath and called 'Heah' to the guy. There was no sound. Papa stood up and turned on the shower. He gasped as the cold water washed away the pee and woke him from his drunken stupor. 'Heah,' he called again above the rush of water. No reply. Papa turned off the shower and yanked a towel from the rail. He dried himself roughly, tucking the damp towel round his waist.

'Heah.'

Nothing.

Papa padded down the hall and into the living-room. Nobody there. He tried the bedroom, the kitchen. Nobody.

'Heah,' he called again. He was alone. At first Papa thought the guy had just gone home when he'd fallen asleep in the bath. That was all there was to it. It happened. He'd had guys conk out on him. Once he thought he was getting the blow job of his life until he realised the guy's head was a dead weight in his lap. He'd fallen asleep.

Papa switched the kettle on for coffee. It was then he recalled seeing a drawer open in his bedroom. He went back to the room and over to the bedside cabinet. Papa could see nothing missing from the drawer. He closed it. He looked around the room and went into the living-room. Small things began to grab his attention. Wee gaps in his rows of CDs. The way his jacket lay on the sofa. Papa checked the pockets. His wallet and mobile phone were missing.

'Fuck,' he said to himself. He was shaking. He went over to the old 1940s sideboard and opened the drawers there. He rummaged through them. Right away he noticed a few items missing – a watch and a ring. The watch was a present from his old firm, the ring had been his father's.

In his bedroom Papa hurriedly put on his clothes. Halfway through dressing he went briskly to the front door and fixed the bolt and chain, frightened the guy would come back. He had found his house keys and car keys behind the sofa and wondered whether they had fallen out of his jacket when he took it off or when the guy frisked it. When he was fully dressed Papa sat hunched on the sofa, mumbling to himself. He was in that strange place between drunkenness and sobriety. He tried to piece together the events of the evening. He had gone to Delilah's, drank like a fish, talked to everybody and trusted everybody.

Memories came back in flashes. He remembered kissing a man on the stairway. That was all, just kissing. But it wasn't the guy he came home with. He remembered, too, sitting in a booth with two lesbians talking about old movie stars. Then he remembered his pick-up. He remembered odd things about his behaviour. The hesitancy of his speech, the way he took his arm at the elbow and had guided him out of the pub and into a taxi. He had been sober and serious. There had been something methodical, purposeful, about his behaviour.

After he had cancelled his credit cards, stammering down the mouthpiece to the 24-hour call centre, Papa made himself a cup of strong coffee. He sat with it in his living-room, perched on the sofa. He felt lonely. Papa prided himself on having a busy social life and wasn't normally lonely. But things like this made him feel lonely. Not just bad things but good things too. He wanted to say to someone 'Wasn't that hilarious?' or 'Isn't that terrible?' He rang Mama, crying down the phone. She came over.

'Did you call the police?' asked Mama, holding Papa's hand.

'It never occurred to me.'

'You've been robbed,' said Mama. 'I think you should let the police handle this.'

But Papa wouldn't phone the cops or let Mama phone them. He told her about the golden shower and his blackout and then his discovery of the theft. Mama listened quietly, shaking her head.

'You guys are playing with fire,' she said.

'I get drunk,' said Papa.

'I know you do,' said Mama, sternly. She petted his hand. 'You lose your judgement. But if that ring means anything to you, phone the police.'

'It was my daddy's ring,' said Papa, crying again.

'You need to take more care of yourself,' said Mama.

Her arms made a strong, sure ring around her friend.

'My mother can fuck a broomstick.'

Caroline would always say that whenever her lover Denise suggested Caroline tell her mother she was a lesbian. It would usually start with Caroline going on about her mother, how she'd rejected her as a child, had never shown her any affection, and had ruined her life. Caroline even said she thought her mother might be autistic. You couldn't get eye contact with her. Denise was tired of her moaning, though she didn't want to tell Caroline this. But Caroline had been on this mother-bashing trip for a while. Her favourite book was *Toxic Parents: Overcoming Their Hurtful Legacy and Reclaiming Your Life.*

She used to tell Denise stories about her mother. Once, when Caroline was eight years old, she was in the school play. She was really excited and had begged her mother to come and see it. Grudgingly, her mother had gone but after the show had shook her head and told Caroline she had looked silly, 'standing there like a block of wood.' Caroline had been a tree in the enchanted forest.

Another story from Caroline's rosy childhood was that her mother used to jam her fingers in a bedroom drawer. If Caroline did anything 'naughty', her mother told her to put her hand in the drawer of her bedside cabinet and then close it on her wee fingers. Denise said it sounded like *Carrie.*

The other story Caroline was fond of telling was how on her twelfth birthday her mother had hit her over the head with a jigsaw. Denise was puzzled. Wouldn't a jigsaw be too flimsy and just break? Caroline explained it was still in the box.

At first when Caroline told these stories Denise tried to look sympathetic, sighed and shook her head disapprovingly. But after the hundredth time she couldn't bear to listen. Denise knew that some people had shitey parents – her own father was a tyrannical alcoholic – but she felt adulthood brought its own responsibilities and you couldn't blame your parents – toxic or otherwise – for everything. Barely a week went by without Caroline trashing her mother. Denise felt that Caroline needed to break the hold her mother seemed to have over her. She felt that Caroline should let her know that she was gay, in a relationship, and had found her own way in the world. But Caroline would only say, 'my mother can fuck a broomstick.'

'I wish you'd let go of this victim thing.'

'Victim thing?'

'You're a grown woman, not a helpless child anymore.'

Caroline would fall silent for a while then come back with something like, 'One of these days I'm going to walk into a police station and tell them the whole fuckin' story.'

'What?' Denise would ask. 'That you're a lesbian?'

It had become a source of tension and conflict between them, Caroline's bitterness towards her mother.

They were sitting in a booth in Delilah's one Saturday afternoon after a shopping trip. They had mainly been window-shopping but Caroline had bought a blouse in Next and Denise had bought a few things from the Body Shop. Delilah's was quite relaxing at this time of day. They played mellow music and had kind of billed Saturday afternoons as chill-out times. Caroline and Denise drank warm, milky coffee and chatted. Joanie came over from the bar and told them that tonight Delilah's was having a special Ellen Degeneres night. Channel Four was hosting a coming out party and broadcasting the episode where Ellen finally comes bursting out of the closet. Delilah's was showing the episode on a big screen with free glasses of wine, chocolates and party hats. The girls said they were keen and took a flyer from Joanie but they had already decided between themselves to have a cosy night in to watch the show. Denise loved Ellen but Caroline didn't really 'get' her. However, Caroline said she would love to get her mitts on Anne Heche, Ellen's lover. She had seen her in *Volcano* and said Heche really got her lava flowing.

They had gone to Safeway that morning to get the weekly shopping and had bought some wine, crisps, tortilla chips, grapes and chocolate. They intended to pig out as Ellen came out. It had been a tough decision. The idea of being in a gay bar with a lot of other gay people, celebrating together, was very appealing. But Caroline felt that this was a time to listen and reflect and feared that things would get too rowdy and trashy in Delilah's. So they decided they would be home birds that night and celebrate their lesbian love together.

Back at the flat Denise made dinner. They sat almost in silence at the table, in candlelight; almost in silence because now and then Caroline made an appreciative noise about the food and also because in the background were the poignant and plaintive tones of kd. Denise enjoyed these moments of togetherness, when they didn't have to speak; they could just share a meal or a song or a movie together.

Later, as Caroline did the washing up, they talked about the impending *Ellen* episode.

'Laura Dern's in it,' said Denise.

'Laura who?' asked Caroline.

'Laura Dern. She was in *Blue Velvet*. And *Wild At Heart*. She was great in *Wild At Heart*. Her and Nicholas Cage were star-crossed lovers?'

'I don't think I saw that.'

'How about *Jurassic Park*? You must've seen that?'

'Oh right. Aye, I know who ye mean.' Caroline washed the soapsuds off the dinner plates.

'So is she one of the girls?' Caroline would always say 'one of the girls'. It pissed Denise off.

'Naw, I don't think she is. But she's playin' a lezzie tonight.'

'I heard Oprah's in it.'

'Oprah?'

'Oprah Winfrey. She's in it tonight.'

'Playing herself?'

'Naw, she's playing Ellen's therapist.'

Denise began drying the dishes.

'I didnae know Oprah acted.'

'She was in *The Color Purple*.'

'Wasn't that Whoopi Goldberg?'

'Oprah was in it too.'

'And Demi Moore.' Denise put down her dishtowel.

'Demi Moore was in *The Color Purple*?'

'Naw,' Caroline laughed, 'she's in *Ellen*. Tonight.'

Denise put the dishes away and then put her arms around Caroline.

'It's going to be quite a night.'

They set out the snacks on the coffee table. There were tortilla chips, crisps and grapes, all in bowls, and a box of chocolates. Two bottles of wine and a couple of glasses stood in the middle of the table.

'We'll never eat this stuff,' said Caroline.

'You'll feel peckish later. It's on quite late,' Denise assured her. She began looking for a videotape they could tape over. She found one that had some *Star Trek* episodes on it. Denise was a Trekkie but was willing to make the sacrifice so that she could tape the coming out night.

'We don't have to tape it,' said Caroline. 'After all, we're watchin' it.'

'I want to tape it,' replied Denise. 'For posterity.'

Ellen was at the Channel Four *Coming Out Party*. She was guest of honour. There had been rumours that she would be there, but Caroline and Denise had thought she'd probably give it a miss and maybe send a taped message. But she was there, looking lovely.

'I think she's adorable,' gushed Denise.

'She's okay,' added Caroline, 'for her age.'

First on the evening's itinerary was a documentary called *The Real Ellen Story*, which was all about the run up to the now infamous lesbian episode and the repercussions for the show and its star in the States. It seemed that the shite had hit the fan after the initial euphoria about the 'outing' episode. The TV company hadn't properly promoted the series and ratings had dropped. Execs and critics alike had expressed concern that the show was 'too gay' and had become a weekly trailer for lesbianism. Denise shook her head, exasperated.

'What is it about heterosexuals?' she asked aloud. 'Tell them you're a lesbian and that's all they can think about. You stop being a person and become a dirty word to them.'

Caroline nodded and poured them some wine. The documentary also touched on Ellen's personal life, her new-found love with Anne Heche.

'It won't last,' said Caroline. 'Showbiz marriages are a fuckin' joke.' Denise knew Caroline was only saying this because she had the hots for Heche. Towards the end of the documentary Ellen was shown making an emotional speech to the assembled cast and crew of the show, on the last day of the shooting. They had been through a lot together and Ellen paid a tearful tribute to them. Denise and Caroline felt a bit tearful too.

At last the moment they had been waiting for arrived. Denise opened the second bottle of wine as the show began.

'We're drinking too fast,' said Caroline.

'Fuck it,' said Denise. 'Special occasion.'

Things seemed to move quickly in the show. It wasn't long before Ellen and Laura Dern were sitting at opposite ends of a sofa in Laura's hotel room. Denise thought about the first time she and Caroline had been alone together. She remembered the awkwardness and fear she felt that night. Caroline had met Denise's brother on an accountancy course and he introduced her to Denise. He had been an unwitting Cupid. As soon as Denise and Caroline set eyes on each other something happened, something special. In the *Ellen* show, Ellen had initially denied she was gay and fled from Ms Dern's hotel room. That wasn't what happened with Denise and Caroline. They had gone back to Caroline's flat, drank some wine and made love. Denise remembered trembling the first time she kissed Caroline.

Ellen consulted her therapist, Oprah, about her confused sexuality, and ended up announcing she was gay over an airport terminal microphone. Denise and Caroline applauded at that moment, exhilarated. Later, Ellen told her friends she was gay and they went to a lesbian coffee house where kd lang was waitressing and singing dykey protest songs. Denise, being a devoted *Ellen* fan, loved the episode, but was more inspired than moved. Caroline, on the other hand, wept openly. The more Denise tried to comfort her, the louder she sobbed. Denise had never heard anybody cry so loudly or so long. At one point she even asked Caroline if she should get a doctor. Caroline half-laughed, half-cried at that. Eventually Caroline calmed down and mumbled incoherent apologies. She blamed the drink.

'There's no need to apologise,' said Denise. They switched off the TV and curled up on the couch together, listening to kd again.

'This is the life,' said Denise, dreamily. 'Wine, women and song.'

Caroline spoke for a while about the *Ellen* show and the feelings it had stirred up in her. She said that for a long time she had hated the idea of being a lesbian. All through her twenties she had struggled with it, going out with guys and denying who she was to herself and others. Denise had never heard Caroline speak so openly about this. She listened quietly as Caroline went on. Caroline even told her about a guy she was engaged to. They used to have sex back at his place on a Friday or a Saturday night, usually once a week. Once, said Caroline, her head resting on Denise's shoulder, had been more than enough. Eventually the guy met somebody new and Caroline pretended to be upset. People had been good about it. They said Mr Right would be along soon. Tell him not to fucking hurry, Caroline had thought to herself. A year later she had met Miss Right, Denise, and everything changed. But she hadn't told her mother that her flatmate was her bedmate.

As the night wore on Denise felt the wine taking effect. She volunteered to make coffee and left Caroline snuggled up on the couch. She brought the coffee in on a tray and had to shove some of the crisps and tortilla chips out of the way to make room on the coffee table.

'I'm going to have a serious hangover,' said Denise.

'Me too,' muttered Caroline. 'Thank fuck it's Sunday.'

Caroline was brushing her teeth in the bathroom when Denise came in wearing her pyjamas. Caroline rinsed her mouth and inspected her teeth in the mirror. Denise put her arms around her.

They both looked in the mirror.

'I'm glad we're gay,' said Denise. She smiled at Caroline in the mirror. 'Look at us. We're Ellen's degenerates.'

Caroline put her hands over Denise's hands and leaned her head back slightly.

'I'm going to tell my mother,' she said, her voice rich with relief.

Strangers in the Night

One of the things about Delilah's was you got passing trade. Strangers blowing through Glasgow, some of whom didn't care what they said or who they fucked. There were three of them dotted along the bar one dull, dreich Wednesday night. The wind whipped up so hard one of the exit doors had to be jammed closed; it was banging open and shut so much. Eventually the wind died down but the rain kept coming. Jeannie the cleaner was going to have her work cut out for her in the morning, what with all the puddles and muddy footprints all over the cream-coloured tiled floor.

It was a quiet night, because of the weather and it being mid-week. Two young dykes sat in a booth crying and kissing and crying again. An older man, kicking sixty, sat at a table reading a wank mag. Joanie had seen them all before. But the three faces at the bar were novel. There was a guy who looked about thirty, wee and squat, with tufts of hair sprouting out of his shirt at the neck. He was balding and his hair was cropped to fine fuzz on his round head. Further to his left was a young black guy. He wore a suit and Joanie saw the orange silk tie he had discarded peeking out of his jacket pocket. He was handsome, Joanie thought Sidney Poitier, and he exuded a quiet confidence. He had asked for a bottle of beer with a low, London accent. To his left was a man in his late thirties. He had strawberry blond hair and a ruddy face. He had the beginnings of a blond beard, obviously hadn't shaved for a couple of days, and Joanie saw hair like threads of gold flash across his jaw and chin. He wore a wedding ring and that always puzzled Joanie. You didn't know whether a man had a husband or a wife. He had a sexy, mischievous look about him.

The taped music meant there were no silences to kill. The blond man sighed.

'I don't know about you guys,' he said, wistfully, 'but I could really go a fuck tonight.'

Joanie plunged two pint glasses in the washer and lifted them out again. The black guy drank from his bottle of beer and gave no reaction. Crop top shook his head, disapprovingly.

'I don't do sex,' he said, decisively. 'Not that up the bum stuff anyway. It's dirty, dangerous, smelly and fuckin' disgusting.'

Joanie dabbed at his hands with a dishtowel and smiled. 'That's what makes it fun,' he joked. He was trying to lighten the tone a little.

'Well I like to fuck,' said the blond, nonplussed. 'I'm old enough to remember what it was like before AIDS. I had my first fuck at seventeen. My boss at the garage where I worked took me back to his place and rode me bareback. When he shot his load I shot mine. Best feelin' in the fuckin' world.' He lifted his glass and drank. Joanie saw his Adam's apple rise and fall. He had spoken so frankly, with such a presumed intimacy, that Joanie felt a sudden closeness, like the guy had taken him into his confidence.

Behind the strangers, the two dykes were crying again, holding each other across the table by the sleeves. They weren't making a noise but Joanie saw the wet faces, crumpled and earnest, glowing in the light.

The wee hirsute guy shook his head again. 'If an arsehole was made for sex, you wouldnae have tae supply yer own juice. I mean look at this.' He picked up a packet of lube that was in a wicker bowl on the bar. They always supplied free johnnies and lube in Delilah's.

'Look at this,' said the celibate. 'Why do you have tae juice up yer arsehole? I'll tell ye why. It wisnae meant tae happen. Not up the bum. No fuckin' way.'

Joanie was getting annoyed with the wee spoilsport. He stood opposite the guy, palms on the bar. 'I have a lady friend who swears by lubrication. If she doesn't use lube her fanny's so dry sparks fly when her husband tries tae hump her.' The black man let out a laugh then. He asked for another bottle of beer.

Joanie didn't mind what somebody's sexual preference was – consenting adults and all that – but he hated the dogmatists who tried to put people on a guilt trip. He felt there were enough people telling us simply being queer was dirty. He gave the black guy his beer and then his change. He looked thoughtful, and Joanie didn't have to wait too long for his opinion.

'If two people want to get together and explore their bodies, enjoy their bodies, then that's fine by me.'

The blond smiled, looking straight ahead, fingers encompassing his pint glass.

'So what turns you on?' he asked, blue eyes blinking.

The black guy cocked his head to one side, as if he was imagining doing what he liked doing.

'I like to hold a man's ass,' he began, 'a buttock in each hand, hold his bare ass and slip my wet lips slowly over his boner. I like to suck.'

Joanie was serving the older guy who had finally cast aside the horny mag. Joanie knew his face, suspected he was married. The new guys were quiet, imagining the blow job. The older guy went back to his table and picked up the mag. It seemed everybody was horny tonight.

'So you like sucking,' said the blond. He had rolled up his shirtsleeves, forearms adorned with golden hair. Joanie wanted to brush his fingers over it. 'I go for that too,' said the blond. 'I had a threesome once. In an Edinburgh hotel room. I had a cock up my arse and a cock in my mouth. I thought I'd died and gone to heaven.'

The black guy smiled. 'Now that's what I call room service.'

Joanie was busy restocking the fridges. He didn't know whether to laugh or leap over the bar into Blondie's arms.

The short guy had a mean look on his face. 'You'd think nobody had heard of AIDS around here,' he growled.

Blondie picked up a condom packet from a basket at his end of the bar and skited it along to the prude. It whizzed along and landed at his elbow. Joanie looked up from the fridge, a cold hand adjusting his wig.

'I suppose you'd have us all stuck in a monastery,' he piped up.

'Naw,' said the wee killjoy. 'Just thinkin' with yer brains not yer balls.'

The rain was battering against the windows and Joanie wasn't expecting much more in the way of custom. It was just as well, seeing as he was on his own tonight. The management kept hiring cute twenty-year-olds that lasted two weeks at the most, out of their pretty faces on Ecstasy. The blond started up again.

'I use my brain,' he retorted. 'I use my brain all day. But sometimes when you get home at night after a long tedious day, sitting on a cock seems to be the only sane thing to do.'

Joanie stayed crouched with the fridge door open. He needed to cool down. After a deep breath he got up and stood at the bar.

'Are ye gettin' it regular?' he asked Blondie, nodding at the gold ring.

The blond studied the ring, as if he were admiring his reflection in it.

'Oh no,' he said. 'This is just to piss the straights off. I had a boyfriend at the start of the year but this is September. You know how those things are.'

The black guy picked at the label on his bottle of beer. 'So you're shopping around?' he asked. The blond nodded. The wee guy ordered another drink. The blond leaned forward and looked down the bar at him.

'So what turns you on? I mean if fucking's out of the question?'

The wee guy looked exasperated. 'Use your imagination,' he snarled.

The black guy let out a laugh again.

Sometimes it was on the quiet nights that you really got your eyes opened. Without the rumbling, mumbling beehive of a Friday or Saturday night to hide behind, brave and revealing words could be heard. Joanie had lounged at the bar like a lazy priest while married men had trashed their long-suffering wives, lesbian mothers had given him blow-by-blow accounts of their custody battles and titanic struggles against a homophobic justice system, rent boys had told their hard-luck stories, spurned lovers had bawled at the bar and bitchy queens stung each other with their waspish wit. Now it looked like Blondie had set a raunchy tone for the rainy evening.

'My ex liked having his balls licked,' said the black guy suddenly. Joanie poured himself a soda water and lime. The blond looked straight ahead, but Joanie knew they could see each other in the mirror behind the bar.

'What about his arsehole?' asked Blondie.

'This summer I was in Gran Canaria and a guy with a stud in his tongue gave me the rimming of my life.'

The wee guy's face crumpled in disgust. 'This is like one ay those dirty phone lines,' he complained.

Joanie laughed. 'At least this doesn't cost ye a pound a minute,' he said, winking at the wee man.

'The arsehole,' declared Blondie. 'The arsehole is a temple of delights. Tickled, licked, fingered, fucked. My arsehole's brought me so much pleasure. So much joy.'

The black guy raised his bottle. 'Here's to joy,' he said, smiling.

Blondie raised his glass and downed the last of his beer. He ordered another.

The older guy left. Joanie saw him tucking the wank mag inside his coat, but guessed it wouldn't stay dry for long. A couple who had been sitting through in the backroom came through and picked up some more beers. The two young dykes were holding hands. The rain ran down the windows.

'So I suppose we've all to fuck ourselves to death is that it?' queried the wee man, with venom.

'What a way to go,' said Blondie, laid-back in his lewdness. The black man smiled, conciliatory.

'This may not be the easiest time to be gay, mate. But why give ourselves a hard time?' Joanie nodded at the black man. He hadn't seen enough black people on the Glasgow gay scene. It was no surprise. They'd had a cabaret singer in the backroom one night who made jokes about the sexual prowess of 'nig-nogs'. The depressing thing was only two people had complained about her and one of them was Joanie himself. Joanie said her next booking should be by the police.

'Everything's sex,' whined the wee man, raising an open hand in front of him, as if he were asking for his change.

'If only,' sighed Blondie. 'You go to work and break your back, you come home, there's crap on the news, you're on your own, you need a thrill for fuck's sake. Where's the thrill in life? That's what's wrong with this country. There's no joy.'

Joanie hadn't known much joy himself lately. After his American beau had done a bunk he'd been unable to capture a feeling even close to love. It felt as if he couldn't trust his own feelings anymore. He looked over at the moany-faced wee guy and thought he might have a point. Men, gay or straight, seemed more at ease talking about fucking than feelings.

'I haven't had it in three weeks. My balls are bursting,' said Blondie.

The black guy and Blondie looked straight ahead. Joanie knew they were looking at each other. It had been a while since he'd had sex. But he believed that no sex was better than bad sex. He was tired of waking up beside somebody he didn't like the look or smell of. He thought he'd better go over and ask the girls if they wanted another drink. Not that Delilah's did waitress service, but on a quiet night it was something to do.

They were crying again, holding hands and sniffling.

'Are you okay?' asked Joanie, tenderly.

The girls shook their heads. 'I can see that,' said Joanie. He didn't want to pry.

'Can I get ye anything?' he asked.

'Could I have some paper hankies?' one of them asked, in a wee wavering voice.

'Sure,' said Joanie. He brought them a whole box, planting it in the middle of the table.

At the bar the three men stood like gunfighters in an old Western. Joanie wiped the bar with a clean yellow cloth. Joanie made some small talk with the black guy; he was up in Glasgow on business, doing a course, and was going back to London on Friday.

'You guys should come back on a weekend,' suggested Joanie. 'If yer looking for action ye'll find it here in Delilah's. Always accommodating.'

The wee one puffed with indignation. 'I've been in better shite houses,' he snarled. Joanie gave him a stern look. 'You're as miserable as the weather,' he told the wee man. Joanie couldn't understand why some miserable people wanted to make everybody else miserable. He was the opposite, making valiant attempts to be cheery when he was depressed.

The guys ordered more drinks. A couple of people trudged in out of the weather, hair plastered to their heads, bought drinks and went through to the backroom to dry out. The tearful twosome left to do their crying in the rain. It had been a long night.

It was near closing time. The blond guy and the black guy had finally got down to first names and looking at each other. The wee man was marooned at the other end of the bar. Joanie went through to see what the boys in the backroom would have. When he came back to the bar the sucker and the fucker were gone, only the short guy remained, elbows on the bar.

'Did they leave together?' Joanie asked him.

A mixture of resignation and contempt puckered the wee guy's face. 'What d'you think?' he asked.

Joanie thought that they had left together, to go some place, a hotel or Blondie's flat, to fuck. He thought of purplish palms on a sweet peach, and moist lips descending a boner towards a golden fleece.

'Disgusting,' muttered the lone stranger. But Joanie just hummed *Ebony and Ivory* as he poured some more drinks. He saw nothing wrong in two guys getting together, to hide away from the hurt awhile, holding onto each other, finding harbour in flesh and bone.

Here Comes the Bride

There had only ever been two hen parties come into Delilah's that anybody could remember. The first one was headed up by a tall, frizzy haired woman with big saucer eyes who, on realising she had ventured into a gay bar, shrieked, 'This is a fuckin' poofs pub. We'll get AIDS!' before frog-marching the hen party out. The other party were a lot more sociable and insisted everybody cough up some cash and kiss the bride.

While two hen parties were a matter of fact, an after-the-event wedding party was something else. They cut quite a dash the night they dared to enter Delilah's. The bride wore a white dress, a veil, the works. The groom wore a kilt, revealing hard-on inducing hairy legs. Bridesmaids galloped about in ridiculous hats and the best man, also clad in a kilt, mooned at a howling audience through in the backroom. It all seemed good-natured fun.

The trouble started when the bride went to the bar and lifted her beautiful lace veil.

'It's a man,' said a wee guy with wavy hair and wavy hands. Necks craned at the crowded bar.

'No way,' said Bobbie. 'Look at that figure, that's a voluptuous woman.'

The wee guy pursed his lips and shook his head. 'The bride's got balls,' he insisted.

Joanie was serving the bride, who was buying two long vodkas for her bridesmaids and a mineral water for herself.

'Still or sparkling?' asked Joanie.

'Sparkling,' beamed the bride, eyes twinkling. 'I like yer hair,' she said, pointing at Joanie's copper coloured wig.

'It's not real,' whispered Joanie, 'but I am.'

The bride smiled a big white-toothed smile. Joanie gave her the drinks, took her cash and gave her the change. The party

WATERSTONE'S BOOKSELLERS
13 - 14 Princes Street
EDINBURGH
EH2 2AN
VAT NO: 710631184
Tel No: 0131 556 3034/5
Refunds or exchanges will be given if
goods are returned within three weeks,
accompanied by a valid receipt.
Mon/Tues/Wed/Fri 9am-8pm Thurs 9am-
8.30pm Sat 9am-7.30pm Sun 10.30am-7pm

217 CASH-1   8127 0102 005

DELILAH'S   QTY 1   9.99
9781903238547
TOTAL GBP   9.99
CASH   10.00
CHANGE   .01

VAT No GB 710 6311 84

31/07/02   13:45

were given a free round on the house when they came in but that was as far as the hospitality could go. The bride winked at Joanie and went off with the drinks. Joanie thought she was pissed when she came in but she seemed to have sobered up a bit. Switching to water seemed like a sensible move. Joanie's eyes followed the bride through to the backroom and he caught a tantalising glimpse of the firm flanks of the best man before he let his kilt drop again.

The wedding party seemed to swell and ebb like a tide, its energy coming in frenetic bursts punctuated by moments of wistful melancholy. The bride went back on the booze, thumping the bar and asking for a 'long lodka'. Now and again one of her bridesmaids would fidget with her veil or the skirts of her dress, as if the ceremony were still to take place. The general excitement began to die down as Delilah's accommodated the party. Even the charming novelty of the best man's bare arse soon wore off. But the gender of the bride was still the subject of speculation.

'It's a man,' insisted the wavy one.

Joanie shook his head. 'Take it from me,' he said, 'she's for real.'

Not only was the bride's gender in doubt, but her sexual orientation was too. A cigar-smoking ash blonde perched in one of the booths swore that she knew the bride when she used to rock'n'roll. She said she'd sat beside her at a kd lang gig at the Royal Concert Hall. It was definitely her, swore the cigar-smoking sleuth, but she had a crew cut and DMs on then. Her companion nodded resignedly.

'It wouldn't be the first time a sister had sold out,' she sighed. From another booth, Bobbie gave the bride a nervous glance.

A natural separation occurred between the bride's party and the groom's. The bride and her pretty maids all-in-a-row stayed in the backroom singing along to old songs, while the groom, best man and their pals barricaded the bar and kept Joanie running around like a blue-arsed fly. One of the guys kept asking Joanie if he was a man or a woman and Joanie kept replying, 'Bend over and I'll tell ye.'

But they were generally good-natured, which was more than could be said for some of the regulars. The guy with the wavy hair said straights shouldn't be allowed in Delilah's, whether they had a drag queen in tow or not. A couple of women marched out of the backroom complaining about 'the tarty hen party'. Others were enjoying the fun. At the bar Papa and Mama got chatting to the groom, becoming something close to surrogate parents, anxious about his drunkenness and the welfare of the bride.

In the backroom the DJ was playing *White Wedding*, *Chapel of Love*, and big lovey-dovey songs for the girls to sing along to. A couple of late teen queens fussed and fluttered around the bride, admiring her dress, trying on the veil, and saying she looked like something out of a fairytale. One of the bridesmaids kept shouting for karaoke, although it wasn't a karaoke night. She would take off her hat, poke at her hair with her fingers, sing a few bars of some indecipherable song, then put her hat back on again.

The groom leant on the bar, and spilled beer, soaking the elbows of his jacket. There was something about the sweet, cherubic, glaikit look on his face that reminded Mama of Jack Lemmon.

'Are you okay?' she asked, putting her hand momentarily on his brow, as if gauging his temperature. He nodded. Papa stood at the other side of him. Mama gave Papa a don't-you-dare look but Papa screwed up his mouth and shook his head as if the thought hadn't entered his mind.

'How long have youse been married?' asked the groom, looking first at Mama and then at Papa. Mama was about to explain that they were just good friends when Papa said 'Twenty years' and winked at Mama.

'Twenty years?' asked the groom 'That's amazin'. Are ye still in love?'

Papa smiled. 'Aye,' he said.

He glanced at Mama, prompting her with his eyes.

'Very much in love,' relented Mama.

'I hope I love ma wife for twenty years,' sighed the groom. 'A hunner years even.'

Papa then went into a routine about how to look after a lady. It made Mama laugh, but there was a lot of truth in what Papa said. He was a gentleman and she liked going out with him. The fact he was gay somehow simplified things. Fortunately they had quite different tastes in men.

'You have to listen to a woman,' said Papa Spenser. 'Opening doors and lighting cigarettes and helping her into her coat and walking on the outside lane are all very well, but a woman likes to be listened to. Most men just don't listen to women.'

Mama looked at the groom, who seemed to be listening intently to Papa.

A woman with a miniskirt and a maxi-mouth was over at the bride's table, chatting her up. She had a tight tee shirt on and looked as if she was trying to breastfeed the bride. Bobbie spied on them from a booth, eavesdropping on some of the loud-mouth's shite patter. Luckily, the bride appeared unimpressed. Bobbie was glad she was off the long vodkas. It was just then that one of the bridesmaids took a dizzy turn at the table, her face as white as the bride's dress. She was helped up by the bride, who volunteered to take her to the ladies. The fanny-pelmeted admirer slunk back to her corner. As the bridesmaid lurched to the stairwell she lost her hat. Bobbie, ever chivalrous, saw her chance and swooped down on the hat like a bird of prey. She crept up the stairs after them.

One of the groom's party was sitting down at a table near the front door. He was enjoying the attentions of three regulars who were camping it up and making jokes about who the best man was. He told the guys that the bride and groom had only known each other a few months and the whole thing was a whirlwind romance.

'I've had a few of those,' said one of the punters, licking the beer-froth from his thick moustache. One of the guys, a wee man with a puny bare chest framed by a leather waistcoat, was feeling the groom's pal's knee under the table. He looked at the straight man with big come-to-bed eyes.

In the ladies room the bride and Bobbie flanked the ailing bridesmaid. Each of them held the crook of an arm as the bridesmaid retched into a hand basin. When she had finished, Bobbie ran the tap on the vomit and the bride helped the bridesmaid to another basin, where she drank from the cold tap, the bride holding back her hair. She swilled the cold water around her mouth and let it pour out. Then she drank some more water and swallowed it. She stood up straight, the bride holding her by the arm, and took some deep breaths.

'How're ye doin'?' asked the bride, gently. Her maid simply nodded and headed for the door. The bride made to follow but Bobbie said 'Wait.' She waited.

Mama had ordered a Coke for the groom, whose head was hovering an inch above the bar. She gave Papa an exasperated look. Papa grinned.

'It's a big night for him,' he said.

'At this rate he won't remember any of it,' sighed Mama. She propped him up, one hand on his back and the other on his chest, and placed the glass in front of him.

'I think you've had enough of the hard stuff,' she said.

'Oh you can never get enough of the hard stuff,' said Papa mischievously, pinching a boy's bum as he minced past.

The best man, who had been sleeping at a corner table, had woken with a start and regained his old energy again. Leaning across the corner of the bar nearest the bathroom, he had grabbed at Joanie's wig as he washed glasses. Joanie's lightning-quick response would have impressed a master of kung fu. He grabbed the best man's wrist with a wet hand and they struggled over the wig. Joanie managed to retrieve it but curling strands of hair like copper wire sprouted from between the best man's knuckles.

'That's no way to treat a fuckin' lady,' snapped Joanie, and finished cleaning the glasses. The best man let out a devilish laugh.

The boaking bridesmaid was safely back in her seat and singing along with the other girls. The room, which had been spinning earlier, had slowly come to a stop. She looked down and noticed a smear of puke on her shoe. She attacked it with a paper hanky then started asking people if they knew a good taxi number to phone.

Upstairs in the ladies loo, Bobbie and the bride looked each other over.

'I think I know ye from somewhere,' said Bobbie tentatively. The bride fidgeted with the lacy cuffs of her dress.

'Where?' she asked.

'My wildest dreams,' said Bobbie. She wanted to move towards the bride but her DMs were rooted to the spot. The bride laughed nervously.

'That's a silly thing to say,' she said.

Bobbie felt that the rubber soles of her shoes must have melted to the floor. She pulled a carton of cigarettes from her shirt pocket. She opened the lid and proffered one to the bride.

'I don't smoke, thanks,' said the bride. Bobbie hesitated, then decided she wouldn't have one either.

'Yer dress is lovely,' she said. 'Is that the wan ye got married in?'

The bride smiled. 'Of course,' she replied.

'It's just that most brides change intae something else,' said Bobbie.

'Evening wear.'

Bobbie smoothed back her short, sleek hair and tried to think of something else to say.

'So where wis the reception?' she asked.

'In a hotel round the corner,' said the bride.

'Whose idea wis it tae come in here?' probed Bobbie.

'Mine,' said the bride, and came slowly towards Bobbie, as if she were actually floating.

The groom seemed to have lost all power in his legs and Papa had to hold him up with both hands while Mama got a bar chair and they negotiated him into it. He was asking if they had any children.

'No,' said Mama, getting in quick before her homo for a hubby came out with any more crap.

'You can adopt,' said the groom, patting Mama's hand consolingly. It made Mama smile and want to cry at the same time. In the backroom the girls were singing *Love Me Tender*.

It was while Joanie was chatting across the bar to Mama that the best man made another grab for the wig. He stumbled off with it held triumphantly in the air. Joanie came round the bar with an indignant shout of 'Heah!' He chased the best man round the tables in the backroom, then back to the front bar. The thief scurried round behind a table and shoved the wig on, hopelessly askew.

'How dae I look?' he asked. Joanie moved his weight from foot to foot, like an anxious goalkeeper wondering which way the ball would come. He made a leap for the best man, his right arm knocking glasses off the table. The best man fell then, and Joanie snatched back the wig and put it on. The best man giggled and bent over the table; his face resting to one side, forehead tipping up the pink heart ashtray. Joanie adjusted the wig. Then he lifted up the best man's kilt and playfully spanked his bare cheeks.

Bobbie and the bride were leaning against the wall, between the sinks and the hand dryer. Bobbie was nuzzling the bride's neck, intoxicated by her perfume. She could feel the bustle and rustle of the dress, like she was dry-humping a giant meringue. The bride pulled Bobbie's head up with both her hands and they met mouth to mouth. The bride slipped her hands down Bobbie's back and into the back pockets of her jeans. They were both moaning, gasping, abandoning themselves to the moment.

Bob the bouncer stood in the doorway with the bridesmaid.

'Has ma taxi been yet?' she asked, anxiously.

'Naw,' said Bob the bouncer, eyes fixed to her cleavage. 'I'll let ye know, hen.'

She grabbed his arm briefly and kissed him on the cheek, leaving a smudge of lipstick. Bob watched her stumble back into Delilah's and wondered if she had a boyfriend. He popped his head out into the street. It was drizzling now, nearly midnight, and no sign of a taxi.

The bride arched her back and opened her mouth, leaning against the wall.

'Oh God,' she said, as Bobbie licked her breasts. Then Bobbie began to sink slowly down until her hands were pulling up the bride's skirts.

'I want a divorce!' bawled the bride, as Bobbie's head disappeared underneath her dress.

Smoking a Joint: When Harry Met Gary

The smell was unmistakable. Harry was smoking a joint. Not that drug taking was particularly unusual in Delilah's. People took E or speed. There was an element of discretion in that. To sit there and brazenly produce a joint the size of a small dog, light it, and disappear in a puff of smoke was a fucking liberty. It was also groovy. People looked around. They wondered what was going to happen. Joanie got a whiff of the dope from where he stood at the bar. He knew he should take action of some kind, march over to the table and demand that Harry extinguish the toke. Delilah's could lose its license over shite like that. Joanie decided to let it slide, the way he was feeling tonight, he could do with a smoke himself. Joanie liked nothing better than a smoke before a fuck. Harry smoked the joint.

'Is that dope?'

A young man with dark glasses sat down next to Harry.

'Naw. Somebody musta farted. Or smuggled a skunk intae the pub.'

The young man laughed nervously and adjusted his shades, which were slipping down his nose.

'Ma name's Gary.'

'Ma name's Harry.'

'Pleased tae meet ye, Harry.'

'Gary.'

Gary watched Harry savour the joint. It was too cool. A couple of punters began to back off a bit, poofily fanning at the smoke and giving little coughs. Harry nodded at them and looked at Gary.

'It's only a toke. Ye'd think I'd set the fuckin' pub on fire.'

Gary giggled. He pushed the shades back up his nose again and drank his bottle of beer.

'It's good here innit?'

Harry didn't look very enthusiastic. He began to appreciate how young Gary was. Late teens.

'Fancy a drag?'

He pushed the joint to Gary's lips. Gary puffed, and sucked at the joint like a baby to a booby.

'Good eh?'

Gary smiled and nodded. Harry took the toke back.

'You know I see aw the steamers an' the speed freaks an' the E posse an' it makes me laugh. This is the only thing that's cool. This is the pipe of peace, Gary. The pipe of peace.'

'Can I get some more?'

Harry gave Gary another few puffs of his joint.

'Nothin' alleviates the stresses an' strains of this poxy planet better than this.'

Gary began to look pale. As a ghost. He suddenly felt very nauseous. Harry looked him in the eye. You didn't need a degree in dopeology to see that Gary was having a major whitey.

'Oh,' said Gary. That was all he was capable of saying, but Harry knew what he meant.

'I think we should go tae the toilet, Gary son.'

They rose as one, Harry extinguishing the toke in the pink ashtray. He ushered the ashen-faced Gary through the bar and upstairs. Joanie moved in to clear away the ashtray and its evidence.

Harry took Gary into the toilet. By this time Gary had extended his vocabulary from 'Oh' to 'Oh God.' Harry propped him up against the wall beside the sinks. He ran the cold tap and dabbed at Gary's face with a wet paper towel.

'You're okay. You're okay, Gary. Jist took a wee whitey.'

There were a couple of guys in the toilet. They were intrigued.

'What're you doin' wi' that chicken?'

'He's jist took a whitey.'

'Put his head between his knees.'

'Put his head between *my* knees.'

'I'm gonnae be sick.'

Harry helped the groaning Gary over a sink. He moaned and groaned. An older guy put a hand gently on Gary's back.

'There, there, pet,' he cooed.

He dried his hands at the drier and marched to the door. He turned to look at Harry, who was helping Gary up from the sink.

'Drugging chickens, whatever next?'

He shook his head and left. Harry knew the bitchy old queen was just noising him up. Gary began to recover. He moaned some more, then leaned against the wall. He smiled at Harry.

'I'm sorry.'

'Don't be.'

'Ah gave ye a showin' up.'

'Nae ye didnae. Have you ever smoked grass before?'

Gary nodded.

'A coupla times.'

'Feelin' better?'

'Aye.'

Gary turned back to the sinks. He turned on the cold water tap and scooped up handfuls of cold water to drink. Harry watched him sup the water. He was a good-looking boy. He could see him better now that he'd taken those stupid sunglasses off. Or they'd fallen off.

'Where's your glasses?'

Gary looked up, wiping his hand on his trouser leg.

'I don't know. They must've fallen off.'

They had a look for the shades in the toilet but there was no sign of them. They were standing at the cubicle door when Gary suddenly kissed Harry. He took Harry by surprise. Harry put his arms around him.

'I'm auld enough to be your da.'

Gary kissed him again, undeterred. He seemed to have made a good recovery from the whitey, the colour beginning to return to his cheeks. The resilience of youth, thought Harry.

'I've got an idea,' said Harry. 'You smoked my joint. Why don't I smoke yours?'

They smiled and bundled each other into a cubicle, Harry snibbing the door behind them. He enjoyed the smoke.

Heavy Losses

That Saturday night was the first time I'd been to Delilah's for ages. Some places hold too many painful memories for me. But I felt I had to go there after I heard about the Admiral Duncan bombing. I wanted to remember friends and lovers I had lost. I wanted to go back to the place where they had been so alive.

First Kevin died, then Marie and then Sandy, all within the space of a year. That was four years ago. Now they're talking as if you could live forever with HIV.

We spent a lot of time in Delilah's, just after it opened. We treated it like a second home. We got quite proprietorial about it. It was our pub, and we had our seats. We'd sit there three or four nights a week. We'd make up names for people we'd see, people we fancied or were curious about. Kevin would stand at the bar gossiping with Joanie, to the point where it was useless sending him up for a round. We'd die of thirst.

I was seeing Kevin in those days. For the first few weeks of this fling, (that's all I could really call it) I used to get quite jealous. On our nights out he spent more time talking to other people than he did to me. But after that unsettling period I came to understand that this was just Kevin's way. He was naturally nosy. He had to find out everything about everybody. That's where the connection with Joanie came in; the bitchy drag queen was a mine of useless information. No, that's not fair. I liked Joanie, but going to Delilah's, the scene in general, was like living in a goldfish bowl. Privacy just wasn't possible. Kevin and Joanie used to talk about what people were wearing and shite like that. One hilarious evening they both dragged up in identical dresses and wigs and called themselves the Hairy Marys. They spent the night telling dirty jokes and we laughed ourselves hoarse.

One time Marie and I were under a table looking for one of

Kevin's contact lenses. Joanie came over shouting 'Penny a skelp' and smacked our arses with one of his poofy platform shoes. We never did find the lens and Kevin ended up staggering around with one eye closed, saying he was getting double vision. It was after that he got these trendy Giorgio Armani specs. Everybody thought he looked great in them except me. But I'd tired of Kevin by then and he of me. I wanted someone I could be serious with and I still don't know what he wanted.

In Delilah's, Marie was more like me. She was into spectating. She wasn't what Kevin described as a 'personality', someone who was always drawing attention to themself. I'd always thought Marie was gay. One time I stood holding her coat and bag outside Club X for half an hour while she had her neck bitten by a Goth dyke who looked like Morticia from the Addams Family. I tended to judge Marie by the company she kept, which was fairly dykey. But Marie was bisexual. She apparently caught the virus from a guy she had been seeing, some guy from London called Richard. I knew she'd been going down there but I didn't know he was the major attraction. The Richard affair had been going on for years. Marie ended up moving to London and I never saw her again. She came up twice, but I missed her. I think that was the start of everything unravelling. Shortly after, Kevin dropped out. We heard that he was in love and Joanie talked of being maid of honour at his wedding. There had never been a queer wedding in Delilah's and Joanie was cruising for one. Joanie told us the whole romance and it seemed that Kevin had finally found a place for all that energy to go. Again, I felt jealous. It was a fleeting feeling; the feeling of being replaced. But then I felt happy for him. I'm happy for anybody who finds love.

I'd seen Sandy around on the scene for a few years. He was one of those faces that grow familiar if you're a regular. I used to go out on the scene all the time. Once, at a karaoke night, we got talking and then started something. Sandy and I never actually fucked, it just never happened. But we had some good fun together, and I felt comfortable in his arms. When he tested positive, I was the first person he told. He had the actual, full-blown thing. He told me he had suspected it for awhile but was too scared to test. I felt a bit paranoid about it. He told me first, and then his mother. 'Two people I love but haven't fucked,' he said, unsmiling. That night I sat in his living-room with my arms around him. It aroused so many emotions in me: fear, sadness, guilt, anger.

I had already watched Kevin die. A part of me wished the news had come too late and I'd have been spared seeing him, broken and almost unrecognisable. That's pure selfishness because he had wanted to see me. He held court from his hospital bed. I expected him to be funny and brave, but he was serious. More serious than I'd ever known him to be. Yet it wasn't a melancholy seriousness; it was just that I was so used to him being crazy and frivolous and full of fun. We sat and talked at his bedside. I never really said what I wanted to say, I was too scared of the feelings it might let out. Even at that desperate ending, I couldn't shake off my reserve.

Marie had a friend called Chris who still lived in Glasgow. She was an English Lit lecturer at one of the further education colleges. I didn't know Chris well. I'd only met her a couple of times in Delilah's. Marie had once pulled me up for not speaking to her women friends. 'Is it because they're not sexually relevant to you?' she mused over a cheap pint of Beck's one hazy happy hour in Delilah's. I'd replied with what I think is the truth – I'm no good at small talk and I hadn't spent enough time with her friends to get to know them. Besides, I don't think you should necessarily be friends with everybody your friends are friends with, if you get my drift.

It was Chris who told me about Marie. I had bumped into her one Saturday in Buchanan Street and she shook like a leaf and blurted out the news. We went for a coffee and sat crying across a wee round table. I noticed some people looking over, maybe thinking we were a couple breaking up or something. We sat talking about Marie. By the end of it, I felt Chris had described a completely different person from the Marie I knew. I wondered if Chris had been in love with her. We swapped phone numbers and said we'd keep in touch, but we haven't. We only had one connection, and that's a painful one. Her death didn't seem real, it was such a bolt from the blue. On the bus home I thought of Marie with the Goth dyke under the neon sign at Club X.

So Sandy phoned me. I hadn't seen Sandy for a while. I'd been living the life of a celibate hermit. The deaths of Kevin and Marie hadn't made me determined to go out and live life to the full. They had kind of deadened me. I'd phoned Sandy a few times, but he had sounded distant on the phone and said something about seeing someone else. Our thing had faded away into acquaintance, with Sandy half-joking that I was cramping his style. That was another wound inflicted, Sandy going.

I stayed in on Friday, after I'd heard about the bomb going off, digesting the news. I actually found myself in tears at one point. There was a sudden sense of vulnerability, of being in danger.

On Saturday I read about the bombing in the *Guardian*. There was a front-page report with photographs taken in the aftermath of the explosion. Men stood around in shock, their lacerated arms held in odd positions. You could see the doorway of the pub, smoke billowing over ripped cables, and on the floor a man crawling, looking like he was trying to escape the carnage.

That night I decided to go to Delilah's. I had thought about it all that day. I had thought about Kevin, leaning across the bar to do his double act with Joanie, and Marie, nursing her pint of cheap Beck's and taking me to task over something or other. I even thought about phoning Sandy, forgetting he too was gone. I thought about how the nail bombing campaign had linked those two obvious bedfellows, racism and homophobia.

I had a shower using a bar of aromatherapy soap. It was Neroli and I was getting pleasantly used to the smell. When I got dressed I drank a couple of cans of lager. The thought of going into a bar sober and alone has never appealed to me. I shoved on a dance anthems CD. It was trash but strangely uplifting. It went down nicely with the beer. It was nearly ten before I left the flat.

Delilah's looked the same. It had only just been painted the last time I was in and that sickly yellow was looking in need of a new coat. It was as smoky as ever, and through in the backroom the music was pumping. I bought a pint of lager at the bar and negotiated my way into a corner where I could put my glass on a wee ledge. It was a good vantage point. The clientele seemed younger but there was still a good range of ages and styles. Two old guys of about sixty stood along from me. One of them coughed and something clattered out of his mouth. He looked at the floor, mystified, while his pal laughed. I looked down at the manky floor and saw a denture, a pink gum plate with a false tooth, shiny with saliva, lying against the wall. I pointed it out to the guy, but I wasn't about to pick it up for him.

The mood seemed upbeat, although I heard a couple of young guys talking about the bombing at one of the booths. There were a couple of Asian guys in, standing at the entrance to the backroom. One of them seemed to be mouthing lyrics to the music. As I looked around I began to see a few familiar faces. Guys I used to fancy, a couple of whom I'd slept with, a friend of Marie's, and finally, surfacing at the bar with a huge honey blonde wig, Joanie. I tried to attract his attention but he couldn't see me from where I was standing. I decided to finish my drink then catch him at the bar.

At that point three had been reported dead and as much as seventy injured. Some had terrible wounds. I looked at the punters in Delilah's, here despite that carnage, determined, alive. I drank my pint quickly. I needed it. It had been a hot day. Then I went to get another drink. It was three deep and a big tall guy was using his superior height to muscle his way in. I waited, then when a couple of young queens in front of me moved slowly away from the bar, clutching what looked like a dozen bottles of alcopops, I stepped into the gap and put my hand out, wrapped around a fiver. Joanie came over and put his hand on mine. We smiled.

Normally I go straight to bed after a drinking session but that night I sat up and played some music low. I needed to think, and to remember. I thought of my friends and family and hoped they knew I loved them. I wasn't brought up to go round telling people I loved them. I thought of all the lies I'd told so people wouldn't know I was gay. These were wounds, too, these lies, these silences, avoidances.

I thought about the wounds, the endless wounds that ripped away at my right to live and love my life, the petty hate crimes that passed for decency or public opinion, the bombers with their stinking bibles, their poisonous bigotries, their smug prejudices.

I was nowhere near that bomb. But I felt the blast.

Rory's Kitchen Drawer

The kitchen drawer in Rory's flat was crammed with papers and objects, old bills, instruction leaflets, guarantees, receipts, and was jumbled up with buttons, pens, Sellotape, and tacks. There were even a few johnny bags (unused) amongst the mess. Don stood in front of the open drawer like a mesmerised child.

'Fart in a trance.'

Don turned to look at Terry, who was carefully packing books into cardboard boxes.

'We'll be here forever if you just stand there like a fart in a trance.'

Terry was a fussy queen, but Rory had appreciated his organising skills. When Rory, before he died, had asked Terry to take care of things, Terry had agreed immediately. Don was glad he hadn't been put on the spot. He knew that some people coped with grief by burying themselves in practicalities. He had watched his sister scrub their parents' house like a demented Stepford Wife for two days after their mother died. Terry was like that. His manner at the funeral had been so officious he had pissed everybody off.

Don had always been a broody kind of guy. Opening the drawer in Rory's lovely, bright, sunflower-yellow kitchen to see the little bits and pieces that bulged and dragged in a rough mass as he gave the drawer a final yank, he was just so sad. It was the very impersonality of it. He and Terry had already packed a box full of letters and photos, some they would destroy and some they would keep. That had been tragic, but strangely comforting. The anonymous flotsam and jetsam in the kitchen drawer were something else. The guarantees. There was one for a vacuum cleaner, an iron, a toaster, and a portable TV.

'Check this, Don.'

Terry held up a slim paperback.

'*Giovanni's Room*. James Baldwin. This was a wee present from me.'

He read from the flyleaf.

– To Rory. Lots of love and a happy thirtieth. May 1990. Terry. Kiss, Kiss.

Don was silent. Terry sat hunched over one of the boxes with the Baldwin in his hand. For a moment, Don thought he was crying. But then he saw Terry place the book carefully into a box and go onto the next shelf, steady and purposeful. He was one particular poof. Don hated shopping with Terry because he was so fussy about things. If he liked a shirt or a jacket or even a pair of underpants he couldn't just grab it, take it to the counter and crash the cash for it. He had to rake around until he found out exactly what it was made of, the washing instructions; he would even tug slyly at the seams to check the stitching. Once he had emerged from under a rail of shirts in Gap and declared emphatically 'I'd never wash that at forty degrees!'

Of course he had to try everything on. Don had hovered in countless shops whilst Terry preened himself in the changing rooms much to the chagrin of store security guards. One had even joked about setting off the fire alarm to get him out of a changing room. Terry was unrepentant.

'I know I'm a fussy cow, but I've yet to regret a purchase.'

Don put both hands in the drawer and rummaged about in an effort to appease Terry. He began to drop the obvious rubbish into a plastic carrier bag at his feet. He knew he should simply turn the drawer upside down into the bag and go back to the lounge to help Terry. He was stalling. It had all happened so fast.

Terry had got a call from Rory to say that he was ill and, as Terry had commented cryptically, 'wasn't going to get any better.' Rory seemed to go down pretty quickly. Terry had naturally become his confidant and executor.

Don had imagined Terry stationed constantly at Rory's sickbed, wearing a big black cloak and scribbling away with an old quill pen. But it was what was needed; someone to defuse the emotional time bomb (that was ticking louder with each passing day) with an increasingly tedious list of Practical Things That Needed To Be Done. Once, when Terry was discussing the need to put Rory's house on the market, Don had seen a solitary tear trickle down Terry's face. Terry had quickly brushed the tear away and said, 'Tasks now, tears later.'

Don had always fancied Rory. He had never particularly liked the man, too posh and pompous. But he was so effortlessly handsome. It was the lack of effort that rankled. It had been Rory's genetic destiny to be gorgeous and he played on it. Don had never fancied Terry. But Terry had been a loyal friend to Don. A pain in the arse, but loyal. You needed him, he was there. He didn't always say the right thing, he didn't always do the right thing, but he was there and he was on your side. Loyalty, Don felt, was a rare treasure he had seldom found with friends or lovers. Things changed too much, that was it. Friends became acquaintances became strangers. Lovers left, interminably they left. After one night or one year, they left. There was nothing wrong with changes, Don welcomed changes, but it was all so fucking transient. He looked down at the kitchen drawer and thought of Rory reduced to ashes and his flat like a shipwreck yielding up its contents.

'Finished!'

Terry stood with his hands on his hips and cocked his head, peering into the kitchen. Don emptied the drawer into the plastic bag.

'Me too.'

They drove home with the books and CDs and bric-à-brac they had retrieved from the flat. Terry was still intent on speaking strictly business.

'I'll go over tomorrow and gut the place. Bit of elbow grease. There's a couple coming to view it next Monday.'

Don was quiet.

That night Terry and Don went to Delilah's. They used to go there with Rory. There had been some kind of connection, some kind of inexplicable bond between Terry and Rory. Don tried to think what it was as he sat in a booth with Terry. There was a kind of emotional coldness about them. Coldness. That was too strong a word, too judgmental. They just didn't give much away. Terry had once confided in Don that a man had broken his heart when he was twenty and he'd never really got over it. Without trust, he said, you can't love.

Don checked out the crowd in Delilah's. It was Friday night, a young crowd. Skinny young guys who seemed ten times more confident than he'd ever been at their age. Or maybe he was just tired. He was tired of Terry. His caution, his brisk, no-nonsense, businesslike approach. Life's not tidy, Don wanted to tell him. It's a mess.

'When did we last laugh?'

Terry eyed him suspiciously and took a frugal sip of his rum and coke.

'My oldest pal just died. I don't get the joke.'

Don worked on his pint of lager. Terry drummed his fingers on the table and stared wistfully out of the window. It began to rain and the street outside shone blue. Across the road they could see the posters on the derelict building flap and peel.

From where Don sat he could clock Bob the Bouncer at the front door, through the glass of the interior door. Don fancied Bob. He was sexy in a caveman kind of way. He was a good-looking guy and the fact he was straight made him irresistible. Don wasn't so sure Bob was totally straight. He had once overheard Bob say to another bouncer friend something about it didn't matter, man or woman, as long as it had a hole.

'You staring at that Bob again? He'll lamp you one.'

'He can get me in a half nelson anytime.'

'You'd run a mile.'

Don looked at Terry. He looked tired and sexless and lost. Terry had said he was celibate. He'd had enough of it all. Don thought, maybe Terry had just got tired of looking. Don hadn't had it in six months. He hadn't honestly missed it that much. His last encounter had been pretty disastrous – a drunken young queen who had puked on his bathroom floor and snored like a giant. When he thought of Rory now, a beautiful big bear of a man who had withered and died so young, he didn't feel so horny.

'I'm going to powder my nose.'

Don watched Terry weave elegantly through the raucous

customers that crowded the main drag, and upstairs to the loo. He took the opportunity to eye up the talent away from Terry's punitive gaze. The younger set had been joined by some smart-suited office-types. They looked like shop-window dummies. A biker with hair down to his feeble excuse for an arse drank a whisky in one go and fled. Maybe he was in the wrong place. Maybe they all were. Joanie danced behind the bar, wearing a huge copper-coloured wig and chandeliers for earrings. Don remembered seeing Rory here. It was in Delilah's where he had first set eyes on Rory. He had said to Terry, Adonis Alert. That was what he'd always say if he spied a handsome man.

'That's my pal,' Terry had snapped, and snorted indignantly. Don had only recently started hanging around with Terry and harboured a forlorn hope that he'd get a boyfriend out of Terry's social circle. He had thought Rory had potential, but from their first conversation it was clear that there was only one man in Rory's life – Rory. Emptying Rory's kitchen drawer into a rubbish bag was as intimate as they had got. And that, decided Don, was curiously intimate.

Eventually Terry came back from the loo and sat brave and red-eyed in front of Don.

'That toilet's a bloody scandal. The dryer's broken, there's no paper towels, there's a bull dyke sniffing glue in one cubicle and a wank-off party in the other.'

Don leaned forward and brushed Terry's hair lightly with his fingers.

'You've been cryin'.'

Everybody was talking about Section 28. Some people were calling it Clause 28. One picky pansy was even calling it Section 2A.

'I don't care what it's called,' said Joanie, sorting his wig at the big cruising mirror behind the bar, 'it's homophobia, that's what it's called.'

It was a Saturday afternoon and it was almost impossible to have a decent conversation for the rabble of shoppers. Section 28 had been dominating the news for weeks. The Scottish Executive, that vanguard of queer liberation, had decided to repeal the Section, much to the horror of homophobes everywhere.

'I'm a teacher and I'm gay,' said Roger, a prim looking queen at the bar. 'Does that mean I'm illegal? My very existence is illegal? Because I like to think I'm a good teacher. And good teachers are going to have an influence on their pupils.'

Joanie was stocking the fridge with alcopops.

'You'll be okay as long as you stay in the closet. That's where they want us all.' He closed the fridge door. He never drank alcopops himself. He'd seen some of the younger queens get out of their pretty little faces on them and even had to order a few of the rowdies out of the pub, they'd got so wrecked. He turned to join in the conversation again. Roger was giving his famous faggots of history speech that ran from Alexander the Great to Jimmy Somerville. 'We've given so much to them,' he opined. 'Yet look what we get in return. Abuse and ridicule.'

Joanie nodded thoughtfully. A big, gangly, intense queen leaned forward on the bar.

'It's been open season on queers for years,' he said. 'First we were the gay plague. Now we're coming to get your children. Talk about social exclusion. We're living in a fuckin' dictatorship!' He banged a bony fist on the bar at the last point, rattling the empty glasses.

Joanie had seen the posters on the billboards around town.

Photographs of 'concerned parents' and some crap or other about what their children were being taught in schools. There was a 'Keep The Clause' campaign and it was in your face.

'What goes on in ma bed is ma fuckin' business,' said Joanie.

The intense queen shook his head. 'That's a red herring, the whole sex thing. It's the social fact of homosexuality they hate. That's why the clause talks about forbidding local authorities from 'promoting' homosexuality and presenting gay relationships as pretend family relationships. They just want to think of us as fucking in the bushes. That's what turns them on. They don't want to accept that we're just as normal and boring and fucked up as they are.' The bony fist banged on the bar.

The intense queen and the teacher began a big discussion about whether discretion was the better part of valour, or whether loud and proud was the only way to play it. The teacher said he had to keep firmly in the closet. 'I don't want to be lynched and lose my livelihood.' The intense queen gave him a look somewhere between pity and scorn. 'That's how the Nazis got away with it,' he said. 'When they come for me I'm going to make sure I'm kicking and screaming.' Joanie didn't doubt it; he was waiting for the fist to come down on the bar again.

It was just after two and Bobbie came in with an old pal and some new clothes she'd bought.

'Was that you shopliftin' in Buchanan Galleries again?' quipped Joanie.

'The only things I steal are women's hearts,' retorted Bobbie.

Bobbie ordered drinks for herself and her pal. She overheard the guys at the bar talking about Clause 28, and the referendum against the repeal of the Clause. Joanie said he'd received his form but hadn't done anything with it. He thought the whole thing was bogus and he didn't feel he should even grace it with a response.

The intense queen said there was going to be a ritual burning of the ballot papers by 'gay activists and democrats' and invited Joanie to come along. Bobbie said she'd shat in a shoebox and posted it to the Freepost address. Her pal guffawed at that and they went off to a booth.

The pub was getting busier with the Saturday afternoon set, brunchers and browsers. There were faces Joanie saw on a Saturday afternoon that he never saw any other time.

'I hope none of you travelled into town on one of *those* buses,' said the intense queen to a group of pals who had bunched up at the bar. A wee guy with sticky-up hair and a nose ring replied.

'I'd sooner ride my own mother than one of those buses,' he rasped. 'I'm not going to be dictated to by tabloids and millionaires.' The intense queen nodded his approval. Before long the wee guy's pals had disappeared as he and the intense queen put the world to rights.

Roger, the teacher, chatted to Joanie as he gathered his shopping things. 'I'm all for gay liberation,' Roger said, 'but I'd be out of a job if I went public.'

Joanie smiled reassuringly at him. 'We all do what we can,' he said. Roger attempted a smile and left. Joanie continued serving what was now a steady stream of customers.

Papa had come in about three o'clock but only stayed for one drink. He was meant to be going for dinner and then to the theatre with Mama, but Mama's bleeper had gone off as they were having coffee in the Italian Centre and she'd been called away to a different kind of theatre.

'What d'you think of this "Keep The Clause" campaign?' Joanie said. Papa said he believed in equality before the law, then asked Joanie if he'd like to go to the theatre with him but Joanie couldn't get the time off.

'We just can't get the staff these days,' he moaned.

Papa left alone, despite the attentions of a young guy with some very old chat-up lines. Joanie checked out the two gay liberationists at the bar, who were now busy trashing the Catholic Church.

'The Pope's not too old to come over my knee,' he heard the wee guy say, deadpan. 'I mean I was raised a Catholic and it makes me fuckin' sick tae hear them.' He went into a big rant about the terrors of organised religion. 'A johnny bag is not the Antichrist!' he yelled.

'Absolutely,' said the intense one, banging his fist on the bar.

As the afternoon wore on into the early evening, punters joined the debate, putting in their penny's worth. A trendy young guy who said he was an art student asked Joanie if he would like to model for him – he wanted to do his own posters. Things like 'I'm a grandmother. They take it up the bum, you know,' and 'Gay used to mean happy. Now it means blowing a boner in Kelvingrove Park.' Joanie said he'd be happy to oblige. He even came up with some ideas of his own. He offered to drag up as 'Sandra Bollock' and hi-jack a bus.

'I want to be Keanu,' insisted the art student.

'You keanu if you weantu,' retorted Joanie.

Joanie had to do a split shift that day due to another no-show from one of the skinny malinky boys that the clueless senior management kept imposing on him. He had a snack in the wee café across at the next block as he couldn't be arsed going home and back into town. When he arrived at Delilah's for the seven-to-twelve shift, Joanie was surprised to see the two liberationists still in the pub.

The intense queen said they'd been for a Chinese meal and decided to return to Delilah's to continue their plot to overthrow the wicked kingdom of Homophobia. The wee guy was full of ideas, each one more fanciful than the last. Joanie thought there was something quite cute about the two of them and wondered if their poofy politicking was only about changing the world or whether it was really an advanced form of foreplay for the brainier bentshot.

Somehow Joanie got through another night in Delilah's, but it was not without its dramas. At one point a group of studenty types got a bit out of hand, shouting orders at Joanie like he was their slave and putting their dirty hands up his dress. Joanie told them he wouldn't mind so much if they weren't so fucking hackett. So then they started singing Bitchy Queen to the tune of *Billie Jean*. Joanie was glad when Bobbie came in and bawled them out, although she ended up being called a flat nose for her trouble.

'Why don't ye chuck them out?' Bobbie asked him at the bar.

'If I had tae throw everybody out that gave me a bit ay lip,' replied Joanie, 'I'd have tae buy myself a mouth organ and a whiskery old dog for company. Because this place would be empty.'

Bobbie sympathised. 'You've been on yer feet all day,' she said soothingly. 'Are you the only person that does any work here?'

Joanie said he'd tried speaking to the management. 'It's no good,' he complained. 'They keep hiring daft wee boys with faces like pop stars and arses like peaches who don't know Guinness from gonorrhoea.'

He remembered few things after that. One was trying to unblock an upstairs lavvie with a plunger, a mop, lots of thumps on the flush button and enough salty language to stop a sailor in his tracks. When he finally got back to the bar and faced the ensuing riot, he told them somebody had better phone the Navy as he thought they'd lost a submarine. Another thing he remembered was pleading with Bob the bouncer not to beat up a boy who kept putting his sweaty hand down the back of Bob's trousers. It was one of those nights when everybody was feeling everybody else up.

Joanie said that Delilah's could give Sodom and Gomorrah a run for their money, but somehow or other he got through another crazy Saturday night. The reason he could only remember parts of it was because he ended up in a lock-in with Bobbie and the liberationists.

The three punters were already pissed and they lost no time in getting Joanie in the same condition. The wee guy had more crackpot ideas than you could shake a prick at. He said he was going to start a 'Keep The Claws' campaign. It would urge gay men everywhere to grow their fingernails for the cause of gay liberation. 'So we can scratch homophobes' eyes out,' he shrieked. The intense queen was drunk enough to laugh now, but it was a scary mad laugh which, coupled with his fist banging on the table, was kind of unnerving. Bobbie was in fine form, saying she was going to chain herself to the railings of the Scottish Parliament wearing nothing but her Doc Martens.

'If that doesnae frighten the shite oota them, nothing will,' said Joanie.

The wee guy said he was going to change his name by deed poll to Guy Fucks and dedicate his life to face powder, treason and plot.

At one point the four of them were dancing on the tables to some old Kylie songs. The intense queen even got into a heated debate about who was the most magnificent Minogue, Kylie or Danni. It was all drunken madness and rage and joy and then Joanie felt the place start to spin. The four of them agreed to share a taxi although they lived at opposite ends of the city. The last thing Joanie remembered was singing *Glad To Be Gay* in the hackney cab and endlessly falling off the fold-down seat and endlessly being helped back onto it by the other three.

Joanie finally got up out of bed at two thirty on Sunday afternoon. Later, after a bath and some vomiting over the lavvy pan, he retired to the couch with a cup of strong hot tea and the ballot paper he'd found amongst all the rest of the shitty junk mail that seemed to come through his door like an avalanche. Joanie looked at the ballot form. He wondered if he had a shoebox handy.

And I Love You So

Greg sat at the bar with his bottle of Bud. It was a shite place to sit. You had to keep craning your neck to see anything. That wasn't strictly true – there was a large mirror behind the bar. But looking at that meant you saw not only what was going on behind you but also your own flushed, lonely and terrified face. It was shite, but he was too scared to move, plus the pub had got a lot busier now so there wasn't much room to move anywhere.

He wasn't the only barfly. There was a row of them seated right along the length of the bar. Everybody trying to get served had to lean over them or squeeze in between them. Greg drank his Bud and hoped somebody would talk to him. Somebody nice. Not the scary guy at the far end of the bar that was giving him heavy eyeball. Greg pretended he didn't know him. He did know him. The guy had chatted him up in Club X once. Greg had sucked his cock in a cubicle. He'd fled after that, hoping he'd never see that cock or its owner again. He'd just ignore him. He looked in the mirror, avoiding his own dial but watching the clientele swell and ebb behind him. At one point someone was feeling his arse but when he looked in the mirror to see who it was they were gone. The phantom feeler.

The night wore on and the beer kicked in and Greg could see himself upstairs in the bog on his knees sucking creepy cock. It was then he was rescued.

'Mind if I sit here, son?'

It was the voice of a big man in his early forties. Greg shook his head and the man sat on the stool beside him. He was nice looking. He looked really out of date, more like a matinée idol from a 1950s B-movie. Very handsome. Very square. He offered to buy Greg a drink. Greg plumped for another Bud. The man ordered a Coke for himself. The big smoothie. He got talking to Greg. He said his name was Jim. Greg thought he looked like a Jim. Homely and handsome. He seemed to move closer to Greg as he spoke until Greg thought he was going to fall into his lap. He had light blue eyes. Sad eyes.

They were driving back to Jim's place. Greg was game for it but he didn't realise Jim lived in deepest Stirlingshire. He said it was a half-hour drive. Greg began to regret saying he'd go with him. Not because he wasn't attracted to him, it was the distance they had to go. The roads were quiet. It was late. Jim seemed to be a capable and competent driver. He spoke of his life as he drove. Now and again he would give Greg's thigh a squeeze with his big left hand. It was proprietorial. Greg thought of them naked, doing it.

Jim told of a live-in love affair he'd had with some guy. They had met in one of the gay bars in Edinburgh. They had only known each other for a few weeks when the guy moved in with Jim. It was the guy's idea. To Greg he sounded like a bit of a chancer. The guy put Jim down in front of his friends. He'd take his money. He was a real fucking leech. Jim could see that now but at the time he was too in love. The guy was good looking and was good company, but he had a nasty streak and Jim thought he could change that. He had showered the guy with love and affection. Jim tolerated the put-downs, the missing money, and the tantrums. He wasn't alone anymore. He had somebody to love.

Then one day he came home to find a note on the kitchen table. The guy had fucked off, with a lot of Jim's stuff. Jim was devastated. He went round a couple of places where he thought the guy might be staying. One of his pals said he'd gone to England. Another wouldn't answer the door and told Jim to fuck off through the letterbox. Jim had broken his heart over the guy. He had to take sick leave. He lost weight. Eventually, he said, he'd got over it. Greg thought it didn't sound like it. Jim's voice had started breaking a few times during the story.

Jim was quiet for a while. It gave him time to collect his thoughts and for Greg to digest the story. Then he started reassuring Greg that it wouldn't be too long now until they got to his place. They were passing through countryside. Greg noticed a big wide, open field to the left of them. This was where Jim would bury him, he thought. He turned and looked at Jim, who had his eyes on the road. It would be okay.

After an eternity they finally reached Jim's house. They went inside and Jim gave Greg a can of beer out of the fridge. He fluttered about switching lamps on and off and fidgeting with his CD player. He was trying to get the ambience right. He tentatively reached for a Shirley Bassey CD. Greg nodded. A whirl with Shirl was cool by him. His host sat beside him and commandeered his thigh again, his big hand moving slowly along it and back again. He told Greg a story about his father.

It seemed that Jim's father was waging some kind of vendetta against him because of his sexuality. Jim had told him he was gay years ago. His father had immediately disowned him with that no-son-of-mine shite. At first it had been a case of the silent treatment whenever he went over to his parents'. His da would sit there gazing straight through him. Things had got worse after his mother died. He'd tried to mend things, but his da was having none of it. He didn't want an olive branch; he wanted a big stick with a nail in it.

His da had done all sorts of crazy things. He'd make abusive calls in the night or ring and put down the phone when Jim answered. He'd sent a couple of sick letters. He'd slashed the tyres on Jim's car and scratched the paintwork with a penknife. Jim hadn't got the police. After all, it was a family thing. Jim said he loved his da and hoped he'd make it up with him. They'd got on well before he found out Jim was gay.

These were his two stories. The thing about the lover who'd trashed him and the thing about his homophobic da. Jim looked at Greg with his sad eyes and moved his hand onto his crotch. Greg put a hand up to Jim's sweet face, then ran his fingers through Jim's hair. It felt funny. The hair began to slip. Jim took Greg's hand gently away.

'I wear a hairpiece. I'm sorry.'

'It's okay.'

'You don't mind?'

'Naw. It's fine.'

Before Greg had time to say anything else Jim was kissing him. Shirley Bassey was singing *And I Love You So,* and they went to Jim's bedroom.

In the morning, Greg felt too tired to move. He looked at the clock. It was 7am. He turned and looked at Jim, who lay with his back to him. Jim's wig had shifted to one side but it was still attached to his head. There was a tantalising glimpse of a bald patch underneath. Greg went back to sleep.

He woke to the sound of Shirley. *And I Love You So* again. Jim came into the room and asked him if he wanted tea and toast. He was in the nude. Greg said he'd like tea and toast, aye, that would be nice. Jim flapped his balls and cock with his right hand. Not in an overtly sexual way, but as if to say check the packet, would you like some more? Greg watched Jim's bare arse disappear down the hall. He was going to do a naked number on him. Greg didn't really like nudity per se. It was fine in bed but all this walking around naked was a bit embarrassing. It was even worse when Jim returned bearing a tray with the tea and toast, still in the buff.

'Put somethin' on.' Greg couldn't help himself.

'I'm comin' back intae bed.'

Jim carefully put down the tray on the bedside cabinet and climbed into bed next to Greg. They both took some toast off the tray.

'There'll be crumbs everywhere.'

'Fuck it.'

Greg bit into his toast. Then Jim moved in on him. He took Greg's hand away from the toast and began eating at the toast that was hanging out of Greg's mouth. Greg remembered that scene in *Lady and The Tramp* where they were eating the same spaghetti, two dogs or whatever. Jim munched at the toast, shoving his face into Greg's and kissing his toast-filled mouth with extraordinary passion. There's a name for this, thought Greg. Autoerotic asphyxiation. He struggled free, choking.

They were dressed and sitting in the kitchen. Greg was drinking a glass of water. He'd just told Jim he didn't want to see him again.

He'd lied and said he was still involved with someone; he didn't want to fuck him about. He just didn't want to see him again. There were a few reasons but he didn't want to tell Jim them. There was the wig thing, the toast thing, the exhibitionism, the age gap, the fact that he lived fuck knows where. Jim had crumpled with disappointment. He sat at the table, across from Greg. He wrote his name and phone number down on a piece of paper. He shoved the piece of paper across the table towards Greg. He looked at Greg with his big, sad, nobody-loves-me eyes.

'If you know anybody you think'll like me, give them ma number.'

Jim gave him a lift to the local bus station. The atmosphere was frosty during the short drive and Greg was glad to get out of the car and away from him.

A couple of months later Greg saw Jim in Delilah's again. They pretended not to know each other. Jim looked even more handsome than he did before. He wasn't wearing his wig. Greg hoped he'd told his da to fuck off. He wished he'd phoned Jim now. But that was because of the drink, and being at the bar again, in Delilah's again, on his own again.

The Threesome Real

Colin wasn't actually picked up by the guy in Delilah's, but he'd seen him there. Amongst all the familiar faces, his was the unfamiliar one. He was skinny and looked a bit evil. He kept looking at Colin; kept grinning at him. Colin even moved a couple of times but he kept showing up. Colin thought the best times to change your position were when you were going to the bar for another drink or when you went for a piss. You just went back and stood or sat somewhere else. You didn't have to sidle along like a bashful crab to avoid somebody. Go for a pee or a pint and you've made your escape. Colin preferred standing because he was short. When he sat down he couldn't see much at all. Standing, he was in with a shout. Delilah's was busy that night. It was a Sunday and a karaoke night. It was heaving through in the backroom but Colin steered clear of that. Why couldn't they play some decent music? Karaoke was crap. The shite singers were embarrassing and the good ones were usually ugly show-offs. He'd once said to Joanie at the bar why didn't they pack in the karaoke for a while? Joanie had shrugged.

'It gets the punters in.'

When Colin came back from the toilet he felt his legs weren't working. He hated that, when drunkenness had affected your body but your head was all too aware. He tried to walk straight. He managed to get back to where he'd left his pint just in time to see a barman swipe it. He'd had enough. He made for the door.

'Heah.'

It was a man's voice. Colin had the uneasy feeling he was talking to him. He kept on walking. The man caught up with him. It was the skinny man from Delilah's. He was walking beside Colin now.

'I saw you in Del's.'

'I saw you.'

'On yer tod?'

'Aye.'

'Same here. I'll get ye up the road.'

'I'm okay.'

The skinny guy was looking at Colin with that smile of his.

'D'ye fancy comin' back? I stay just aff the Vicky Road.'

Colin couldn't help smiling.

'See. Yer smilin'.'

The next thing, the guy had hailed a taxi and was ushering Colin into it. Colin looked at his face. He wasn't bad looking. It would be okay. As long as he got up early. He had work in the morning; he worked in an accounts office. They were talking about sending him to college day-release to get a qualification.

He followed the guy up the close. One of the stairhead lights was broken. It was dingy. There was a smell of cat piss. The skinny guy fumbled with his keys and Colin saw he was even more drunk than he was. Eventually he got the right keys in the right locks and they were in. It was a tiny flat, really a bedsit. There was a hall with a bathroom, but just one big room that seemed to be a bedroom, living-room and kitchen in one. Colin sat in an armchair and the guy fixed them drinks. He said it was whisky but it smelled strange and tasted funny. By this time Colin felt he was sobering up a little. He was glad of another drink, any drink. So he drank it. He didn't like the flat. It was claustrophobic. He felt as if he'd been locked in a cupboard. The skinny guy was sitting on a chair facing him. He was smiling his smile. He stared at Colin.

'Somethin' happened to you. When you were young. Somethin' bad. I can tell.'

Colin shook his head.

'You don't know me.'

They drank their drinks. The guy went up to the window and drew back one of the curtains. He looked out for a while. Then he came back and sat in the chair. He left the curtain open.

'A pal of mine might be comin' up. For a wee while.'

'That's okay.'

The skinny guy looked indignant.

'Of course it's okay. It's ma fuckin' hoose.'

Colin didn't like his tone but it was late and he was drunk and he'd just have to make the best of it. He hoped they'd go to bed soon and get it over with. It could only have been a couple of minutes later that the doorbell went. It was the pal. The pal was a big man. He looked dirty. He wore an old anorak and had two manky dogs with him. The dogs were wild and chased each other round the room, occasionally stopping to jump up on Colin and lick at him with their big slabbery tongues. Eventually the big guy laid into the dogs with a leather leash. They whimpered and cowered in a corner. The big guy poured himself a drink and glanced briefly at the skinny guy. They went into the hall. Colin could hear them talking quietly but couldn't make out what they were saying. The dogs looked at Colin from the corner of the room. They had stopped whimpering. They looked as if they were using all their strength to keep quiet.

The skinny guy came back in with a proposition. A threesome. Colin shook his head. He said he didn't go in for that. In fact, he didn't have any major moral objections to a threesome, but the thought of that dirty big bastard near him made him want to throw up. He tried not to show his revulsion. If he hadn't been so drunk he'd have run. He stayed. His host was clearly annoyed at the rejection of his unique hospitality; he muttered and went back into the hall to break the news to his pal. Colin went to the sideboard and poured himself another drink. They'd be asking if the dogs could fuck him next.

Both guys came in but said nothing. The big man put the dogs back on their leashes and shoved on his scabby anorak. He gave Colin a sly look. The guys went out again. Colin heard the front door close and his host came back in. He sat opposite Colin and lit a cigarette. He appeared calmer now. He spoke to Colin.

He said that he'd had a troubled childhood. There had been family problems. Things had happened. Things he didn't want to talk about. He had been in care from when he was twelve until he was sixteen. He'd been a bit of a delinquent, he said, but he'd got himself sorted out since then. This was his own place. He knew it wasn't much but it was all he could afford. He had two jobs – he needed them to pay his mortgage. He worked as a hospital porter and as a barman. He smoked, and blew the smoke in clouds above his head. Even then, all Colin could smell were those dogs.

They went to bed. They didn't have to go anywhere to reach it – the bed was in a corner. They both sat on the bed as they undressed. The guy pulled down Colin's pants and looked inquisitively at his cock. It was as if he was measuring it up, and made a dismissive grunt. They climbed into the bed, which smelled of old cheese. They put their arms around each other and began to kiss. It was going to be okay. The guy then started poking and prodding at Colin with his hard-on, bouncing it off his thighs and between his legs. Then he said he was too drunk and turned his back on Colin.

It was good it was over. Colin hoped he'd wake first in the morning. He would go home and wash the stink off him and get into work. He knew he was going to have one hell of a hangover. All he could think about was getting home and washed and forgetting the whole thing had ever happened. He looked at the light spilling across the bed from the street. The curtain was still open. He looked at his pillow. There was a big stain on the pillow, like a tea-stain. He could smell rising damp. Looking up, he noticed the ceiling was stained too.

Later he woke and his face was in the pillow. It was still dark. He felt fingernails digging into him. His body was being moved, shifted in the bed. He wasn't sure if he was dreaming at first. Then he could hear voices. The big man held him down while the skinny one fucked him. Then they swapped places.

He never told anybody.

Yerma's Yearning

Eventually Maureen gave in. Karen had been going around like Yerma for months. Like Lorca's Yerma, she seemed capable of anything. She was desperate to have a child. Maureen felt if she didn't go along with this then the relationship would have ended, and she didn't want that.

Karen had been broody for ages. A colleague of hers at work had recently had a child. In fact it appeared to Maureen that Karen had gone through a kind of hysterical pregnancy alongside her colleague's bona fide one. There was nothing about this woman's pregnancy Karen did not know. One day she got off the phone and came running into the kitchen screaming, 'Her waters have broken'.

'Why don't you just fuck off with a man?' Maureen had barked at her.

Motherhood wasn't something Maureen had contemplated for very long. Once, when she was a student, she had convinced herself she was pregnant, wept into her pillow, and then spent a long dark night of the soul reconciling herself to a few years pushing a pram while her contemporaries got first class honours degrees. But it had been a false alarm. For one thing, it would have been an immaculate conception. After the initial panic, she was clear in her mind that penetration had not taken place. She had gone to bed with a PhD student called Philip, after a drunken night in the Student Union. They had been naked and rolled around Philip's bed. But there was no penetration. Years later Maureen had heard that Philip was living in North London with a bus driver. A male bus driver.

Delirium after a bogus bonk was the nearest Maureen had got to pregnancy. However, she had gone on to have sex with men. She had always had safe sex and some of it had been almost pleasant. Maureen looked back on it as her 'straight phase.' She knew a woman who swore by the necessity for a 'straight phase.' This woman said it was a kind of rite of passage for a lesbian. She said it had two distinct advantages – (1) it meant you could be absolutely sure you were a lesbian and (2) nobody could say that you were a lesbian because you were too ugly to get a man. Maureen thought that was a load of shite. Her 'straight phase' had been dictated by peer pressure, pure and simple.

Maureen and Karen knew several lesbian mothers, all of whom had been in relationships with men when their children were conceived. That was one thing, thought Maureen. But to coldly calculate having a child whilst being a lesbian was something else.

'You make it sound like a crime.'

Karen sat in an armchair with her hands under her sweatshirt, in fists at her belly, as if she were physically trying to look pregnant.

'It's just so calculating,' said Maureen.

'It's not calculating. It's considered. I've thought this through really carefully and I want us to have a child.'

Maureen dug her nails into the cushion beside her.

'Us?'

'We're a couple aren't we? Couples do things together.'

Maureen shook her head in exasperation. Karen leaned forward, pulling the belly of her sweatshirt out a little more, and gave Maureen a reassuring smile.

'Do you feel inadequate because you can't inseminate me?' she asked softly.

'Karen,' said Maureen, 'I don't want to inseminate you. Strangle you, yes. Inseminate you, no.'

As was usually the case, a long silence followed this exchange, Karen pulling her feet up onto the armchair and assuming the foetal position.

Karen's yearning for a child was no mere voice in the wilderness. She had sounded out a friend of theirs, Jack, a gay man who wanted to be a daddy as much as she wanted to be a mammy. The two couples, Maureen and Karen, and Jack and his partner Fred met in Delilah's to discuss it.

'They're not mutually exclusive,' said Karen decisively. She looked pleadingly at Jack for back up, as she did the whole evening.

'What aren't?' Maureen wasn't going to make it easy.

'Lesbianism and motherhood.'

'And the world is round,' retorted Maureen.

'I don't see why I should have to sit here and justify a basic natural instinct.'

Jack looked at Maureen, sympathetically.

'She's made up her mind.'

Maureen leaned across the table, her lit cigarette inching towards Jack's eye.

'She's made up her mind. But who's goin' to change the nappy and collect the kid from school?'

Fred intervened.

'This baby's going to have four parents, Maureen. I think, between the four of us we can manage to raise a child.'

'Don't patronise me.'

She settled back in her seat and stubbed her cigarette out in the small pink ashtray.

'Don't all look at me as if I'm Herod or something. I just think there are practical things we need to talk about here.'

'Such as?' asked Karen.

'Where will it live, who'll look after it, how much will it cost?'

Jack drank from his bottle of beer. Fred sipped at his mineral water. They looked at Karen.

'We'll work these things out. I'm not the first woman to have a baby, y'know.'

'You're Miss Obvious tonight.'

Jack attempted to smooth things over.

'What we need to do is clear the air. None of us are getting any younger. Karen wants a child. She really, really wants a child. And it's something I've been thinking about a lot, haven't I, Fred?'

Fred nodded gravely.

'Karen and I want to try for a baby. We'll be the mum and dad. We'll share the care. But we hope our partners will stand by us and help and support us.'

Maureen tried to take the edge out of her voice.

'When are you starting to try?'

Karen looked pleadingly at Jack, who said nothing. She looked shyly at Maureen.

'We've been for tests.'

'Tests?'

'Y'know. Like HIV.'

'Oh that old thing!' said Maureen sarcastically. 'Really, Karen, you're a queen of the understatement.'

Karen again fixed her eyes on Jack, looking like a bewildered puppy. Jack accepted the challenge.

'We're going to try the natural way.'

'Am I fuckin' hearing things?'

'We didn't want all that hassle with test tubes and syringes and all that.'

Maureen turned her attention to Fred.

'Fred, are you into this?'

Fred shrugged and then nodded.

'I just want Jack to be happy.'

'That's very self-sacrificing of you,' said Maureen. There was a short pause in the proceedings. Fred went to the bar to get another round of drinks in. When he came back, Maureen spoke again.

'I'm not trying to be a spanner in the works or anything. I just want you to have thought this through. It's such a big fuckin' step. The repercussions are enormous.'

Karen put her hand on Maureen's arm.

'We have. We've thought it through.'

Maureen took a swig of her Tia Maria and Coke and then looked over at Fred.

'So Fred,' she asked, trying to sound jovial but only sounding like a bitter old lemon, 'how do you feel about your boyfriend shagging my girlfriend?'

Soon after this initial meeting efforts at procreation began. The attempts were made in the spare bedroom of Jack and Fred's house. Jack had made sure everything in the room was fresh. He bought a lamp from Habitat that gave off a soft, gentle 40 watt

light. Karen had been christened Miss Ovulation by Maureen. She
was as prepared as prepared could be. But on the first evening of
passion everything seemed to go embarrassingly wrong. At one
point Karen thought she'd have to kill Jack to make his cock go stiff.
When he finally got a hard-on it was a long time coming. As for
Karen, she giggled and farted and even screamed with laughter at
a feeble attempt at foreplay before becoming very quiet and still
once Jack finally got to work. She was so stiff and immobile that if
it hadn't been for her laboured breaths Jack guessed that this must
be what necrophilia felt like.

In the afterglow, Karen turned away from Jack and lay rigidly at
the far end of the bed. Jack's face was burning with a mixture of
embarrassment and exertion. They both hoped she was now
pregnant. She wasn't.

Maureen's behaviour throughout the long haul towards that
golden moment was reprehensible. She swore, she sulked, she
went for days without speaking to Karen. But Karen and Jack were
unstoppable.

'Do you think it's easy for us?' Karen asked Maureen, sharply.
Maureen gave her the silent treatment. Karen sat down beside her
on the sofa.

'It's pretty arduous. I think it's putting a strain on all our
relationships. But it'll be worth it, Maureen. In the end, it'll be
worth it.'

Lovers fight, and Jack and Karen were no exception. They tried
to adopt a cool, professional approach to their sex sessions but this
proved increasingly difficult. There were times when Jack couldn't
quite 'cut the mustard' as Karen put it. Jack blushed at the use of
the Americanism. He suggested he take Karen from behind.

'Okay dokay,' said Karen. 'That way you can pretend I'm a guy
and I can pretend you're a dildo.' They both giggled at that; a rare,
light moment punctuating the sweaty tension that dominated
their procreative proceedings. Jack had no problem cutting the
mustard this particular evening. In fact he closed his eyes and felt
every thrust take him closer to heaven. He groaned with pleasure,
to the quiet fury of Karen. What made her furious was the

knowledge that she was about to come and could do nothing to stop herself. She trembled and gasped and finally said, 'God,' as they came together.

Later, Karen sat on the edge of the bed in a dressinggown of Jack's which she had adopted. She spoke in a wounded whisper, as if she had been winded by remorse. She said she felt ashamed and compromised.

'You came,' said Jack, coldly.

'So did you,' whispered Karen.

'That's the whole fucking point,' said Jack.

Karen said then that perhaps this supposedly natural method of conception hadn't been such a good idea after all. She said she knew of a woman who provided free fertility treatment no questions asked. It was artificial insemination. There might be risks but at least they wouldn't have to keep going through these gruelling episodes. Jack didn't respond to this. They sat despondently on either side of the bed. They both felt terrible. It had been such a great fuck.

Whilst Maureen grew more difficult and distant, Fred was a mountain of strength. He behaved like a meticulous madam, ushering her favourite lady of the night to a rich and generous houseguest. Yet he was never intrusive. He respected the privacy of the mare and her stallion, closing the stable door and bolting into the lounge where he listened to Sondheim and sipped malt whisky. Karen and Jack grew closer to him, praising his tact and his tenderness. Secretly, Fred wanted more than anything to watch them at it. In any respect, his sex life with Jack had improved immeasurably.

'Don't be such a cold fish,' urged Karen, attempting once more to put her arm around Maureen's naked form in bed. Maureen shrugged her off and sat up, holding the bedclothes protectively against her.

'The audacity of you,' she hissed. 'You come in here – smelling of cock – and start groping me. Are you surprised I'm revolted?'

Karen burst out laughing, it was either that or cry.

'How long is this going to go on?' pleaded Maureen. Karen shrugged.

'I honestly don't know. It's one of Nature's great mysteries.'

'Well, I wouldn't know anything about Nature,' said Maureen, 'being a pervert. Being a lesbian, which if I can remind you Karen, is what you used to be till you started shagging a man.'

Karen took a hold of one of Maureen's hands.

'I love you, Maureen. Please bear with me on this. It's important to me.'

Maureen looked impassively at Karen, her hand going limp. The whole thing was impossible.

Jack and Karen deliberated about other options before resuming business as usual. Karen decided there was no harm in trying to be tender and affectionate with each other. She reasoned that it would make the sex easier and more productive. She had read in a trashy magazine in a dentist's waiting room that the mood you were in when you conceived a child affected the temperament of the child. So if you were nervous or angry the child would be nervous or angry. But if you were relaxed and loving then the child would be the sweetest baby born and would become a well-balanced adult.

She began to think pleasant thoughts while they were doing it. She thought of sunlight flashing on a beautiful blue sea. She thought of Maureen's lips brushing the fuzz of her fanny. She thought of Kim Basinger in *LA Confidential*. She thought 'I am happy' and 'Life is wonderful.'

'It's okay for us to enjoy it,' she reassured Jack.

'But we're gay,' he replied, anxiously.

'Of course we are,' said Karen. 'But we're friends – working together to achieve something. Something that will bring us so much happiness.'

She put her arms around Jack and beamed, 'We're making a baby.'

Karen began going into baby stores and checking out the clothes and toys. She even bought some things and took them home, sheepishly, furtively. She thought of hiding them from Maureen, then decided to be open about her purchases. Maureen found the blue romper suits and blue vests and socks.

'Now that's what I call forward planning,' she commented cattily, holding up the offending articles.

'No harm in forward planning,' sighed Karen.

'What if it's a girl?'

'Then it's a girl.'

'But these are boy's things. They're blue.'

Karen looked resignedly at Maureen.

'Since when have you thought gender should be colour-coded? You ought to know better, Maureen.'

Maureen threw the baby clothes in her face.

'It's like living with a big baby already, the way she carries on.' Karen rested her head on Jack's big hairy chest. Her fingers gently stroked one of his nipples. It was pierced and Karen traced the silver ring with her forefinger.

'It's been hard work,' said Jack, softly. He held some of her rich, auburn hair in his fingers.

'I think it's going to happen soon,' Karen said dreamily. Later, when Karen had gone and Jack was in the bath, Fred came into the room and closed the door behind him. He smothered his face in the rumpled sheets, his heart thumping.

The day Karen learned she was pregnant her heart was filled with conflicting emotions. She was jubilant, but also scared. She suddenly felt incredibly vulnerable, as if someone so much as brushing against her would knock her over. Then she felt an incredible strength, as if she were now invincible, immortal. She wanted to work through these feelings privately before telling anyone. A day's grace would help her regain her composure. Then she would tell them. She would tell Maureen first, then Jack, who would tell Fred.

It was a long day with the lonely secret of life in her. At the end of it, she lay in bed and thought of how she felt grown-up, on the edge of something momentous, something astonishing. She slept peacefully. But Maureen was restless. She knew that Karen was pregnant now. There had been a look in her eyes that night she had never seen before. When Karen had sat with her hands in her lap and looked with a flicker of a smile at her, Maureen had thought of the Mona Lisa, the Virgin Mary.

In the living-room, Maureen cradled a cup of camomile tea, now that it had cooled enough to drink. She sipped at the tea and set it down on the table in front of her. She didn't feel angry with Karen. She knew now why she had been such a bastard about all this. It wasn't the baby. She didn't really mind children and thought that maybe sometimes they would be nice to have around. No, it was something else entirely. The thought of forward planning. The thought of a long-term future with Karen. This was what had bothered her and broken any peace of mind for her. She couldn't see a future together for herself and Karen. Her face twisted with sudden tears and her hand shook as she reached for the cup. That was the thing. She didn't love her any longer.

Delilah's was having a drag night. It wasn't Joanie's idea; it was a management notion. They thought they needed something to break up the karaoke nights and quiz nights and endless drinks promotions nights.

'What're you wearing?' Bobbie had asked Joanie, the week it was announced.

'Maybe I'll dress as a man,' replied Joanie. He wasn't too hot on the idea. It wasn't something that made him run to his dressing-up box.

'You're scared somebody'll rain on yer parade,' said Bobbie, who wouldn't be drawn on what she had up her sleeve, or down her trousers.

Joanie was ambivalent about the plan. The feeling reminded him of an event in his schooldays. By the time he reached the age of fifteen he'd got used to being slagged for a being a 'bentshot'. In fact he sort of prided himself on being the class poof. He'd come to view himself as some kind of mascot. Then a new boy had started at the school and had joined his class. He wore preposterous flared trousers, skin-tight tee shirts and had shoulder-length hair loaded with three tons of hairspray. His voice was higher than a hippie at a hash party and he could mince for Britain. When he swanned along the school corridors ten boys snaked behind him trying to get the walk right. They never could. Joanie got so jealous he started wearing lipstick to school.

It wasn't until the day before the drag extravaganza that Joanie really became excited. Then it dawned on him he had to be Dusty. The hair, the eyes, the voice, it could only be Dusty. Joanie had a brassy backcombed wig that he hadn't worn for ages, false lashes and plenty of pale pink lipstick. The dress was harder to do. He'd seen Dusty in an old TV show wearing a dress with long sleeves, doing all her traffic policeman hand moves. That was the look.

He'd gone to a wee second-hand clothes shop off Byres Road that specialised in retro gear. It was called Backlash and was a favourite haunt of Joanie's. He'd got some gems there – a pair of pink thigh-length boots that Bobbie called his Penelope Pitstop's; a velvet trouser suit; cocktail dresses so fabulous that whenever he wore them he ended up with a cock on his tail; ridiculous hats – from pillbox to panama; hot pants and some cool shoes. He didn't have time to browse through the Briggait. If there was a Dusty dress to be discovered, Backlash was the place to start looking.

It took an hour to find what he wanted. He had tried on three outfits. There was a beautiful pink safari suit that he would have loved to wear but when he donned it in the pokey wee changing room it just didn't fit. The trousers were flying at half-mast and the jacket pinched him under the arms. The next thing he tried on was a magnificent red evening dress. The Goth-chick shop assistant nearly swooned when she saw Joanie in it. 'You look like Liz Hurley,' she sighed. But Joanie didn't let flattery go to his head. Red wasn't his colour and nor was it Dusty's. Besides, the dress was too conventional, too classy. They finally found the groovy number they were looking for, third time lucky. Joanie thought it had a fantastic cut, the shoulders were slightly puffy, the sleeves swelled out like bells and it reached to his ankles. It was lemon-coloured cotton and was an impressive fit. To the amusement of the Goth chick, Joanie tried out a few Dusty moves to test the sleeve action. Then he gave the assistant a satisfied smile. 'I'll take it,' he commanded.

It wasn't till he got home that Joanie could really appreciate the dress. It was always tricky trying on things in shops. There was never enough time to check the fit and how it moved. Joanie had bought a few things that looked great on him when he was standing still but as soon as he took a step in them he felt like a sack of potatoes. The Dusty dress was like a dream on him. Joanie found himself taking quick wee steps in the dress, speeding down the hall, spinning around the living-room with his arms outstretched as he and the dress got to know each other.

Finding shoes to match was the next step. Joanie wasn't a fan of high heels. They were fine if all you were doing was walking from your front door to a waiting limo but they were no use for bar work. He did have a pair of vivid yellow high heels with glittery straps but he felt like a wee lassie in her big sister's shoes when he tried to walk in them. He settled for a sturdy pair of flat-heeled pale green shoes. The dress was so long that he could have got away with DMs.

Joanie had a good collection of wigs but some wore better than others. His backcombed wig was just right for Dusty and was light enough to groove around in. When Joanie clocked the full ensemble in his mirror he felt increasingly enthused about the drag night. He hoped that this enthusiasm would be infectious and the night would be a success.

It started slow, as these things often do. It was a Friday night gig so people were having to get home from work and get into costume. There were no prizes for best outfit, it was simply an event night. But they had a great DJ who played all the diva disco stuff and lots of promos for homos at the bar; all bottled beers were a pound.

Gradually, the punters began to arrive. Not everybody dressed up but it worked out at about 60/40: six dragsters for every four stick-in-the-muds. Two dykes were the first to arrive. Caroline and Denise were dressed as Boy George and Pete Burns and were half-pissed. Their friends, the Marx sisters – Karl and Groucho, quickly joined them. Karl had a big bushy beard and kept asking people if they wanted to feel it. The first of three Madonnas arrived. He was an early Madonna, with bleached blonde wig and black lacy gloves, sporting a big crucifix. The guy actually looked quite like her. He jumped about yelling 'Holiday! Celebrate!' and wouldn't let up the whole night. There was a Marilyn Monroe who sashayed around like he owned the fucking place; two Shirley Basseys who swore that diamonds were forever; a glitzy, showbizzy chap who declared she was Liberace but who kept being mistaken for a glam rocker; a Liza Minnelli aka Sally Bowles, and two more Madonnas, one with a conical bra and fishnet stockings, the other dressed as a geisha. One of the star turns for Joanie came in the form of five young girls who passed themselves off as Westlife. They kept putting on phoney Irish accents but were pretty good singers.

It was gone ten before Bobbie arrived. She had gelled back her hair, sported a Hawaiian shirt, white chinos and huge moustache, and introduced herself as Magnum P I. She even gave Joanie a card which read 'Magnum P I (Pussy Investigator)'. They admired each other's outfits as more punters arrived. A spiky-haired dyke floated past carrying a violin. 'Nigel Kennedy,' explained her friend, Charlie Chaplin. A tall stately Cleopatra – who was heard to remark 'Forget the milk, just bring me some ass' – was accompanied by a formidable Morticia. There was a Bill Clinton and Monica Lewinsky. Bill brandished a big cigar and Monica had a large stain on his dress.

Bobbie downed a bottle of beer at the bar. 'This is kinda confusing,' she said. 'I think I've just fancied a guy.'

'I know,' sighed Joanie, blinking panda eyes, 'you can't tell the boys from the girls these days.' Joanie was more laid-back as he had some new staff onboard. He reckoned they probably wouldn't last the pace but they gave him a head start. He hoped to enjoy the party. Just then Papa and Mama arrived. Papa was a magnificent mini-skirted Cher with a gorgeous black wig and biker jacket. Mama was a Vegas Elvis, with a knockout white spangly suit and a be-bop wig. Joanie was delighted they'd made it and told them so. They laughed and complimented each other. Joanie was tickled by Mama and Papa's arrival. It wasn't only their costumes that were a hoot. It was the whole attitude. Papa stood hand on hip, chewing gum and fluffing at his wig. Mama strutted like she was the king of all she surveyed. She curled her top lip and spoke in a totally incomprehensible American drawl. Papa blew a big pink bubble of gum that burst and stuck to his lips and chin. Bobbie patted at her big broad moustache to make sure it was still there. They ordered three bottles of beer and told Joanie they were going into the backroom to check out the other dragsters.

Music was courtesy of DJ Diva's Diva Disco. There was Madonna, Cher, Donna Summer, Kylie, Sister Sledge, Bananarama, Diana Ross, The Three Degrees, Destiny's Child, and Janet Jackson.

DJ Diva was a ballsy blonde in a leather catsuit. She played around the club scene in Glasgow and Edinburgh but this was her first Delilah's gig. She stood at her rig-out pulling on and off a pair of big black headphones and doing a sexy wiggly dance. At first she was the only dancer in the joint. Everybody was talking so loud you could hardly hear the music. The drag seemed to have acted like strong drink on the punters, and erstwhile prudish customers were now goosing everything within a half-mile radius and shrinking violets were suddenly coming up roses. Westlife were huddled together, thick as thieves, each guzzling a different flavoured alcopop. Monica was smoking Bill's cigar. Morticia was drinking a Bloody Mary, which he claimed had real blood in it.

Papa and Mama stood in a corner, looking gallus and groovy. They both seemed much younger in drag, like the coolest dudes in Hollywood High. They clocked the Madonnas, who were strategically placed at three opposing corners of the backroom. Geisha Madonna looked serene in his kimono and cubist black wig. Early Madonna looked all arsenic and black lace, hopping about as if he was getting ready for a prizefight. Big bazooka Madonna was poking everyone with his conical bra. Bobbie waved to the rock legends then went to check out the talent.

She went in a booth with another bottle of beer. DJ Diva was playing The Three Degrees' *When Will I See You Again?* Bobbie thought it was a sad song, full of the uncertainties of love. But she was determined not to brood on broken dreams, old flames that had burned her confidence. She swigged her beer and patted at her moustache. Delilah's was getting busy and she thought of how hot it must be getting inside DJ Diva's leather catsuit.

Joanie was serving at the bar. It was getting hectic but the new starts seemed to know their stuff. He knew he could knock off early and enjoy the party when he wanted to. He was washing glasses when he heard a creepy voice say 'Good Evening'. He looked up to see a vicious-looking vampire with red eyes glaring at him. 'My name's Dracula,' said the vampire. 'Cunt Dracula.' She smiled and her plastic fangs slipped out of her mouth. She caught them and slipped them back into place. 'I'll have a vodka and cranberry juice,

Dusty.' Joanie grinned, pleased she'd sussed out who he was.

Cunt Dracula was the last of the dragsters to arrive. After that it was the randan brigade, looking for a cheap drink before they hit the clubs. Joanie served a few rounds and then explained to the other bar staff that he had a hot date with the son of a preacher man. He excused himself and inched his way through to the backroom. Papa and Mama had found seats at a wee table. Joanie picked up a chair and joined them. He waved to Bobbie who was busy looking butch in her booth. She waved back but didn't budge.

Joanie had brought some more beer that he shared with Papa and Mama. Monica came over to their table, puffing a cigar.

'Do any of you guys know the best way to get rid of a spunk stain?' asked Monica, earnestly.

'Rub the affected area vigorously with a big bar of green Fairy,' advised Joanie, blinking under the weight of a ton of mascara. Monica disappeared in a poof of smoke and Mama coughed in disapproval.

'This is amazing,' said Mama. 'I thought we'd be the only three dressing up.'

Joanie smiled. The group turned their attention to the DJ's kit, where Westlife seemed to be arguing with DJ Diva. Joanie went over to see what all the commotion was.

'It's her,' said a Westlifer, pointing at DJ Diva. 'She won't play *Uptown Girl*.' Another one butted in. 'We want tae dance. We've been practisin' aw week.' Joanie had a word with DJ Diva, who insisted that Billy fucking Joel wasn't on her diva playlist but agreed to play it strictly as a one-off.

The Westlife girls were a star turn. They did some line dancing, three steps to the left and kick, and three steps to the right and then kick. Joanie got up and joined them, to the delight of the crowd. DJ Diva, knowing she was onto a good thing, followed it up with la Springfield herself, *Son Of A Preacher Man*. Joanie, Westlife, and what seemed like the whole pub did all the Dusty moves. The Shirleys Bassey were displaying some serious wrist action. Marilyn Monroe and Liberace were clapping in time. The early Madonna seemed to be using his crucifix to re-enact a scene from *The Exorcist*. Boy George and Pete Burns were shaking their hips and their hair like there was no tomorrow. Even Morticia, who stood on a table with her arms crossed over her chest, was seen to be tapping her toes. They all danced to Dusty, penned in by palls of smoke and walls of heat, bathed in the smell of a hundred perfumes and perspirations.

Later, Joanie wound his way through the throng and up the stairs to the toilet. He passed a pissed-looking Bobbie, who was having her neck bitten by Cunt Dracula. In the loo he met Papa, putting on some lipstick at the sinks and humming *I Got You Babe*. Joanie pinched Papa's arse and waited for an empty cubicle. A door was flung open and out trooped three Westlife girls. An acrid smell hit Joanie like a left hook.

'Either someone needs to change their sweaty socks,' said Joanie, 'or you girls have been sniffing poppers!' The girls giggled and ran.

When Joanie got back downstairs the party was at its peak. DJ Diva was blasting out a Kylie medley that had everybody on their feet. Papa and Mama were dancing in the middle of the backroom like it was their own private rock 'n' roll party, Monica and Minnelli were high-kicking like they were auditioning for the Moulin Rouge, DJ Diva was stamping up and down like a cross between a cheerleader and a dominatrix. Joanie's dress was torn under the arm, his wig was singed by uncontrollable fags with uncontrollable fags, and his false lashes were falling off. Looking towards the bar, Joanie could see some surprising liaisons. Torpedo-titted Madonna and marvellous Marilyn Monroe were winching each other to safety and Karl Marx was finally getting her beard felt, trembling in Bill Clinton's clutches.

The night slowly but surely came to an end. DJ Diva played out with The Weather Girls, which saw Cleopatra jumping on a table till he broke it, then the bar closed, and one of the staff turned up the lights – provoking a melodramatic scream from Cunt Dracula, who flapped out of the bar like a demented bat. Bobbie sighed with relief and peeled off her moustache.

Joanie found himself at the door with Bob the bouncer, flanking the exit and bidding goodnight to all and sundry.

'Goodnight, Dusty,' said Morticia. Bobbie stuck her moustache back on and grabbed hold of Joanie, giving him a manly goodnight kiss. Papa and Mama stood behind Bobbie, beaming.

'That was a drag!' laughed Mama.

Framed in the doorway of Delilah's, Joanie waved off the last of his guests.

'See what you guys are missing?' he called out.

'Holiday! Celebrate!' came the raucous reply.

The Driving Seat

There were two reasons Bernie got so pissed. He hadn't brought the car and his legs were shaking. He hadn't brought the car because it would mean hanging around Glasgow's gay scene sober. He couldn't handle that. His legs were shaking because he couldn't handle anything anymore. It had all got too much for him. He had felt terrified standing there against a pillar in Delilah's, resting his pint on a wee ledge. He was terrified in case someone he knew had seen him come into Delilah's, someone who would tell everybody he was a poof. He was terrified that someone from work would come in and spot him. But what the fuck would they be doing there anyway? Logic wasn't a part of this. It was sheer fucking terror. He was frightened somebody would speak to him. He was frightened nobody would speak to him. He decided he would drink away the fear.

He drank five pints in a row. He was drinking too fast. When he went to the toilet he was conscious of a stagger in his step. It was one thing your legs shaking but another when they stopped working altogether. One time in the toilet he had overheard two young guys talking. He was amazed at how poofy they sounded. How poofy they acted. How did they get through school? How did they get through the day?

Bernie didn't want to stay but he didn't want to go home. Besides, the alcohol had finally given him a bit of bravado. His legs weren't shaking anymore. If guys looked at him he looked back. He was a poof, what a-fuckin-bout it? He turned to a man beside him.

'Whit's the best place tae go?'

'Whit?'

'Whit's the best dancin'?'

'Club X is okay. It's dark an' its lively an' yer guaranteed yer hole.'

Bernie laughed at that and downed his pint. He'd heard of Club X right enough. It was quite discreet. There wasn't a big pink neon cock outside it or anything. Just an X sign. X as in anonymous. He would go along to Club X. He had every right.

There were two bouncers standing at the entrance of Club X. That was par for the course at a lot of city centre places. It was no big deal. They looked like ordinary common or garden bouncers. Bernie even fancied one of the stocky, sexy bears. As he walked towards the entrance he tried to walk straight. He didn't want to get a knock-back for being drunk; that would be a brass neck. He halted momentarily at the doors, expecting to be cross-examined by the bouncers. All they did was nod and say 'Right mate'. Bernie went on. He came to a descending stairway. He could see there was a counter on the landing below, and a cloakroom. There was a queue on the stairs that was a bastard. The stairway was floodlit and he felt too drunk to wait. A young guy in front of him turned to face him.

'Hi ya. Want a flyer? '

He handed a flyer to Bernie.

'It's two pound aff wi' a flyer. '

'Thanks, pal.'

Things were looking up. People seemed friendly enough. It was just this fucking queue. It began to move. Slowly, step by painstaking step, it moved. Bernie gave a weary sigh. The young guy who had given him the flyer turned around again.

'Cheer up. This means it's busy. The busier it is the better it is.'

Bernie nodded. He would get lost in the crowd. Anything that aided anonymity was to be applauded. The queue snaked forward down the stairway. When he finally got to the till he found it was four quid with a flyer and six quid without. The young guy was right enough. Bernie decided not to put his jacket in as there was already a queue forming for the cloakroom. What was the score with these queues?

He wandered into the darkness of the club interior. It was busy. There was a square bar, which you could attack from all sides. Two small dance floors. There were seats and tables and wee cubbyholes. It was pretty dark. What Bernie really wanted to do was find the toilet before he peed his pants. He asked somebody at the bar who gave him a haughty look and pointed. Bernie followed the direction of the finger. The toilet was big and spacious with a large metal urinal. He peed there, glad there wasn't another fucking queue. He washed his hands and pushed the button on the air dryer. He glanced in the mirror and was surprised at how good he looked. He had felt like shit and was encouraged to see he looked human. He went back through to the disco.

Bernie bought another pint at the bar. The stagger from Delilah's to Club X, then the shuffle down the floodlit stairway had left him restless and thirsty. He wasn't sure what to do, whether to make an arse of himself on the dance floor or head for a cubbyhole and down his drink. He chose the cubbyhole option. He sat on a bench seat. He was alone in the alcove apart from two young lovebirds in jeans and white tee shirts that looked as if they were trying to swallow each other whole, and good fucking luck to them.

Bernie decided he would enjoy himself. Now that he was settled here. He wasn't long there when a man joined him. He didn't even say 'Mind if I join you?' He boldly planted himself beside Bernie on the bench seat. The guy was big and heavy with a face only a visually impaired mother could love.

He put down a pint of beer on the table in front of them and made a great show of lighting a cigarette and blowing smoke rings. He turned to address Bernie, who thought he looked pissed. That made two of them. His head appeared to be rolling off his shoulders.

'I'm Dan. Who're you?'

'Bernie.'

'Pleased tae meet you, Bernie.'

He spoke like a robot, trying to gain control of his drunken mouth. He grabbed Bernie's nearest hand and shook it warmly. He had clearly made up his mind that he was going to hump Bernie. Bernie didn't mind. This was an exploratory trip. He wanted to be a poof. To hear poofy voices, to see young guys winching each other, to be cruised and cruise. He was too drunk to care or to fight off Dan if he came at him.

Dan started chatting to him. He made remarks about men that

passed by, pointed out a woman who was really a man, and a man who was really a woman, and gradually his arm, big and clambering, crept across the back of the bench seat until he had a hold of Bernie. Dan looked at him with a weird combination of resignation and lust. It was as if he was saying they were stuck with each other and there was nothing they could do about it. He was right. Why else had he come here, Bernie asked himself. To be with a man and see what it felt like. That was all he wanted to know – what it felt like.

He left the club with Dan when they finished their drinks. Dan walked ahead of Bernie and opened the door of a car and got in. He opened the passenger door from the inside for Bernie. He got in and put his seat belt on. Dan started driving. He drove for about a minute then stopped at traffic lights. He turned to Bernie.

'Can you drive, pal? Ah'm too drunk.'

'So am I.'

'We're fucked then.'

He started driving again.

'Why don't we abandon the car and get a taxi?'

Dan shrugged and smiled.

'Fuck it.'

Bernie was too drunk to be scared. Dan drove like a hyperactive five-year-old in a toy car. Eventually they got to Dan's place. Bernie was amazed they'd made it alive. They staggered out of the car and went upstairs.

The place was so clean you could've eaten off the floor. Bernie was glad it wasn't a dive. Dan dragged him into the kitchen, filled up the electric kettle and switched it on. He asked Bernie if he wanted tea or coffee, but they didn't wait for the kettle to boil. They hurtled into Dan's bedroom.

Bernie felt like a wee animal being overpowered by a bigger one and dragged into its den. Bernie wanted to keep his pants on but Dan pulled them off and over his feet in one brutally efficient move.

Dan hauled the duvet over them and they were both naked, in each other's arms. Bernie closed his eyes as Dan rolled on top of him. It was like being on a scary roller coaster ride. Bernie held on tight to Dan in case he flew off. Dan moaned and groaned and moved his big arse up and down. He kissed Bernie's face and neck and chest and belly and cock and scrotum. He caught Bernie in his arms and rolled over in the bed till Bernie lay on top of him. Bernie wasn't sure what to do. He started doing what Dan had done to him, move for move, Dan roaring like a lion as soon as Bernie put his lips to his throbbing big boner.

After a while of this kissing and rolling around, they lay quietly together. Bernie lay with his eyes shut and his arms around Dan. He felt good. He felt he had finally achieved something here. Something he had wanted to do for a long time. This was the first time, lying here with a man. They slept.

Dan woke him early. At six thirty. Dan got up and began shoving his clothes on. Then he began to pick Bernie's clothes up off the floor and started throwing them at Bernie, who sat up in bed, bewildered.

'Get dressed,' Dan ordered.

Bernie slowly put his clothes on. When he stood up to fasten his trousers, he felt nauseous.

'Can I use your toilet?' he asked.

Dan nodded. Bernie went to the toilet. As he stood pishing into the pan, his eyes caught sight of all the toiletries on the ledge beside the bath. There were skin creams, perfumes, make-up and sanitary towels. Then when he went to wash his hands and face at the sink, he noticed a plain gold ring on a wee ledge beside the toothbrushes. Bernie felt sick and wanted to be sick, to get it over with. He hung over the sink but couldn't do it. He went back into the bedroom where Dan was making up the bed. He turned and looked at Bernie.

'I want you out of here in five minutes. Ma wife's home at seven.'

Bernie stood stock-still.

'Move!'

He moved.

When Bernie got back to his place he took two paracetamol and a glass of water, pulled off his clothes and climbed into bed. It felt good to be in his own bed. He felt as if he'd been away from it for years. Sleep came quickly. He slept fitfully and woke up about noon. He needed to pee, and to drink more water. Then he sat in the living-room. He didn't open the curtains. He thought of putting the TV on, then decided he couldn't bear the noise. He thought of making himself some breakfast, then felt sick at the thought of it. He thought about Dan. He had a strange longing then for him. He wanted to be taken in his big strong arms again, carried into his bed, under the duvet. To feel Dan's big body rolling over him. Then Bernie thought of how quickly and coldly Dan had got rid of him. How he'd felt scared at the way Dan had looked at him. It was as if nothing had happened between them. As if Bernie was an intruder that Dan had surprised. Bernie began to take stock. Dan was an ugly big bastard. He was also married, something he didn't have the courtesy to mention before they'd done this thing. Bernie felt ashamed all of a sudden. Ashamed and cheap. He felt terrible for what he had done. He'd worked himself up to this, doing it with a man, and had ended up kissing a married man's cock and being thrown out with the rubbish. He heard a car screech outside and remembered the drive to Dan's. Both of them drunk and unable to drive. How dangerous that was, how wrong. Bernie found himself crying then and wasn't sure why exactly. It was shame and guilt and feeling sorry for himself. It was also relief that he was home in one piece. He covered his face with his hands.

Later Bernie sat in the kitchen drinking coffee. He had put some laundry in the washing-machine and listened to the noises as it worked through the wash cycle. He drank his coffee and reflected on the night before. He felt better now. He felt he had made a step forward on a journey he was destined to make. He was a poof. Just like those boys in the toilet in Delilah's. Just like the lip smacking lovebirds in Club X. Just like Dan, wife or no wife. For too long, Bernie decided, he had been scared to live like he wanted to live. He decided it was time to get into the driving seat and take control of his life.

Struck by Lightning

At my time of life you take what's coming to you. Usually, it's an old man in a torn car coat, smelling of lager and urine in equal measure. I answer to sixty but am actually perilously close to seventy. The temptations of celibacy are almost irresistible. Almost. The thing about this particular game is that you never know your luck. Take last Saturday for instance. I was sitting here, at my usual place, at the far right corner as you enter Delilah's. When I say my usual place, I mean whenever I'm in this god-forsaken dump. It's too young for me. Most of the clientele are in a drug-induced state of hysteria. However, it has to be said that a significant number of them are quite beautiful. I come as an observer rather than a participant. I sit over here in the corner and imbibe as many gin and tonics as I can possibly bear. I am rarely disturbed. But I had the most extraordinary fortune last Saturday.

A young man approached me. Barely twenty, I would say. Pencil slim. Model looks. He appeared from nowhere and sat down beside me. I caught my breath, at his beauty and his impertinence. At the point of asphyxiation I let out a tremulous gasp.

'You okay?'

Unable to find my voice, I simply nodded vigorously. The young man gave me the once over. I gave him the twice over. He began a conversation with me. Something about how noisy it was. How smoky. He was too beautiful to look at. I wondered if he was some kind of performer. A budding young actor perhaps. Or the lead singer in a pop group. It transpired he was a student at University, studying Politics and Economics.

'Brains as well as beauty,' I quipped.

The impetuosity of youth being what it is, it wasn't long before we got to the bottom of things. He lived in a student hall of residence and would not be able to accommodate me. But he plainly wanted to spend the night with me. I told him he could

132

come back to my place. I feigned nonchalance, pinching myself. I should explain that I live with my mother. She is almost ninety, a fact of which she is unnervingly proud. She is a light sleeper so stealth is essential when returning from the hunt. As we came up the drive to the front door I turned to my beautiful young beau and held a phallic forefinger to my pursed lips. He smiled and nodded.

Once safely ensconced in the lounge, we had a nightcap. I had another gin and tonic and my child bride had a whisky. He began to speak frankly of sexual matters. He liked to suck, but not to fuck. He liked hairy chests, did I have one? I felt embarrassed. My chest owes more to Debbie Reynolds than Burt. I hoped this whole evening had been more than cruel flirtation and that he would stand and deliver. But he spoke with the sureness of beauty. He was direct and to the point. He liked older men. He made some amusing reference to wine. I was, apparently, vintage. I asked him if he intended popping my cork. He needed no further encouragement.

We mounted the staircase to my room. In a trifle, we were naked and thrashing under the billowing sheets. He was nubile to the touch, skin smooth as silk. He began at my neck and worked his way down over my hairless chest, down past my belly, until he swallowed my pride. He licked, he kissed, he nibbled, he sucked, he blew. He made a meal of me. I came convulsively, my back arched in gay abandon. I reciprocated, or would have had he not ejaculated as my lips gave his prick a preliminary tickle. He blamed my moustache.

We lay entwined and spoke softly for a while. Then we drifted off to sleep. I dreamt my mother had come into the room, discovered we naked lovers, and brained the both of us with her ivory-headed walking stick.

When I woke in the morning I was quite alone. My young buck was gone. I looked for a note but there was none. I had half-hoped he'd have left a contact number. My mind raced. Had I dreamt the whole thing? I looked at my cock and could make out a small love-bite. I could smell his aftershave on me. He had said it was called

Be. Then, as so often the morning after, I was seized by paranoia. I suspected robbery, and possibly murder. I looked about me. Nothing seemed amiss. I hurried downstairs. Everything seemed to be in order. Then I thought of my dear mother. I had a fearful vision of her, strangled in her bed; her rings hacked brutally from her arthritic fingers. I dashed into her room. She was sitting on her commode, reading a magazine. I excused myself. Having exhausted all the negative possibilities, I was now free to gloat about my conquest. I went into the bathroom and studied myself in the mirror. I had held a vain hope that somehow beauty was contagious and I had been stunningly transformed by my intimacy with a god. Crestfallen, I let my dressinggown fall from my shoulders. If anything, I looked older and plainer than ever. It had been a late night and I had drunk too much. I ran a bath and submerged myself. I replayed the details of my night of debauchery. The smoothness of his skin, the eagerness of his lips.

It was here that I was sitting. To observe, not participate. How can I explain the inexplicable? It was as if I was struck suddenly by lightning.

Ben liked the expression. Get laid. It was better than fucked or shagged or screwed. It was an Americanism.

'So what happened last night?'

'I got laid.'

Sandy wanted to know all the ins and outs. She would tell Ben the gory details of her sex life and expected him to reciprocate.

'Again?'

Ben smiled at the incredulity in her voice.

'Ben, yer a cow.'

'It never rains but it pours. I don't know whit it is, Sandy. I'm fightin' them aff wi' a stick.'

'You must be doin' somethin' right. What's yer secret?'

'Wish I knew.'

Ben and Sandy had met for a few drinks in town. Sandy was going on to meet a girlfriend in a new bar that had opened up in the Merchant City. Ben was going on to Delilah's. They sat in a booth and gossiped. Inevitably, they turned to sex. Sandy was currently single. She had been going out with a fireman who, she assured Ben, knew how to use his hose. But the flames of passion had flickered and died. Ben had something to tell her. He had been in Bennets the night before and met this guy called Jerry. He worked in a bank in town.

'A sperm bank?' asked Sandy. If it was nothing to do with sex, she'd make it something to do with sex.

Jerry worked in finance. He was a sharp dresser and looked as if he'd just stepped out of a trendy shop window. He'd approached Ben. He was a bit full of himself, but very charming. He said he hated the scene and had just come in that night to escape a tedious works' night out. Ben wasn't sure about Jerry. He found smart men slightly intimidating. Ben was a denim queen. He went back to Jerry's place.

Jerry lived in a ground floor flat just off Great Western Road. They sat in the spacious kitchen and Jerry made them coffee. Ben wasn't used to this. Normally he'd be down to the nitty gritty by now. This was definitely upmarket stuff. Ben wondered if they were going to do anything at all. He had been asked back for coffee and it just might have been literal. They drank the coffee. Ben was unemployed but told Jerry he was a landscape gardener. It was daft, lying. Especially if the man wanted to see you again and you had to string the lie along. Ben had worked for the Parks Department but that was over a year ago.

They eventually went to bed. The sheets were fresh, as if Jerry had changed them that day. They wanked and sucked cock and fell asleep. Ben didn't feel comfortable with the whole situation. There was something too reserved and mechanical about Jerry. He couldn't relax.

Next morning they sat at the kitchen table again, with coffee and toast. Jerry had the radio on. He said he was meeting his sister and would have to go out. After they got ready he gave Ben a crumpled piece of paper with his name and phone number on it, written in pencil. Ben said he'd call.

'You should call,' said Sandy.

Ben shrugged.

'I don't know.'

That had been the Friday night and this was Saturday night. Sandy said he'd started the weekend with a bang. Sometimes she'd shake her head and look disapprovingly at Ben when he told her of his sexploits but she was into it. She liked talking about sex with a man she had no sexual connection with.

Ben had got laid again. He'd got his hole, as Sandy liked to announce at the top of her voice in the pub. He'd met someone in Delilah's. Bob was his name. He was a housing worker, up from London for the weekend. He had silver hair and a pockmarked face. Lovely blue eyes. He'd stood beside Ben and felt him up. It was tacky but Ben liked the up-front approach. They went back to Ben's.

Ben lived on the fifteenth floor of a tower block in Sighthill. It was a dive and he couldn't really do anything about it till he got a job. Then he'd grudge spending the money on the place. He didn't like his neighbours. There were two old widowers, a young guy who was dealing smack and a wino who played C & W all the time. There was talk of the flats being upgraded. They were using them to house the asylum seekers that Glasgow was taking. The council said they would install video surveillance and get a concierge service. Ben was glad they hadn't installed video cameras in the lifts yet. Bob had stuck his tongue in Ben's mouth as soon as they had stepped into one.

It took around a minute for them to get from the front door into Ben's bed. They'd got into bed half-dressed and continued undressing each other under the covers. There were two things that Ben wanted to tell Sandy. Two things Bob had done that really annoyed him. The first was he kept asking if he could fuck Ben. Ben hadn't gone in for that for a while and he wasn't about to fuck with a total stranger who was going to bugger off back to London the next day. He kept asking and Ben kept telling him no. The other thing was he tried on Ben's underpants. He made a huge song and dance of putting on Ben's pants and acting as if it was a sexy big deal. Eventually he'd taken them off and Ben had put them back on, to protect his arse from further advances.

'Sounds kinda sexy.'

'You would say that.'

They were talking on the phone on the Sunday night, Ben and Sandy. Ben felt depressed after two nights of drunkenness and debauchery. Sandy said he should count himself lucky. She could barely remember what a cock looked like. If this was the sin, then Ben collected his wages later that week.

He noticed little tiny dots on his pants. He wasn't sure what these spots were at first. Then he realised they were spots of blood. It was the following Saturday he stood in the bathroom with his trousers and pants down, under the light. He looked at his scrotum. There were what looked like little grey-green balls stuck to the sagging skin. He pulled one off and held it up under the light on his fingers. He saw tiny legs moving. It was a crab louse. He had crabs. He'd never had crabs before but this was obviously what it was. He phoned Sandy for advice.

'You have to get a lotion,' she said. 'They plant eggs.'

'Eggs? This is like a fuckin' horror movie.'

'D'you have anything else? Like a discharge?'

'Naw.'

'You didnae fuck?'

'Naw.'

'I'd go to the VD clinic if I were you. Just in case.'

Ben got an appointment for Monday. They confirmed the crabs and prescribed a lotion. He was to put it on his scrotum and leave it on for two hours. That would do the trick. They took a blood sample as well as a wee scrape from his cock. They asked him if he wanted an HIV test but he said no. Ben supposed they would test the blood they took anyway, anonymously. He didn't want to know about it.

The lotion stung his scrotum. He had to pick the dead eggs off his pubic hair. They hadn't spread anywhere else. Sandy had said these crab lice could crawl up to your armpits and over your hairy arse.

Ben wondered who had given him the crabs. Was it Jerry? Surely he was too clean and fresh and smart to have crabs? That had fuck all to do with it. The smart money was on Bob. There was that pantie trick. What the fuck was that all about? The guy probably had a crab fetish. Kinky cunt. It wasn't about blame. He'd slept with two guys in a row. The AIDS poster came to mind. Sleep with one person and you're sleeping with all their ex-partners. Those crabs had probably originated on Plato's balls.

He hadn't fucked with them. If someone had crabs and you got naked with them, that was you.

He met Sandy the following Friday. He thought she'd be a pain in the arse but she was sweet. Ben was in penitent mood.

'I'm gonnae clean up my act.'

'Don't kill yerself. You're young, you're single, you're sexy. These things happen.'

She told him another story about the fireman.

Ben never phoned Jerry.

John felt the letter in the inside pocket of his jacket. He felt it sort of rustle and crackle as his jacket rubbed against his shirt. He was scared of losing the letter. Yet he also had a sudden vicious urge to destroy it. To rip it up into a hundred tiny pieces and throw it to fuck. Or burn it. Ask somebody for a match or a lighter and torch the thing, watch it blacken to cinders. But shite doesn't burn. And that's all this letter was from start to finish, shite. He thought of opening it up and holding it over the lit candle on his table, to make a ceremony out of it.

His face had burned when he had read the letter that morning. His arms had shook. He couldn't believe such an offensive weapon could have been so callously shoved through his letterbox. He thought he should sue the Post Office for attempted murder. He knew the handwriting on the envelope immediately. It was from Cary, his boyfriend. He recognised that meticulous, mutinous hand. It was the ultimate Dear John letter. Not only was the age of chivalry dead, but a stake had been driven through its noble old ticker.

The letter seemed like such a physical thing. It was a material fact, there in black and white. The prick had even put his address in the top right hand corner of page one, as if John had forgotten where he lived. He'd been there. They had slept there together. He had sucked Cary's cock in that flat. He had been there but was never going to go there again. It was a nice flat. It was dark because Cary was a real Blanche Dubois about lighting. He was always talking about 'ambience'. How ambience created mood. Ambient lighting. Ambient music. He thought it was classy. John thought it was calculating. But there was a beautiful, ethereal quality about Cary's place, the pretentious cunt. It really was a chill out zone. It was a haven.

'It's kinda sci-fi'.

Cary had looked at him with surprise.

'Sci-fi?'

'Aye. Like one of those old sci-fi movies.'

'It's the lighting. I've worked on the lighting.'

He certainly had. There were uplights, spotlights, dimmer-switches, what looked like hi-tech versions of lava lamps, candlelight, fuck there was moonlight through a skylight.

'I just meant it's kinda space-age.'

'Space age?' said Cary. 'We've had the space age for thirty years.'

'I know. It's nice. I like it.'

John had only two forms of lighting in his house. A hundred watt glare or a forty watt lamp out of Woolworth's. Take your pick.

It revealed something about Cary's character, thought John. This whole ambience trip. He wanted to control his environment. To mould it to his liking. He was a hedonist. He was also into E in a big way. Cary wanted pleasure from his environment and the people in it. But man cannot live by pleasure alone, thought John, morosely. He shifted in his seat just so he could feel the rustling paper of Cary's rejection slip slide dangerously close to his heart. Truly, the pen is mightier than the sword, mused John.

The lighting in Delilah's was diabolical. It was rumoured to have been designed by the Gestapo. A furious big drag queen had once smashed some of the lights with the heel of his stiletto and was frog-marched out shouting for sunglasses. But they had created a darker place here at the booths where John sat. In candlelight, the gentlest light of all.

He started to play with a cardboard beer mat on the table. He began to unpick it at a corner, peeling back the top layer of cardboard. He tore the thinner piece of cardboard into strips, imagining it was the letter. Then he started picking at the label on his bottle of beer. He dampened the paper with some beer that had been spilled on the table and he scraped off most of the label. He looked at the scraps of paper and cardboard on the table and felt self-conscious at the mess he'd made. He gathered the litter into a bundle and sat it neatly on the ashtray. He needed the toilet.

John stood outside the two cubicles. There was a guy peeing at the urinal. At least he was peeing at first. But when he had finished peeing he just kept standing there, glancing over at John. He eventually jolted his head back as if to summon John over. Just as he did this one of the cubicle doors opened and two sheepish looking young guys came out. John hurried in past them and snibbed the door. He was relieved that the only thing the cubicle smelled of was some fancy aftershave the boys were wearing. He took off his jacket and placed it carefully on the dirty floor. He pulled off some of the toilet roll, wiped the black plastic toilet seat with it, dropped the paper into the pan, then unfastened his trousers and let them drop. He hitched up his shirt and sat and shat. The cubicle didn't smell so nice now. John gave a heavy sigh as he crouched on the pan. He could see the letter sticking out of his jacket pocket. He was tempted to wipe his arse with it and flush it down the pan. He wiped himself with the toilet paper and pulled the plug.

When he came back out of the cubicle the guy who was kidding on he was doing the pee was still there. There were a few other guys in the toilet, one of whom hurried past John into the cubicle he'd just vacated. John went to a washhand basin and washed his hands. In the mirror he could see the urinal man looking over his shoulder. He thought for a moment he should pick him up to take his mind off the letter but dismissed that as a bad idea.

Back at the seat nothing had changed. His neat pile of litter was still carefully balanced on the small pink ashtray. He started picking the label off his new bottle of beer then he stopped himself. The candle was ready to burn out when a barmaid appeared. She replaced the candle, emptied the ashtray and took away the empty bottles. John looked around at the growing clientele. He wondered if their partners had dumped any of them that day. Or perhaps some of them would meet a new partner tonight. But not John. He wasn't even thinking about that. He couldn't have slept with anybody or been near anybody tonight. He sat there and tried to evaluate his relationship with Cary. It had been mainly a sexual connection. He had never truly felt close to Cary, who was too busy swallowing E and surrounding himself with ambience to convey any genuine feelings. John felt that maybe Cary was his E. He was a pretty dope who gave him a high. But it couldn't last. It couldn't endure. Highs never do.

What would he do with the letter? He had a few ideas. Instead of destroying it, he could treasure it. He could get it framed and build a shrine around it. He could get it laminated and stick it up on the wall like a certificate of rejection. He even thought of writing something on it and posting it back to Cary. But there was something too banal, too final, about Cary's letter that any response would be futile. He'd had the last word.

John felt in his pocket for the letter. He took it out and opened it up delicately. He began, once more, to read it.

German Shepherd

A man wearing a leather jacket was holding court at a booth in Delilah's with some friends. He was telling them about the time that he furthered international relations by sleeping with a German chemist. It had all started in Chapps bar in Edinburgh.

'Wasn't that some kinda creepy leather bar?'

A friend was already beginning to disapprove.

'Chapps was great,' said another, 'I used to go there. They had a dance floor upstairs. Had some wild nights in there.'

'That's right,' continued the man telling the story. 'They had the main bar area downstairs and a wee dance area upstairs. I was only ever in the place twice.'

'Were you alone?'

The narrator shook his head.

'I was with forty lesbians.'

'Forty?'

'Slight exaggeration. I was with this Australian woman I knew. She was straight. A couple of her friends were lesbians. We hit the town one night and ended up in Chapps.'

Another pal returned from the bar with his round.

'That's closed noo, Chapps.'

'Didn't they just do it up and call it somethin' else?'

'Fuck knows. I never go to Edinburgh.'

'Anyway, back to the story. As I've only ever been in Chapps once I didn't know how to get upstairs. It was quite dark.'

'It wis dark in there. Sexy.'

'So I asked this guy. He pointed and told me where the stairway was. He looked at me with his big pussycat eyes – '

'Pussycat eyes?'

'Meeoow.'

'Okay. Okay. I'm just tellin' you. He shows me the stairway and he says somethin' about maybe seein' me up there later. What gets me is his accent. It's a foreign accent. It sounds like he's Swedish or Dutch or somethin'. I don't know. But he's obviously game for it.'

'Obviously.'

'Well just listen and you'll find out. I go upstairs and get more drink in and dance like fuck with the rest of the crew. I mean it was great music. It was housey stuff. This is before techno. It was house music. Fuckin' brilliant.'

'Loved house. Of course queens invented it.'

'It was house stuff all night. Then this guy appears. It turns out his name's Gunter and he's German.'

'Hold it right there. He's a German? The unsexiest race on Earth, the Germans.'

'Just listen.'

'The French and Italians – sexy Europeans. The Germans? Good at stealin' deck chairs. Bad at sex.'

'Let me tell the fuckin' story.'

'Let him tell the story.'

'He's German and his name's Gunter. He works as a chemist. He's about forty. I was only in my early twenties at the time. He's game for it. He starts touching me up while he's talkin' to me.'

'Feelin' yer balls?'

'Aye. He asks me if I want to come back wi' him. To his flat. In Edinburgh. So I says I'll need to ask my pals. I thought I'd introduce him to Annie, the Aussie woman.'

'Good idea.'

'I introduce them and he says hello. Annie says go for it. She thinks he's got a nice face. So then me and Gunter down our drinks and march back to his place.'

'So he lives in Edinburgh?'

'He was stayin' at a pal's. Rentin' a room. It was durin' the Edinburgh Festival.'

'Was it fancy?'

'It was a bit scabby. No' dirty. Just a mess.'

He took a drink of his pint and sighed with satisfaction.

'Okay. So was he a good shag?'

'Let me tell you what happened. We get intae bed and start

the usual stuff ...'

'It's called sex.'

'... then he gets out of the bed and starts fumblin' about in a bag. I was just lyin' there thinkin, what the fuck's he doin'.'

'What was in the bag?'

'I thought it would be somethin' scary. A knife. Or a gun. Or a giant dildo – '

'You wish.'

'But it was this stuff, massage oil. It smelled like, I don't know, roses or somethin'. He climbs back intae the bed and starts massagin' me wi' this oil.'

One of the guys tapped the table.

'Who says the Germans wurnae sexy?'

'He gave me this amazin' massage. It was really fuckin' sensual. But I couldnae relax cause I had freaked when he went intae the bag.'

'A German gave you a massage? Is that it?'

'We were on the subject. Of foreign parts. That's my wee story.'

'You never saw him again?'

'Naw. He gave me his card. Next time I'm in the Ruhr valley I might look him up.'

'Sounds pretty romantic for a one night stand.'

'It makes ye think though. I went back wi' this guy, a strange man, in a city that was strange to me, in that pokey wee room. He could've done me in. Buried me out in the back.'

'It's the risk ye take innit?'

'I mean I hadn't been wi' that many guys then. I was twenty-two. I wisnae that long out the closet. Here I was wi' a big fuckin' German on top of me. But I trusted him.'

'Think of it, how often that happens – '

One of the guys was in a philosophical mood.

' – You go tae a pub or a club and you meet some man you've never met before – '

'Never fuckin' seen before – '

'You meet some guy and you go back wi' him. You're maybe steamin', stoned or whatever – he could've anythin' – the clap, halifuckintosis, the big A – he could be anybody – a serial killer, a Tory for fuck's sake – and you take off all yer clothes and climb intae bed wi' him. And when are ye at yer most vulnerable? Naked.'

'Naked as the day God laid ye.'

'Stark fuckin' naked wi' the Man With No Name fumblin' under the mattress for his flick-knife.'

'Or massage oil.'

'That smells like roses.'

'But that's part of the buzz innit?'

'What I'm sayin' is, like your story about the German poof – '

'Gunter.'

'Gunter. You placed your life in his hands. He could've raped you, beat you up, strangled you. What does he do? The most tender thing you can think of. He massages you. He massages you and you smell like a fuckin' rose. Thanks for that story. It's a lovely fuckin' story, man.'

There was a reverential pause. The storyteller drank from his pint and placed the glass carefully in the middle of the table.

'It just goes to prove. There is a God. And he's a poof.'

That night he lay in bed and thought of Gunter's hands rubbing his back, and smiled. He could even smell roses. But that was just the potpourri on his dressingtable.

Joanie and the Dutch Master

'If that tram driver doesn't improve his diction I'm getting the next plane home,' snarled Joanie, as the Amsterdam tramcar rattled along the lines. He was annoyed that his old pal Mickey hadn't met him at Central station. He had Mickey's address written on a folded-up envelope in the pocket of his jeans but Joanie didn't know Amsterdam and found the tram driver incoherent. It sounded like he was shouting out the names of the stops but Joanie, guidebook and street map in hand, couldn't fathom him out.

'Could you repeat that with yer teeth in?' he pleaded as the tram shuddered by another indecipherable stop.

Looking through the window, Joanie watched the different faces, different races, blur by. He saw an Ethiopian restaurant, a falafel bar, and a sex shop. He heard the bells of the trams and bikes. Looking down at his map he managed to locate Crijnsenstratt. He saw that he was nearly there and alighted at the next stop, swinging his big blue holdall before him as he descended the steps off the tram. According to the map he had to take two lefts, then a right. He nearly got a bike up his arse when he tried to cross the first left.

Finally he got to Crijnsenstratt. There was a wooden door with no bell and no name on it. Then he noticed the silver box at the side of the door, with the names Dunn, Both and Velde beside a square plastic buzzer. Joanie pressed the buzzer. There was no response. He pressed the buzzer again with an angry forefinger. He heard footsteps coming down the stairs. Then the door opened and there stood Mickey, wearing a dressinggown and a towel wrapped round his hair.

'Joanie!' he yelled and threw his arms around his visitor.

Joanie followed Mickey up the narrow, steep, staircase.

'Oxygen, oxygen,' Joanie gasped as they reached the top landing.

They went through a white painted door into Mickey's apartment. Mickey shared the flat with two Dutchmen, Herman

Both and Karel Velde. Mickey worked beside Herman at a call centre operated by a big hotel chain. Karel had several jobs, including working in a theatre and a bar. The flat seemed pretty small to Joanie but according to Mickey it was vast by Amsterdam standards. Space was something that was at a premium in the city. They all had their own rooms and there was a lounge with an open-plan kitchen and a small dining-room.

'This is where you'll sleep,' said Mickey.

'On the table?' replied Joanie.

Mickey said it was a gate-leg table and they could fold it down and put it in a corner. Joanie could sleep on the cushions off the sofa, inside a sleeping bag on the floor. Joanie was beginning to wish he'd booked a hotel room.

The old friends sat on the sofa drinking tea and crunching biscuits. Mickey asked Joanie all about Delilah's and the Glasgow scene, and Joanie dished the dirt on some of their mutual acquaintances. Mickey had worked in a dozen or so bars, gay and straight, but he was enjoying his new line of work – he took reservations for hotels all over Europe. When he'd left Glasgow two years before he'd tried to persuade Joanie to move to Amsterdam, but Joanie wasn't keen. He liked Glasgow. It was a dirty, grey, miserable, homophobic dump, but it was also a beautiful city, full of great, warm people. It was home, which was the only place any self-respecting friend of Dorothy really wanted to be.

Joanie was in Mickey's room unpacking his bag. He had tried to travel light. He hadn't brought anything draggy apart from an aqua-green trouser suit he'd bought in an Oxfam shop. It was really poofy and ridiculous on him, which was why he liked it so much. As he struggled to find wardrobe space for it he became aware of a presence at the door. Joanie turned to see Herman. He was a big guy, the wrong side of forty, with a walrus moustache. He wore a white vest and faded blue jeans. Bulging beneath the jeans, stretching across his right thigh, Joanie could see what appeared to be the biggest cock in captivity.

'Hi,' said Joanie.

'Hi, I'm Herman,' said the Dutchman with the daunting dick.

Then he disappeared down the hall.

They were in April's and men were springing up all over the place.

'It's getting busy,' observed Joanie.

'It's 'cause you're here,' said Mickey, with a wink. They had gone past the main bar through to the wee circular revolving bar at the back. Joanie liked the concept and wondered if a revolving bar could work in Delilah's. Mickey said he didn't like it; he'd rather move in a bar of his own free will. After awhile Mickey said he wanted to go home. He'd been out late the previous night and had been ill that morning, which was why he hadn't made it to the station to meet Joanie. As Joanie had four more nights to spend in Amsterdam he didn't mind having an early night.

The four guys watched some TV in the lounge before hitting the sack. Karel was tall and thin, with a dry, wispy brush of blond hair capping his long face. He was talkative compared to Herman. Mickey took control of the TV and flicked between channels, to the increasing irritation of Joanie. Later, Joanie said he was hungry and Karel went over to a corner shop and brought back patat and satay sauce. It would be Joanie's staple diet for the rest of the holiday.

Although Joanie slept like a log, snug in the sleeping bag and draped across the couch cushions, he didn't tell Mickey that. He was annoyed that Mickey hadn't volunteered his bed.

'I didn't sleep a wink,' moaned Joanie. 'I think I've dislocated my hip.'

Mickey just smiled and said, 'It's your age, dear.'

He sat in an armchair and watched Joanie roll up the sleeping-bag, fix the cushions back on the couch and then manoeuvre the table back into the centre of the dining-room. Herman and Karel were at work but Mickey had taken time off to see Joanie.

The guys spent a nice day walking around Amsterdam in the warm sunshine. They walked alongside the canals, the Princesgracht, the Herengracht, Singel, stopping to take snaps of each other. They clocked the hookers in the red light district, and went for lunch at De Jaren, a big, modern, airy café. Because it was such a bright day the garden and balcony areas were packed. Mickey seemed miffed but Joanie was happy to sit in the cool spacious interior. They rounded the afternoon off with a few beers in April's.

That night Mickey and Herman had invited a few people over from work. Joanie got rat-arsed and mixed up his drinks and people's names. Magalit, a lovely Dutch girl, became Magaluf. A Brazilian guy, Umberto, was forced to go by the name of Sombrero. Shuki, an Israeli pal of Herman's, was hailed as Sushi. Joanie's last party trick was to bogart a joint and take a whitey. Finally, having been given the evil eye by Mickey, Joanie crawled up the stairs and fell asleep on top of Mickey's bed. When he woke in the morning, Mickey lay under the covers beside him. They lay half-awake, looking at each other.

'You look like shit,' said Mickey.

'So do you,' replied Joanie.

Saturday was Queen's Day and Amsterdam was crowded. Mickey and Joanie made their way through the cosmopolitan chaos, sometimes inch by inch. Everywhere they turned there was music: a groovy Rastafarian DJ playing Bill Withers' *Lovely Day*, a young Dutch girl skipping around a stage singing *I Will Survive*, and DJs in the gay area pumping out rave anthems to the crazy revellers. The quieter streets, away from the centre, were littered with street hawkers selling crockery, old clothes, books, dolls, and food. Joanie bought a four-pack of Heineken from a vendor, and he and Mickey sipped from the cans and soaked up the atmosphere.

Back at the flat, Karel was getting ready to go to work and Herman was getting ready to go to the sauna. Mickey and Joanie sat at the dining table eating pasta and salad. Joanie wanted to go out but Mickey was too tired. He suggested Joanie tag along to the sauna with Herman but Joanie wanted to go to a bar. When Herman and Karel left, Joanie and Mickey drank two bottles of wine and danced to Madonna in the lounge, for old times' sake. Between the booze and the beat all they had to do was smile their survivor's smiles at each other. They had known each other for fifteen years and it felt like fifty.

The next morning Joanie lay on the dining-room floor and waited till he was sure Herman and Karel had left before he got up. When he opened the door to the lounge, he was startled to see Mickey sitting quietly on the sofa, sipping tea. Joanie sat down beside him while Mickey quizzed him on why he'd slept so late. Joanie was depressed. The holiday was crap – he hadn't 'done anything'.

Mickey had a rendezvous with his flatmates and some colleagues from work. He wanted Joanie to come. They planned to hire a boat and sail on the canals. Joanie showered and changed and came down the narrow stairs from the bathroom in full make-up, sporting his aqua green trouser suit like some old Hollywood movie star.

'You fabulous old cunt!' gasped Mickey.

The boat cost eighty guilders for an hour, which worked out at ten guilders each. Apart from Joanie, Mickey and the sailing Dutchmen, there were Shuki, Umberto, Juliana and Pedro, all workmates of Mickey's. It was a dull, overcast day but the air was mild and spirits were high, helped by some space cakes they had munched in a brown café with steaming, hot coffee. Pedro took charge of steering the small white boat.

Joanie loved the hour-long sail, which Mickey said was as smooth as a rent-boy's arse. Amsterdam looked even more impressive from the canals. They admired its narrow buildings, topped by fancy gables; waved and yelled at boating neighbours they passed on the canals; swigged cans of Heineken and sang and whooped under the myriad bridges. Joanie stood up now and again to get a better view and appreciate the sail. At one point he could see the red light district again. The black prostitutes in their white bras and knickers seemed to be moving in slow motion in their shop windows. Joanie thought they looked graceful.

That night they were meant to be going to a nightclub, a queer shop called Troot. Joanie and Mickey stood in the middle of the queue. Joanie had changed out of his trouser suit and opted for jeans and a white shirt. Mickey wore jeans with a tee shirt and a leather jacket. Joanie looked up and down the queue. There were guys in tuxedos and big cocktail dresses and women in evening gowns. A young queen in front of them said something in Dutch to Mickey, who gave a weary sigh.

'What's the problem?' asked Joanie.

'No jeans,' said Mickey. 'It's a special dress code for the Queen's birthday.'

Just then a huge, hairy man in a tutu, with a fairy wand in his hand, stopped beside Mickey. He pointed at his jeans with the wand and shook his head, rolling his big, heavily made-up eyes. Joanie urged Mickey to wait and chance it, but then they saw other denim-clad queers being turned away at the door ten yards in front of them. They accepted defeat and left the queue.

'What a cruel irony,' mused Joanie as they walked along the canal side. 'I, queen of glamour, refused admittance to a club for being too dowdy.'

The city looked prettier at night, or maybe it was just the beer they'd drunk. Joanie gazed at the lights on the canal bridges and sighed.

'Let's go to Soho,' said Mickey, emphatically.

He led the way through the crowded street level bar to the upstairs bar. The stairway seemed to be floodlit, exposing a tatty, old, formerly bright, red carpet that looked to Joanie like it had been found in a rubbish skip outside an old cinema and recycled. They stood at the end of the bar, and after an eternity, managed to get served. They discussed their shared history, their love lives (or lack of them) and Joanie ordered the beers four at a time. On the way home Joanie pissed in a canal. Mickey warned against it, saying the police could fine him. Joanie simply giggled as his pee arced into the dark waterway below.

On Monday Joanie wanted to go to the Van Gogh Museum, and threatened to cut off an ear if Mickey didn't take him. But when they got to the Van Gogh there was an intimidatingly long queue. Mickey suggested they go to the Rijksmuseum as a compromise. Joanie paid them in and they wandered around the huge museum admiring the exhibits. Mickey's favourite was a 17th century snuffbox inlaid with mother of pearl.

'I could keep my johnny bags in there,' he sighed, wistfully.

Joanie admired a three-thousand-year-old bronze Chinese mask, which he thought looked like an ex of his. But his favourite, however, was a Rembrandt. *Hendrickje asleep*, it was called, and was meant to be a drawing of Rembrandt's lover. Joanie thought it was angelic, but Mickey said when it came to drawing, Rembrandt wasn't a patch on Rolf Harris.

They had a nice lunch in De Jaren and then Mickey coaxed Joanie into a sex shop where they gawked and giggled at the various sex aids. Mickey howled at something called a pussy stick. They couldn't quite see (it was concealed by a wrapper), but the label said the stick was to be inserted in the pussy before intercourse to regain 'virgin excitement.' Joanie handled the plethora of vibrating dildos.

There was a red rubber one they both thought particularly fetching.

They spent half an hour in the shop, Mickey trying on some rubber shorts and pouches, before stepping out into what was becoming another sunny afternoon. Joanie said he wanted to do some shopping and they agreed to split up and meet later at the flat.

Mickey decided to stay in that night. He said he had a headache and retired at eleven o'clock, advising Joanie to go to the sauna. Joanie settled down for the night in the dining-room. What happened next was so unexpected that he later wondered if he had dreamt it. He had awoken to find the enigmatic Herman standing above him, wearing only black leather shorts. Herman's face, at least what could be made out in the darkness, was expressionless.

'You want to fuck?' asked Herman, tenderly.

Joanie sat up, leaning on one elbow. He reached through the night until his fingers traced Herman's hard-on through the smooth leather.

'No,' said Joanie, as gently as he could. In the blink of an eye Herman was gone.

Although Mickey was gracious enough to escort Joanie to the airport, he was in a foul mood. Joanie wondered if it was just that sad awkwardness of saying goodbye, or if Mickey was feeling homesick. They kissed at the airport then Joanie marched through to his gate, clutching his boarding pass, not even looking back to wave.

Unpacking that evening, Joanie reflected on his long weekend in Amsterdam. It hadn't been the sexy, sauna-filled, wild weekend other guys often came home talking about. It had been a more refined experience altogether, the only real cruising he'd done was on the canals. Maybe he was getting old. What he couldn't work out was why he'd turned down the horny Herman. He hadn't fancied him, but God knows it hadn't stopped him before. Not so long ago he would've sat on that Dutch Master's cock and sung like a soprano. But Joanie wasn't looking for sex anymore. Or drugs, or rock'n'roll, or money, or fame. The only thing worth looking for was love. It was then that he found the long, thin, parcel at the bottom of his bag. Sellotaped to the wrapping paper was a small white envelope with 'Joanie' written on it. He recognised Mickey's handwriting. He unwrapped the package and smiled. It was the red rubber dildo. Joanie sat on the bed and opened the card.

'Sit on this, bitch,' Mickey had written. Joanie turned the control dial at the bottom of the dildo and felt the rubber reverberate in his fist. He thought of sweet, silly Mickey, of horny Herman, the black whores, *Hendrickje* sleeping, and he blessed them all.

Bobbie and the Womyn

One night Bobbie came into Delilah's with a womyn. They had met at a lesbian disco in Clyde Street. It was a monthly thing, cans and bottles on a couple of long tables serving as a bar, a disc jockey who played scratchy vinyl records that kept jumping or stopping altogether. There had been a dancing free-for-all at the end of it and, somehow in the crowd, Bobbie and the womyn found each other. They had danced to some old punky classics, Siouxsie and the Banshees, the Cure, before ending up locked in an embrace on the creaky, slippy, floor.

Although Bobbie talked a good game when it came to sex, even she was more than a little intimidated when the womyn advanced menacingly on her, sporting a strap-on dildo, in the womyn's cramped one-bedroom flat just off the Gallowgate.

'If I want a cock I'll go an' get a real wan,' said Bobbie.

The womyn had reluctantly taken off the dildo and they made do with what God gave them, searching each other with fingers and tongues. As they turned in the womyn's bed, Bobbie felt she had finally met the one she had been longing for, someone handsome and headstrong like her.

In the morning they sat in the wee living-room with coffee and cigarettes. Bobbie noticed a bookcase in a corner, crammed full of well-thumbed paperbacks.

'I paint, sculpt, devise movement pieces and rage against injustice. What do you do?' the womyn demanded.

She was staring at Bobbie as if she didn't quite believe she was there.

'I work in a fruit and veg shop,' said Bobbie. The womyn nodded; an accepting, supportive nod.

'That's good,' she said, in her strange, strong voice. 'Fruit and vegetables are healthy.' She fixed Bobbie with a look. 'You're a vegetarian, right? Because if you eat dead animals I never want to touch you again,' said the womyn.

'I'm a vegetarian,' lied Bobbie. She rifted and tasted the ghost of last night's Big Mac in her mouth. She quickly dragged on a cigarette.

'I'm a womyn,' said the womyn.

Bobbie smiled. 'I noticed,' she said, admiringly.

'You don't understand,' said the womyn. 'I'm a womyn. It's spelled W-O-M-Y-N. There's no 'man' in it. I'm a lesbian feminist.'

Bobbie looked at the womyn and felt curiously excited.

The womyn had never been in Delilah's before. She despised the commercial gay scene and it took a lot of persuading to coax her in. It was like trying to get a reluctant five-year-old to start school. Eventually Bobbie got her to Delilah's and manoeuvred her into a booth. The womyn took in Delilah's with her sad, searching eyes. Bobbie said she would go to the bar and get the drinks. She wondered if the womyn would feel okay about being left on her own.

'Don't be so insecure,' said the womyn, coldly.

This hurt Bobbie, because she was insecure. She was worried that this sexy, sullen, mysterious womyn would abandon her for somebody else.

They had shared a passionate week together in the womyn's flat (which smelled of rising damp and patchouli). Now and again the womyn would snatch a book from her bookshelf and read a passage to Bobbie. There were tirades against the patriarchy and fragments of lesbian erotica and poetry recitals interspersed with strange, almost menacing, silences and fantastic sex on the womyn's bed with incense and candles and the two of them burning. Bobbie had never felt so turned on or glad to be gay before. But it wasn't all exhilaration. The womyn was strange, intense and possibly a bit too full of herself.

Bobbie stood at the bar, anxious to be served and get back to her new found love. She glanced back to make sure the womyn was unmolested. The womyn had both arms crossed over her belly and was surveying the scene, poker-faced. Bobbie got the drinks, a pint of lager for herself and a rum and coke for her partner. When she got back to the table and sat down, the womyn didn't acknowledge her presence. She was still inspecting the bar.

'There's yer rum and coke,' said Bobbie. The womyn grunted. Then she turned suddenly and stared at Bobbie.

'Is it always this busy?' she asked. Bobbie was glad that there was no hostility in the question. She didn't want the womyn to dislike Delilah's too much. As much as Bobbie liked the womyn, she couldn't really envisage a time when she wouldn't be going to Delilah's. Yet she knew this thinking was crap, as the pub could be taken over and turned into a straight place, or she could move away or outgrow it. She even began to think that the womyn might take her away from all this and she wouldn't need Delilah's any more. She began to relax.

'It's busier at weekends,' she said, responding to the womyn's question. She felt slightly uncomfortable with the womyn looking at her. She seemed to be staring more out of curiosity than admiration. The womyn sipped her drink and gave a weary sigh.

'So this is where you waste your time,' she said, almost to herself. Bobbie tried not to let the comment rile her.

'It's a good place tae meet other women,' she countered.

'It's a man's pub,' retorted the womyn.

'No, honestly, it's mixed. It's usually sixty-forty. Sixty percent men, forty percent women.'

The womyn swept the pub with her fierce brown eyes. 'It looks more like eighty-twenty to me,' she said, coolly.

After a couple of drinks, bought and paid for by Bobbie, the womyn seemed to warm a little. She even bobbed her head to some of the music and smiled. She smiled yet more when one of Bobbie's pals came over to speak to them. Her name was Joyce and she had big hair, big tits and a big mouth. Bobbie liked Joyce but she didn't like the way the womyn was looking at her. Bobbie had never seen her hold a smile for so long. Bobbie tried to make secret, scary eyes at Joyce to get rid of her. Eventually she did leave and the womyn's smile faded from her face. There was a silence, and Bobbie gulped at her lager and tried not to appear jealous.

Bobbie was scared she'd get too drunk and lose control of the situation. Dating was so hard, you had to be vigilant. The early weeks were crucial. It had been a tumultuous first week with the womyn. Bobbie hadn't realised just how much she needed love in her life right now. Drinking and carrying-on and fucking about were all very well but she was getting older. It was harder to pretend to be happy when you got older. The way the womyn had held her, that first night in her bed, had left its' mark. Sure, she was strange, who wasn't? Bobbie felt time would smooth over these teething troubles.

'Who's the drag queen?' asked the womyn tersely, nodding towards the bar. As she had made no attempt to go to the bar, she had only seen Joanie from a distance.

'That's John … Joanie. He's been here since it opened.'

The womyn's displeasure was unnervingly obvious. 'I find that offensive,' said the womyn.

'He doesn't do an act or anything,' said Bobbie apologetically. 'He just dresses up for a laugh really.'

The womyn glanced across at Joanie. 'A laugh? At womynkind's expense!' snarled the womyn.

'Nobody thinks anything of it,' said Bobbie, in a conciliatory tone.

'Nobody thinks. Period,' said the womyn. 'That's the whole trouble with the gay scene. It's just a predatory sexual playground for men. That's why we womyn need our own space. To get away from crap like that.' She nodded over in Joanie's direction. Bobbie struggled valiantly to steer the subject away from Delilah's. She looked at the womyn, who seemed more relaxed now. She had an elbow up over the back of the seat and was looking over at the bar. She turned to catch Bobbie's eye.

'I just hate to see people painting themselves into a corner,' she said, exasperated. She got up and fumbled in her jacket pocket. Then she started walking away from the booth.

'Where are ye goin'?' blurted Bobbie.

'The toilet,' the womyn snapped back.

She headed in the wrong direction, spoke briefly to another

woman, then turned and walked in the right direction and disappeared up the stairs. Bobbie was tempted to follow her. She knew the womyn had a formidable sexual appetite. She was also a new face in Delilah's, that had pulling power in itself. Then there was the way she had looked at Joyce, so obviously flirting, fancying her. Bobbie checked herself, smiled at her own insecurities. She felt a bit light-headed now. The music was good, the atmosphere was buoyant, and she was in with a brand new lover.

Bobbie kept watch for the womyn. Eventually she materialised again. She didn't look over at Bobbie but instead went to the bar. Bobbie watched her being served by Joanie. A tall queen obscured her view and then she was suddenly alarmed to find the womyn leaning over the table, a crazed look in her eyes.

'Give me some money,' she growled. Bobbie fumbled for her purse like she was being held at gunpoint. She handed the womyn a fiver.

'Fuckin' drag queen,' said the womyn, and headed back to the bar. Bobbie saw the womyn and Joanie exchange money and poisonous looks. Then the womyn came back over to the booth. She sat down and put a solitary drink, a rum and coke, on the table. Bobbie looked at the half-inch of beer she had left in her glass.

'Didn't ye get me a drink?' she asked.

'I think you've had enough,' retorted the womyn, nostrils flaring.

Bobbie was too frightened to ask for her change. It wasn't that she was physically scared of her. Although the womyn was lean and wiry, Bobbie felt she could probably wipe the floor with her. She was afraid of being dumped, not thumped.

Glancing across at the bar, Bobbie saw Joanie watching them. He was giving her a strange, pitiful look. Embarrassed, she turned away.

'What happened at the bar?' she asked.

'That freak – that monstrosity – tried to rip me off. The fuckin' prices in here. Rip-off merchants.'

Bobbie almost smiled at that. The womyn hadn't spent a penny at the bar and had moaned all night.

'It's not so bad,' said Bobbie. 'They have happy hours in here. Wan twenty a pint. That's not bad.'

The womyn leaned forward across the table, an incredulous look on her face.

'Happy hours? In this dump? This ghetto?' She sat back and picked up her rum and coke. Bobbie drained her glass and got up.

'Same again?' she asked the womyn, who nodded. Bobbie made her way down to the bar. The alcohol was taking effect. She felt half-cut and decided to get a half-pint this time. The bar was busy and Bobbie fumbled for money in the pocket of her jeans. Now that she had physically moved away from the womyn, she found her perspective changing. It crossed her mind that she might stay at the bar and leave the womyn to her own dour-faced devices. She had put up with enough crap for one night. But then she thought of the womyn's strong, lean body; the passionate and purposeful way the womyn moved the length and breadth of Bobbie's tingling frame, stretched out on the womyn's bed. She thought of the leaping flames of the candles and the womyn's tongue searching her. Bobbie decided she would walk across hot coals to get to that feeling.

'Who's she?' said a voice from behind the bar. It was Joanie, with a quick nod towards the womyn.

'Ma girlfriend,' said Bobbie, forcefully.

'Who rattled her cage?' asked Joanie.

'She didn't have enough money,' said Bobbie, hoping that would explain it.

Joanie took the order and poured the drinks.

'She looked at me as if ah wis somethin' she'd found oan her shoe,' he said.

He gave Bobbie her change. Bobbie gave him a grateful smile and went back to play poker faces with the womyn.

Bobbie tried to make small talk with her but she shrugged each question or statement off with a grunt or a groan. The womyn seemed to loosen up a bit more after the rum went to her head. She became more voluble and even less charitable. She began to pick off Delilah's punters like a sniper.

'Look at that old queen dressed like a teenager,' she said. 'Look at him, mincing up and down. Sad old fuck.' She spotted two young women with their arms around each other. They were singing along to a song Bobbie liked.

'Check those two,' sniped the womyn. 'They should be at home reading a book. Not pissing about in this shithole pretending to be one of the boys. I suppose that's the only way to get anywhere in here. Kid on you're as stupid as the men.'

Bobbie imagined she was on her own, enjoying the beer, listening to the music.

'Look at him,' said the womyn, pointing at a guy who was dancing beside one of the booths near the door. 'God save us from disco divas.'

Bobbie looked at the womyn, and something in her face must have betrayed her feelings. The womyn retreated in her seat, defensive all of a sudden.

'I'm only being cruel to be kind,' said the womyn, with great conviction. 'Someone ought to tell these guys there's more to life than buggery and bad music.'

Bobbie sat on the lavatory pan and tried to stop herself from crying. She couldn't understand why the womyn was being so nasty about everything. She decided she could never go to Delilah's with her again. The womyn was non-scene. She obviously hated it and that was all there was to it.

Fuck it, thought Bobbie, sometimes she hated the scene too. It could be snide, bitchy, lonely; the same old faces and the same old crap. Here was a womyn who was intelligent and passionate. Who was above all that crap. You couldn't spend forever in a queer bar. Here was somebody who could open up new horizons to her. She recalled the womyn kneeling naked on top of her bed, reading from a dog-eared book to her. Bobbie couldn't remember the words now, just the hunched figure of the womyn in the candlelight, babbling.

At first Bobbie thought they were fighting. The womyn's hands were buried in Joyce's big hair, pulling. It looked as if they were biting each other. As she got closer their mouths seemed to connect and stick together. They didn't even see Bobbie pick up her jacket. She headed back down to the bar, unsure whether to stay or go. Joanie came over to her and handed her a half-pint of lager.

'On the house,' he said. Over Bobbie's shoulder he could see the womyn and Joyce locked together like battling insects. 'You win some, ye lose some,' he said. 'You're well shot ay the torn-faced cunt.'

Bobbie nodded, as if in agreement, but a salty tear made its way down her face and curled over her top lip till she could taste it.

The Other World

I had a dream last week about a man I hadn't seen for eight years. I don't know whether he's alive or dead. So I suppose I do believe in ghosts.

Last night I went to Delilah's. There was nothing on TV, I'd just got paid and I felt horny. Maybe horny's not the right word; more depressed and anxious and in need of some kind of release. As soon as I'd stepped into Delilah's I felt it was a mistake. The punters seemed to be getting younger every day. I swear I saw a twelve-year-old sniffing poppers at the bar. A bunch of teenage girls were taking over the karaoke session in the backroom. They said they were the real Spice Girls. They introduced themselves as Fanny Spice, Spunky Spice, Bad Hair Spice, Lager Lout Spice and Finger-Fucking Spice. Then they proceeded to murder *If You Wanna Be My Lover*.

It was a Thursday night so maybe that explained it. It usually attracted the younger crowd. There were some students in, sporting spiky, dyed hair and stinking old men's jackets. One had his lips, nostril and eyebrows pierced.

I had a day off flexitime today so I knew I could get as drunk as I wanted. I duly did so. While I was hard at it a guy came over and asked me for a light. He wore lime green Lycra shorts and had a big, long, orange face. As he leaned over to catch the flame his face turned a ghastly yellow in the light.

'Like the tan?' he asked, waving his cigarette in his hand. 'Gran Canaria.'

I nodded dumbly.

'See ye, pet.' He gave me a suggestive wink and wandered off. I noticed a hole like a fag burn in the back of his shorts.

Delilah's got smokier and noisier. I could've sworn to God that I heard Cher at one point belting out *It's In His Kiss*. I craned my neck to see through to the backroom; the singer was a boy of about nineteen (stone, that is). It was mobbed in the back now, but that suited me fine. The front bar was quieter and you could breathe again, move your elbows, stretch your legs, get served at the bar. I was feeling pissed but I wasn't feeling any better. I hate Delilah's and I hate karaoke and I hate the gay scene and I hate not being young anymore.

It was then I saw a heavily built man in a suit giving me the eye from the bar. He had a square, handsome face, dark eyes and eyebrows. He raised his eyebrows quizzically when he caught my eye. I nodded to him and he came over. He said his name was Ralph and he was a taxi driver. We made small talk for a few minutes – name, rank and serial number stuff – then he said that he knew me from before.

'Before?' I asked.

'In another life,' he said casually.

'Don't tell me,' I said. 'I was Antony and you were Cleopatra.'

He grinned.

'You're no far wrong,' he said. He told me that he had psychic powers and that he knew a number of people who were now 'in spirit'.

'You mean like they're pickled?' I asked mockingly.

'In spirit,' he said carefully. 'They've passed over to the other side.'

'I don't really go for all that,' I assured him. I read my stars in the papers but I know it's a load of crap. I looked at Ralph and decided I liked what I saw. Psychic-psychobabble aside.

'I received a message from Princess Diana last week,' he whispered reverentially. 'She's at peace now.'

I nodded respectfully. 'I'm glad to hear it,' I said.

'She married Dodi in Heaven,' he added, somewhat labouring the point. He lifted his glass to his lips and I caught a twinkle in his eye. I wondered if he was taking the piss. I steered things back to the material world. He told me some stories about his work. He said he used to pick up a straight couple, drive them out into the countryside, and sit on the grass while they shagged in the back of his cab. They were both married, though not to each other, and it was a fifty quid fare.

'How did it end?' I asked.

'They rented a flat,' replied Ralph, drolly.

'Sounds more comfortable,' I reasoned.

'Have you ever had it off in the back of a taxi?' Ralph asked me. I told him I hadn't, that I wasn't an exhibitionist. He looked disappointed and I understood it was a loaded question. I looked at his hands resting on the table beside his empty glass. I decided then that I would go back with him. I wanted those hands on me. He looked at me and smiled mischievously.

'You've made up your mind,' he said.

'About what?' I asked, coyly.

'You know,' he said. 'What're you drinking?'

Ralph bought me another pint, my fifth. I was feeling it now. He was drinking soda water and lime.

'Do you have your taxi outside?' I asked him.

He shook his head.

'But I am driving,' he said, 'if you'd like a lift.'

'That would be nice,' I replied.

Ralph took a couple of the ice cubes out of his drink and plopped them into the ashtray.

'I told them no ice,' he explained. 'Where to?'

'What?' I asked.

'Where would you like the lift to?'

'Your place,' I said, too quickly.

Ralph talked to me about the next world as he drove. He was a slow and careful driver. I didn't mind, except it meant I had to hear more about the other side than I really wanted to. Ralph said he'd been having visions, premonitions and receiving messages, from the other world since he was five years old. He'd looked into his mother's crystal ball and saw a man lying shot in a big car.

'JFK?' I enquired, nonchalantly.

'My Uncle Billy,' retorted Ralph. 'He was a gangster in London. He made the Krays look like the Krankies. A rival put a contract out on him. Of course I saw the vision the day before he was shot.'

'That's scary,' I said. I was so pissed by now I almost believed him.

'Sometimes it can seem like a curse,' sighed Ralph, as we trundled along at a snail's pace. He talked some more about his mysterious powers. He said he had psychic antennae and could tune into people's thoughts. He said it was just like radio waves. He could drive along in his taxi and be contacted by the controller about a fare and nobody thinks that's weird. But in olden days people would've thought it was magic. He said his psychic powers were like this, that there was such a thing as thought transference, telepathy. He said he knew what I was thinking right there. But if he had known what I was thinking he would have shut up and driven faster. He kept on talking about things psychic. He said he could astrally project and that one time he left his body while he was being fucked, floated up above the bed, looked down, and watched himself getting it up the arse.

Ralph's house smelled of cat pish. We were hardly in the door when he wrestled me to the floor. We took off each other's clothes, me nearly blacking out with the smell of the carpet. Ralph rolled on top of me. He had the mother of all bellies and that took me by surprise. He had worn his shirt hanging out over his trousers. Like a maternity smock. I'd been through this before with another guy. It seemed that this was the fashion for the bulkier boy. It was probably a dress code they picked up in *The Fat Poof's Guide To Getting Your Hole*. Ralph had a nice face so I concentrated on that. I struggled for breath beneath him and he apologised about his weight. He said he'd broken his leg, was in plaster for two months, and couldn't get to the gym. We wrestled around on the pishy carpet. I never saw the cats but he said he had three.

In bed we rested in the darkness, lying on our backs. Ralph told me cats were our psychic channels to the other world, can sense ghosts long before we do, and could teach us a thing or two about telepathy. His voice was soft and deep, like he was a big fat cat purring beside me. He said cats had their own language, that a woman had written a book about it, and that he was in the process of learning it. He was quiet for a while and I tried to doze but I felt queasy, and knew my hangover was beginning to take over.

Ralph asked me if I had the second sight. I told him I'd had double vision a few times. He said that I was psychic but that I needed time to get used to my powers. I thought that was a joke. Just before we slipped into sleep Ralph told me that he knew when someone was going to die because he saw 'the death mask,' a skeletal-like face, appear on them. He'd seen it on a lot of people, but he never told them. You should never halt someone's spiritual destiny. 'It can be a curse,' he sighed again and dozed off.

Ralph was one of those frisky characters in the morning. He bounced and wanked all over me. All I could think about was tea and toast. Eventually he came, then got up to put the kettle on. I heard him singing in the kitchen, his voice rich, deep and strong. I felt guilty, smirking at his beliefs. The big pussycat popped his head round the bedroom door and asked if I wanted tea in bed. I said I'd get up.

In the living-room I sat on the sofa eating my toast and sipping at the boiling hot tea. Ralph told me he sang at weddings and other functions. Old folks' homes. He said he loved performing and his favourite song was *Feelings*. He'd adapted the song; had created a new, more up-tempo arrangement. He felt that with the current vogue for more dance-type music he could reach a wider audience by speeding up some of the standards. He asked me if I liked musicals and I nodded, stupidly. I must be the only gay man I know who hates cats and show songs. Ralph drained his cup of tea, went over to the CD player and pressed a few buttons. He picked up a radio mike and I heard what sounded like an electro-version of *Feelings*. He danced from side to side and swayed his head at an imaginary audience. His big sweet face shone with sincerity as I bit into my lip.

With the threat of another song looming, I decided to stall him by asking if I could meet his cats. They were out on the veranda and he said I could meet them some other time. He came over and sat beside me on the sofa. He asked what I thought of his arrangement of *Feelings*. I said he ought to release it as a single. He was doing *Seven Brides for Seven Brothers* at the King's this autumn. He'd get me a ticket to see him.

I decided to make a move before my hangover paralysed me completely. Ralph said he could give me a lift. He made another pot of tea and we sat and listened to his show songs collection. I noticed my watch was missing and Ralph said it was in the bedroom; went to get it for me. He came back with my watch in his hand. Instead of giving it to me, he sat with it in his palm. He closed his other hand over the watch and shut his eyes firmly.

'Are you okay?' I asked. He was silent, concentrating. After what seemed like minutes, he opened his eyes and looked at me with an unnerving intensity.

'Psychometry,' he explained. He told me he could glean things from objects, stuff about their owners. He said it was one of his gifts.

'That's a new strap I got put on it,' I said, concerned that might have affected his psychometric reading.

'That's okay,' he said. 'I got a good reading. You're on the threshold of something. Some kinda turning point. A new romance.'

I put my hand out for the watch. He put the watch on my wrist, trembling as he did so, like a nervous groom with a wedding ring. I looked at the watch.

'God is that the time?' I exclaimed, pretending I had somewhere else to be. Ralph fixed me with a steely stare.

'So when do I get to see you again?'

I began to haver. I said I was busy, that I'd really enjoyed the time we'd spent together, but I couldn't say anything for definite. I even added, ridiculously, that I was in love with someone else. Ralph's face hardened.

'You certainly know how to make someone feel cheap,' he said, coldly. I got up, slightly startled, and walked through to the bedroom to get my jacket. I think he kept talking to me from the other room. I heard notes of his rich, velvety voice sliding between a histrionic version *of Don't Cry For Me Argentina*. I stood at the living-room door with my jacket over my arm. I gathered that a lift was now out of the question.

'It was nice to meet ye,' I said in a croaky, cowardly voice.

Ralph got up and took a few steps towards me. He seemed as if he was about to cry. Then he stared at me, a strange, crazed look in his eye and I felt my heart jump.

'The death mask!' he gasped, and staggered back.

'Oh fuck off,' I said and made for the door.

I felt sick on the bus. I vowed never to go back with another man. I was too long in the tooth for this hassle. It was never, ever worth it. People, men, were too weird. I felt scared, thinking maybe I was going to die, that Ralph did have mysterious powers, and had foretold my imminent doom. In my heart I knew he'd just tried to freak me out because he never got a date.

I filled my flat with sighs of relief. After a shower, I arsed around in my dressinggown. I dismissed all thoughts of the other world and things supernatural. I felt my face with my hands. It felt fine. It was still warm, at least. I decided to look at it in the mirror – the full-length wardrobe mirror in my bedroom. I crept up on myself. I looked at my face. I'm nearly forty and I look it, but I looked okay. A bit tired, but evidently alive. I thought about my mortality. I understood that if not today then one day I would face my death. I knew I was right not to see Ralph again, it wasn't right. I studied my face and wondered if anybody could love it. I've only ever loved two men in my life. One betrayed me and the other one died. I'd like to see both of them again. I don't know if I believe in love anymore, never mind telepathic cats or the other world. I moved closer to the mirror, close enough for my breath to cloud the image.

A Coat of Arms

Jimmy and Alec were just about to leave when Lawrie came in.
Jimmy and Lawrie knew each other well, but not as well as Jimmy
would've liked. He introduced Lawrie to Alec and, before he could be
dissuaded, Lawrie was at the bar buying a round.

Lawrie was beautiful. He had big brown eyes like Maltesers, was
into opera in a big way, and red wine. He was a doctor. Jimmy had
met him in Delilah's last winter. It had been snowing and Lawrie had
come in out of the snow. He had never been in Delilah's before. There
was snow in his hair. There was something different about Lawrie.
That was obvious. He was sophisticated. Debonair.

Fuelled by lager, Jimmy had steamed towards him and chatted
him up. They had become something after that. Not lovers; Lawrie
and Jimmy occupied that grey area between friends and
acquaintances. There was nothing really definite about their
connection. They would call each other up to see a film, a play;
sometimes just go to the pub.

Things had dragged on with Jimmy and Lawrie for a few months.
It was obvious this was going to be a romance-free zone. Obvious to
everybody, that is, except Jimmy. He grew fond of Lawrie, that
fondness where you like the way a person walks, even if they're hen-
toed, or like the warm honeyed tones of their voice, even if they're
talking crap. He had decided Lawrie was simply a slow-burner. It was
a matter of biding his time. Wasn't it better to wait, to let things grow
and develop? After all, Jimmy was tired of the yo-yo knickers, the
one-night stand scene. How much better to make love. So he waited
for something that never came. Jimmy was never very intuitive. He
needed things spelled out.

It was spelled out one night at Lawrie's house. Lawrie had invited
Jimmy over for dinner and as usual, Jimmy saw Cupid hovering in
the wings, drawing back his bow. Dinner was steak served up with
roast potatoes and veg. Jimmy was almost vegetarian by this point

but would have eaten a live lamb if Lawrie had served it. He would have bitten Bambi's balls for a taste of that man. They ate in candlelight. Lawrie had put on a classical CD, Jimmy couldn't remember what – he was strictly a pop man. Dessert was ice cream, followed by coffee and chocolates. Then the wine flowed like some unstoppable, tempestuous river. Red, red wine. It was a Friday night so they didn't have to worry about work the next day – this was a time for play and Jimmy was hoping to sample his host's bedside manner.

He had never actually seen Lawrie's bedroom, although he'd been in his house half a dozen times. Jimmy knew where it was, down the hall to the left. He had seen Lawrie going in there to pick up a jacket or do something else, get something, always closing the door behind him. In retrospect he saw that this thing about the bedroom being out of bounds was a sign of where their relationship was going. No fuckin where. But love, as they say, is visually impaired. Looking into Lawrie's big, brown eyes, once or twice, he thought he saw love.

They sat on a sofa in the living-room and drank and talked. Jimmy decided, in collaboration with the wine that tonight was the night he got into Lawrie's bedroom and into his beautiful arms. Lawrie had lovely skin. Olive skin. Whatever olive skin was, this was it … his soft wavy hair in the lamplight, his Malteser eyes and his olive skin.

'I've been thinking. About us.'

'What about us?'

Lawrie's tone was abrupt, not to say indignant.

'We've – we've known each other a few months now and I was wonderin' – wonderin' where we were goin'.'

Lawrie looked quizzically at Jimmy.

'Where we're going? We're not going anywhere? Are you …?'

'Naw, it's just, are we friends or what?'

Jimmy's hand was in the flame.

'We're friends.'

'It's just – I really like you. I'm attracted to you. I'd like us to go further.'

Lawrie seemed to soften a little. He looked surprised.

'I hope we can be friends. I hope we can be good friends. But I never really thought of you that way.'

Jimmy back-pedalled. Over a cliff.

'I just wanted to clear that up. I mean it's important to know where you stand…'

Lawrie touched his arm momentarily.

'You're a friend.'

Jimmy spent the rest of the evening trying to hide how crestfallen he was. He felt he succeeded. Lawrie didn't seem particularly aware of the effect he had on him. Maybe he had treated Jimmy's enquiry as simply idle curiosity. But the wine made them feel warm towards each other.

At the close of the evening Lawrie offered to call a taxi or fold down the sofa bed. Jimmy said he'd get one in the street, the main street nearest Lawrie.

It was next morning that Jimmy felt the first pangs of shame and regret. It was so obviously not going to happen. Why couldn't he see that? But Lawrie was such a kindly guy; it was easy to misinterpret, put a different slant on things. Lawrie had merely extended a hand in friendship to him and the rest of his anatomy was, like his bedroom, out of bounds. The slow burn had fizzled out.

The guys still called each other up after that. But it was never the same after the Monte Carlo-or-bust night when Jimmy got to know where he stood. On his own, as usual.

Jimmy hadn't seen Lawrie for a couple of months when he walked into Delilah's that night. It was good to see him again. What wasn't so good was the interest he took in Alec. But Jimmy felt more amused than jealous. After several drinks the guys decided to get a taxi up the road to the West End, where they all lived. Then Lawrie invited them back to his for a nightcap. Alec seemed to think that this was a great idea and so the three of them landed back in Lawrie's flat.

'Can I put this on? I love Motown.'

Alec had taken over and hired himself as DJ.

'Aye. On ye go.'

Alec shoved on the Motown compilation CD. Even the Motown was wrong tonight. It wasn't *Misstra Know It All* Stevie Wonder. It was *I Just Called To Say I Love You* Stevie Wonder. To go with the matured music, Lawrie opened a bottle of malt whisky. Jimmy had turned down the offer of a whisky and settled for coffee. The Motowners huddled on the sofa with their whiskies. Jimmy eyed them from an armchair. It was that funny feeling you got when you saw two people meeting for the first time. The curiosity, the playfulness, the fucking flirtation. Jimmy was sure nothing would come of it. Alec had recently acquired a new boyfriend. And, anyway, surely he wasn't Lawrie's type?

The music was okay. Bad Motown was still better than most of the other shite that got played. Somehow he felt himself become detached from the rest of the company. It was late; fatigue and inebriation were setting in. There was no novelty or mystery in his relationship with Lawrie: that had been resolved. Then there was something in the way Alec and Lawrie were positioned on the sofa. It looked like something was going to happen; like something had been implicitly agreed. Alec would be staying and Jimmy would be going. Lawrie's generosity with the whisky was unbounded. Jimmy watched the two guys on the couch. He didn't feel jealous or pissed off, just surplus to requirements. He had to go home.

Jimmy stood up and announced he was going to the toilet. He did what he regarded as the longest pish in recorded history. It was a big one. He felt drunk now. He didn't want to conk out in a chair and snore in front of the guys. He knew he was a snorer. Guys had told him so. It was time to go. When he washed his hands and face in the bathroom sink, the mirror echoed his sentiments.

He went back into the living-room. The music had stopped and Lawrie hadn't bothered to put anything else on. Jimmy didn't know where Lawrie had left his jacket.

'I think I'll be headin' home.'

Alec didn't say anything, just took a sip of his whisky. Lawrie sprang up eagerly.

'I'll get your jacket, Jim.'

He brushed by Jimmy and went down the hall. This seemed so

ungentlemanly, his haste. Jimmy looked at Alec, who avoided eye contact. Lawrie came up behind Jimmy and mumbled something. Jimmy said cheerio to Alec, who was rummaging amongst a pile of CDs. He stepped into the hall and Lawrie began shoving a jacket on him, like an over-zealous waiter, which was fine, except the jacket wasn't Jimmy's. It was Alec's. Lawrie adjusted the collar on the jacket and guided Jimmy towards the front door at breakneck speed.

'This isnae my jacket.'

'What?'

'The jacket. It's Alec's.'

'Oh.'

Lawrie gave an embarrassed laugh. He helped Jimmy out of the jacket and went back down the hall. He returned in two shakes of a rent boy's tail with Jimmy's jacket. Jimmy smiled and took the jacket.

'That's the one. See ye, Lawrie.'

Lawrie smiled. 'See you.'

He closed the door behind Jimmy.

It was a summer night and it was humid. There was a fine drizzle. Jimmy started heading in the direction of home. It was a twenty-minute walk. He'd only gone a hundred yards when he saw a taxi. Spontaneously, he hailed it and got in. The sooner he was home the better. Once home, he made himself another coffee. He was going to take it to bed with him but knew he'd flake out and never drink it if he did that. He sat in the kitchen and drank the coffee and flicked through yesterday's paper. He decided not to think about Lawrie and Alec, not now.

In the morning he thought it over. He sat on the edge of his bed in his boxer shorts. He remembered Lawrie trying to get him into Alec's jacket, in his hurry to get rid of him. He wondered if Lawrie and Alec had slept together. Or maybe they had just had a grope on the sofa. Would they see each other again? He cursed Alec. He was a fucking rat. He was never going to speak to him again. Not for a couple of days anyway. He smiled at Lawrie's mistake. There was something clumsy about him. He'd watched him once in Delilah's struggling with the zip on his jacket. Jimmy wanted to take him in his arms and steady him.

The Duet

The support band was okay but Joanie wished they'd fuck off stage and leave the coast clear for Kylie. It was Kylie he'd paid to see and only Kylie would do. He felt sorry for support bands. He knew it must be hard for them, knowing the bored, inattentive audience awaited the main attraction and had other things on their mind – like getting another drink in the bar or another piss in the toilet. Joanie knew what it felt like to be the support act. Most of the guys he'd dated seemed to spend a lot of time looking over his shoulder, waiting for the main event, the younger, prettier one who'd bend over forwards to please them. He politely clapped the support band then looked at his watch. He had arranged to meet Bobbie at the bar at seven but she hadn't shown. She had her own ticket so Joanie had made his way into the auditorium.

The band finally packed it in and Joanie went to the toilet. He hadn't dragged up tonight. He hadn't wanted to upstage Kylie and the last time he'd come to a concert in full fagalia he'd been frisked and the sexy security guard thought he was packing heat when he grabbed his hard-on. Joanie was frightened he'd go off in his hand.

When Joanie got back to his seat there was Bobbie, clutching a programme and shouting for Kylie, like a wean shouting for her mammy.

'What took you so long?' asked Joanie. Bobbie said she'd fallen asleep on the couch and dreamt that Kylie had broken her ankle and she'd been asked to step in at the last minute.

'See what happens when ye watch *Popstars*?' Joanie retorted.

It was then that the curtains rose revealing an enchanting love boat set. Joanie counted eight prancing dancers. The prettiest pixie in pop was lowered down from the gods on a big silver anchor and launched into *Loveboat* from her *Light Years* album. Joanie gasped with delight.

'It's a fuckin' Broadway show,' he swooned. What followed was a hopping, skipping, jumping, and clapping, bumping, grinding extravaganza that amounted to the poofiest party in town. Kylie was in fine fettle and so were the Glasgow audience.

'I thought there'd be more queers here,' mused Bobbie. She was wearing more than her usual minimal make-up and Joanie thought Bobbie looked strong and beautiful, like Garbo or Dietrich.

'Kylie's church is broad,' observed Joanie. 'Her gospel is love.' And how they loved her. They stepped back in time with Kylie, they spun around with Kylie, they turned it into love with Kylie, and they put themselves in Kylie's place.

The heady highlight for Bobbie was Kylie's cover of Olivia Newton John's *Physical*. It was kind of kinky borderline bondage stuff with the nubile nymphet doing some pole dancing with the boy dancers. She had thought Kylie would come on with some tired old crappy backing band and half-tweet, half-mime to her back catalogue. But the show was snazzy and slick and Kylie's voice was strong, clear and true. It went straight to the heart.

It went straight to Joanie's heart. Joanie and Kylie went back a long way. Like that other hardy perennial, Madonna, she seemed to have been there forever, for all those crazy disco nights with boyfriends and girlfriends and fair-weather friends. She had provided the soundtrack to the crazy 18-Certificate movie that was Joanie's life. *Light Years*, she had called the new album. Light years – light as a balloon and sweet as bubble gum, light as in so far away and out of reach. Joanie knew those feelings well. Hearing Kylie now made him recall how he'd skipped through the eighties, dazzled by the big hair and bright lights of that momentous decade. The first time with a man, sniffing poppers and falling in a faint, crying on the late night bus because of the loneliness and the lovelessness, being queer-bashed on a train and no one coming to help him, waking up in strange beds with stranger men. He'd been called everything from a dog to a disease. But he'd survived those years with a mixture of war paint and wit when the only constants in his life were divas and disappointments.

On stage Kylie was standing on top of a wee white piano in top hat and tails doing an old showbiz rendition of *Better The Devil You Know.*

'Fuck,' gasped Joanie in admiration, 'the ghost of Ginger Rogers.' So the night went on, song after sweet song, Kylie taking staircases Busby-Berkeley style, being held aloft by dancers' palms like a Hollywood heroine. Bobbie and Joanie were on their feet clapping and dancing and yelling and loving it. Joanie wanted to throw flowers on the stage. He wanted to throw himself on the stage. Then she was gone, like a vision, a dream, gone.

They were in a booth in Delilah's with beers. They both felt high after their sail on Kylie's loveboat. Bobbie was looking at her programme and sighing like she had a big schoolgirl crush. Bobbie loved girls and girl groups from the Ronettes to Atomic Kitten. She was pissed off with cadaverous rock dinosaurs and catatonic art students with their pompous dirges that passed for hip and happening music. She wanted three minutes of joy from a pop princess. Bobbie hadn't minded being a girl. She loved singing songs with other girls, daft old Glasgow songs as they played hopscotch or skipping ropes. They used to tie rubber bands together across the fences at either side of the close and jump over them, flashing smiles and knickers. It was only when they'd got into their teens and started obsessing about hackett-looking captains of the school football team with their boners and their b.o. that girls started being hard work for Bobbie, when they stopped singing and started simpering about boys.

Joanie was light years away. He thought about all those years ago, dancing in Bennets to Kylie. Some of the men he had danced with were gone now. They'd died or fled or he'd forgotten them, forgotten their names. He'd go on a Tuesday night, billed as an alternative night, and there'd be guys dressed like Boy George or Robert Smith or Divine or Adam Ant. That's when he'd started dressing up. One night he wore Nancy Sinatra boots and a fanny pelmet minidress he'd found in the Briggait amongst the pish and the trash in the lanes, the Glen Daly LPs and blow football sets, Agatha Christie paperbacks and suede gloves. Those markets and stalls and jumble sales were treasure troves for Joanie then; a mint-green crimplene suit that made him feel like Audrey Hepburn; a black velvet backless dress was another he remembered. A sexy big clone had run his tongue up and down Joanie's bare back till he thought he'd cream his pants.

There was a time when Joanie could count the number of men he'd slept with. But then he gave up that game. All he knew was there had been nights when he was drunk and alone and it seemed the only thing that could keep him from Hell was the heat of a man in his arms. Light years later, working in Delilah's, sometimes it was like watching the movie of your life, hearing your diary being read in public, all those lovers and losers playing those old tunes, making those old moves.

He looked at Bobbie, who was looking across the bar. Bobbie did look good. Her hair was slicked back, like Bowie in his *Low* days. She was wearing grey woollen trousers and a black velvet jacket. She looked one dandy dyke. Bobbie faced him and smiled.

'Sorry,' she said. 'I was miles away.' Joanie said he'd get more drink in.

There was a wee skinny barman covering Joanie's Sunday night shift. Joanie thought he was cute, so skinny he could fall down a stank and climb back out again. But Joanie wasn't one of those older guys who chased boys half their age and wanked over Westlife. The noise and narcissism of the teenyboppers held little charm for him. But it was hard being young. He knew how hard it had been being young, the world against you and your back against the wall. Fuck knows it didn't get much better.

Bobbie sipped her pint. She started telling Joanie about an old girlfriend. This girl had a crazy mullet hairstyle and was a total fashion disaster. They were in their early twenties and used to have snogging sessions in Bobbie's bedsit off Byres Road.

'We would sing in my room, my wee fuckin' room with its cold water tap and black fungus on the ceiling. I had a telly and I remember watching *Top Of The Pops* with this girl, Shirley her name was. We loved that one, *Especially For You*. Kylie and Jason. We used tae sing it tae each other.'

It was then that a scary ex of Bobbie's came in. Bobbie hid her face with the Kylie programme.

'You okay?' asked Joanie.

'X file,' replied Bobbie, from behind the programme. The ex was a married woman who claimed she was bisexual. She'd threatened Bobbie once with a knife. Joanie thought they'd better leave. Delilah's was work so he didn't always want to drink there.

'Let's go,' said Joanie. He got up and Bobbie followed, covering her face with the programme and banging into tables on her way out.

They ended up in an old bar that smelled of beer and sweat and pish and pipe smoke. There was a dartboard in one corner and a medallion man DJ who Bobbie said looked like Des O'Connor, stationed in another corner. He had one of those orange tans Bobbie said her big sister Fiona used to get out of a bottle when she was going out on the randan. It was really an old-timers pub, half-empty, and some of the punters were up dancing.

Joanie clocked the clientele. A couple in their fifties were up doing the twist. They looked a handsome pair. An old guy sat at a table trying to get as much creamy froth from his beer onto his moustache as possible. He kept winking at Bobbie.

'He's givin' me the boak,' said Bobbie.

'It's when they stop winkin' ye start worrying,' joked Joanie.

A woman with greasy hair and a cheesy smile came in with a collecting can and started working the tables. She arrived at Joanie and Bobbie's table and looked down at them, grinning.

'Would you like to help disabled children?' she asked, in a stupid little song of a voice. She had a silver-coloured chain round her neck and attached to it was what purported to be an ID badge. Joanie thought she was probably at it but put a pound coin in the can anyway.

Then they heard a big barmaid shouting, 'Right you! Oot!'. The woman scarpered. Bobbie laughed.

'This is some joint,' she observed. 'Is this what's ahead of us?'

They talked some more about the old days, Bobbie telling Joanie stories from her mixed-up teens, dating guys and fancying their sisters, fancying their mothers. Joanie told her about his roaring twenties in high heels and high hair. They were tripping down memory lane when the DJ appeared at their table, taking requests. Bobbie asked for *Especially For You.*

Joanie went to the bar for more drinks and when he came back the DJ was playing their request. He said it was for the lovely couple in the corner and beckoned them onto the floor with an outstretched hand. Bobbie grabbed Joanie's hand and led him onto the manky dance floor. She pulled him close and they danced slow, holding each other's hands. Joanie could see the handsome older couple gazing admiringly at them. Over Joanie's shoulder Bobbie could see the old guy with the frothy moustache, winking like fuck.

Swing Low, Sweet Chariot

There was a big man with a baseball cap and there was the guy in the chair. There were four steps up to the entrance, then a landing, then two more steps. Then they were through the swing doors, backing in, then turning and cutting a swathe through the busy Friday night revellers. Some people saw the wheelchair and thought they were collecting for charity. One guy shook his head disapprovingly – as if the place wasn't overcrowded enough, you didn't need to be run over by a cripple in a wheelchair. But they carried on up to the bar. The service at the bar was pretty slow that night. Joanie had a night off and so wasn't there to crack the whip. The man and his pushchair pal waited patiently. Eventually a blond bombshell of a barman leaned across and said to the man in the baseball cap, 'Being served?' The man nodded down at his pal who was brandishing the fiver.

'What can I get you?'

'A pint of lager and a pint of heavy please.'

The barman poured the pints. There was a surge forward as more people swept into the bar. The big man was pushed against his pal's wheelchair and the chair moved. The man in the chair put his brakes on.

'You okay?'

'I'm fine.'

The guy in the chair smiled good-naturedly. The big man lifted the pints and took the change. He gave his friend the change and then his pint of lager.

'It's so busy,' he sighed. He adjusted his baseball cap and looked around to see if he could see a space for them to go. A woman tried to squeeze past and the strap of her bag caught in one of the wheelchair's handles. She tugged at it violently, not realising where it had stuck.

'Fuck sake,' she gasped, exasperated.

'Sorry', she said, as the guy in the chair unhooked her. She smiled and hurried on.

'God, it's busy.'

The capped man thought he saw a space and they started moving to a far away corner.

'Excuse me.'

'Excuse *me*!'

There were various pushes and shoves and apologies and curses as they made their tortuous journey to the vacant space in the corner. Once they got there they felt a bit more relaxed. There was a small table where they could rest their drinks. There wasn't a chair or stool but the big man was happy to stand. He could see what was going on. He'd look about him then he'd lean over and speak to his pal. Sometimes he'd crouch down and talk to him that way. People paid them some notice. They were okay looking. They had never been in Delilah's before, not that anybody remembered. Somebody thought they might be foreign tourists but the blond barman shook his head. No one could remember seeing a wheelchair in Delilah's before.

When the big man crouched down some people thought he'd gone and left the guy in the wheelchair. Then he'd bob back up again, over the sea of people. There was some speculation as to what the relationship was between these two guys. A woman with a nose ring and an eyebrow piercing suggested that the big man was a social worker.

'Or some kinda *helper*,' she said firmly. Her friend nodded in agreement, and stared at them again. The big man took off his cap and scratched his balding head. A man who stood beside the wheelchair at the bar when the pair got served was suspicious.

'There's somethin' creepy about it,' he complained. 'He's a good lookin' guy. What's he doing pushin' a spastic around?'

The big man was crouched down again, an arm around his pal, speaking to him. The man at the bar craned his neck but couldn't see what was going on. He turned to the blond barman.

'What're they doin' in here anyhow? Don't they have centres for people like that?'

The barman shrugged his shoulders.

'It's a free country.'

The woman with the nose ring spoke to her friend.

'I knew a girl who worked in a home for the disabled. There was this guy who had no prick, it was jist like a tube. Can ye imagine it? She said there was a woman who had no speech or movement or anything. She communicated by blinking her eyes. You had to go through the alphabet and she'd blink and you'd stop at a letter. That's how she communicated. It was a home for the disabled. She had to spoon-feed them and wipe their arses and everythin'. She said it was terrible. She said wan day she turned a corner and there was a hunchback jist standin' there. I feel sick jist talkin' about it.'

The man at the bar stood on his tiptoes to see where the man in the cap had gone. He was both relieved and annoyed to see him crouching once more beside his paralysed pal. He wondered if they were lovers. He wondered if the guy in the wheelchair could get it up. Or whether the big guy just turned him over and banged his numb, oblivious arse. They were both quite attractive, he decided, right up on his tiptoes now.

After a while it got even busier. People were getting ratty, drinks were being spilled and people were being knocked off balance. They had let in too many people. The woman with the nose ring said she was leaving before she fainted.

'As for that wheelchair,' she said, 'it's an obstruction and a fire hazard.'

She left with her friend. Some other people left too, and the place quietened down a bit. There was more elbow room and it became more tolerable.

The man in the wheelchair looked up at his pal.

'You need the toilet?'

The man nodded.

'I'll ask somebody.'

He turned and looked around, deciding whom to ask. His eyes rested on a big woman with a wild mane of blonde hair falling over her face.

'Excuse me, d'you know where the toilets are?'

The woman swept some of the hair off her face with her hand. She looked with resignation at the man in the cap.

'The toilets?'

'Aye.'

'They're upstairs and they're stinking.'

'Upstairs?'

She nodded.

'Fuck.'

'What is it?'

'It's for my boyfriend. He uses a wheelchair. He can't walk.'

The woman cocked her head to one side and looked over at the guy in the chair. She turned back to the man in the baseball cap.

'I'm presuming it's a piss?'

'Aye.'

The man in the cap nodded. The woman looked thoughtful. She brushed back her hair again with a leisurely sweep of her hand.

'Does he have a bottle?'

'Aye but he cannae just pull it out here.'

'I think I know a place. C'mon.'

She put down her drink and walked over to the guy in the chair.

'The loo's upstairs, pal. But I can take ye somewhere private.'

The guy smiled up at her. 'That'd be great.'

'C'mon.'

She took charge of the chair and began pushing it purposefully forward. His boyfriend followed closely behind. They had to travel a fair distance till they came to a stairway through a back doorway. The woman pushed the guy in the chair through the doorway and made a sharp right away from the stairway. There was a small alcove with a barrel in the corner of it. It was out of sight of the stairway and the doorway.

'Here we are,' she announced. 'You'll be okay here. I'll stand guard at the stairs.'

She walked over to the stairway and lit a cigarette.

'I'll show ye where to empty it,' she added, absently. She puffed at her cigarette. The guy in the cap took a bottle container out of a small bag that was slung over the chair. From her position at the bottom of the stairway the woman couldn't see them, but she heard the sound of the piss flowing into the bottle and the guy sighing, relieved.

Mama's Papa

Mama and Joanie were in a booth, talking about Papa. Mama was worried about him. She'd seen him get pissed a few too many times and slope off with this or that drugged up boy. Mama told Joanie she didn't even think Papa was that interested in younger guys – it was just the attention he liked. As for the boys, Papa was a good-looking guy with money to throw around. These crazy love affairs didn't seem to last any longer than the following morning.

'I wish he would settle down with somebody,' sighed Mama. 'Somebody mature.'

Joanie nodded and smiled ruefully. 'I wish we would all settle down sometimes,' he said. 'But what about you Mama? When are you gonnae love again?'

Mama shook her head. 'I don't do encores,' she said.

Joanie knew the story of Mama's great love. She had married a fellow doctor in her early twenties. They couldn't have children. They lived a life filled with romance. It was all violins and roses. Then her husband was killed on one of his rock-climbing trips and Mama had cried a river. Mama had been widowed ten years and looked like she was hell-bent on making a career out of it.

Joanie never really bought into that once-have-I-loved thing. He always believed love was just around the corner. Mama was only fifty-five and it seemed sad for her to be wallowing in widowhood. She looked good, loved her job, and had a variety of friends, gay and straight, although her friendship with Papa was probably the most interesting of them.

Mama said she met Papa in Frasers, Buchanan Street. Papa had been looking for a tie and had asked Mama's advice. Mama had told him she didn't work there. 'I know,' Papa had retorted, 'but you look like a woman of taste.' Mama helped him choose the tie. That was at three on Saturday afternoon; they parted company at two on Sunday morning, Papa dropping Mama off at her flat in a taxi.

In between times they had wined and dined and roared around the gay scene, Papa being a vivacious tour guide. Papa later swore that Mama had tried to pick him up but Mama laughed this off and said she knew a big jessie when she saw one.

Their friendship had grown since then. They dined together at some of the fancier Glasgow restaurants, saw opera and ballet at the Theatre Royal, cruised and boozed in Delilah's. They were a fine pair.

But Mama worried about Papa. She had been there for Papa through bad times as well as good. Once, when he'd been robbed by a pick-up that'd stolen his father's ring, he sobbed down the phone to her and she'd gone to comfort him. He'd also had a bout of crabs and a dose of the clap. Mama didn't approve of his bed hopping. Her views weren't based on morality, but safety. Bringing strangers into your bed, your life, could be a hazardous business. Picking up a stranger could lead to anything from robbery to rape. She had seen a good doctor friend die of AIDS, and didn't want that to happen to Papa.

'This place is great fun,' said Mama, 'but I wish you guys would slow down once in a while and think before you fuck.'

Joanie nodded, and considered what Mama said. More than anyone, he knew things could get a bit OTT in Delilah's. Some nights everybody seemed to be out of their fairy face on something, from alcopops to Ecstasy. He couldn't remember the names of some of the notches on his belt but he'd cleaned up his act a while ago. Joanie didn't like to judge. It was hard to live your life in the closet and some of the queers he saw surface in Delilah's were like drowning men gasping for air. They had been starved for too long: starved of sex, starved of the right to be themselves, they wanted to make up for lost time.

'A lotta the people that come here don't get a chance tae be queer through the week,' reasoned Joanie. 'They have to cram a week's poofiness into one night.'

True, not everybody was cowering in the closet these days but it could still be tough even if you were loud and proud. It was no fun being the only fairy in the factory. Joanie didn't want to argue with

Mama. She was usually a good sport and if she appeared judgemental it was because she was concerned, not because she was a killjoy.

'I think there should be something called queer leave,' said Joanie, decidedly. 'Y'know, like maternity leave, or like academics get sabbaticals. If they won't let us be queer at work they should give us more playtime. Then maybe you'd see us slow down a wee bit.' That didn't even raise a smile with Mama. She was in a maudlin mood and he would just have to let her work her way through it.

'I wouldn't mind if Papa was happy,' sighed Mama. 'But he's not. You see him in here high as a kite and being the belle of the ball but that's not the whole story. When that boy stole his father's ring it broke his heart. He called me at four in the morning. He cried in my arms. He's not happy.'

'What would make him happy?' asked Joanie.

'Love,' said Mama firmly. 'The only thing that can make anyone truly happy.'

'I've seen him in here dangling a twenty-year-old on each knee. He looked blissfully happy,' said Joanie, trying to lighten the mood.

'I'm talking about enduring happiness,' said Mama, softly. Joanie was getting slightly annoyed with Mama now. Here she was a pretty, intelligent, woman, who seemed resigned to spending the rest of her life alone. Yet she seemed to be pining for a husband for Papa. Joanie suspected she was projecting her own anxieties about being single onto the footloose Papa. They were quiet for a while, listening to the soft music, Joanie clocking the clientele in the backroom, Mama watching the snow fall through the long windows.

Maybe Mama's just got the winter blues, thought Joanie. Winters in Glasgow could be pretty harsh. He knew she sometimes took a winter break. Not every year, but every couple of years. She'd been to Australia last Christmas. She had an aunt there.

'You need a holiday,' said Joanie. Mama gave him a sad smile.

'I like the snow,' she said. 'The snow makes me think of my father.' She leaned on the table, arms folded, and Joanie thought she looked like a neat little schoolgirl.

'One of my favourite memories of my father is of him making a snowman in our back garden. I remember him crouching down on the white lawn, building this beautiful big snowman. It was meant to be a surprise but I was watching from my bedroom window. When he was finished he took me into the garden and pretended the snowman had just appeared. It must have been six foot tall. I remember it didn't have a nose – stones for the eyes and mouth but no nose. Daddy sent me in to get a carrot from the kitchen. He stuck it in the middle of the snowman's face and there it was, the snowman had a nose.' Mama smiled and Joanie thought she would cry.

Joanie felt like crying too. He envied people who had sweet stories to tell from their childhood. His own father was a violent man, full of beer and curses. Joanie spent much of his childhood farmed out to cousins for safekeeping.

'Your daddy sounds like a nice guy,' said Joanie. Mama nodded.

'As far as I remember he was. He died when I was eight. My mother remarried ten years later. I was at med school by then. I was glad she'd found someone. I got on okay with him, but he wasn't my daddy.'

Joanie said that at least she had some happy memories. Mama leaned forward slightly, her voice hushed.

'I visited an old aunt of mine in Sydney last year. My mother's sister. We talked about my father. He killed himself when I was eight. He got up early one morning and took poison. He was found in his car. Some of what happened was kept from me while my mother was alive. But my aunt told me the truth.'

Joanie listened to the story of Mama's Papa. Her aunt had told her that her father had been arrested at a public toilet for 'lewd and libidinous behaviour'. Cottaging. On the Sunday the police had charged him, and by the Tuesday he was dead. Mama's aunt told her that her mother had guessed about her father's sexuality. She regretted never having spoken to him about it. She said that she understood. The aunt had asked of her sister, 'Who else would've understood? Your understanding wouldn't have been enough.'

The aunt hadn't been keen to tell Mama anything, but she had pressed the old woman until she had given her the truth.

'That's awful,' sighed Joanie.

'My father was a kind, gentle, man. I think he killed himself because of the disgrace. He was gay and couldn't live with it.'

Joanie held Mama's hands in his.

'That still happens,' he said. They sat for a few moments like that, then Mama broke free. She gathered her things.

'I need some air,' she said.

Joanie and Mama walked arm-in-arm like sisters, through the falling snow. They moved slowly through the shoppers, the blasts of Christmas muzak from the stores, the buskers, bible thumpers and beggars. They found themselves at George Square, admiring the Christmas lights. They watched children playing in the snow and Mama said a prayer for her daddy, her sweet daddy, who had built a beautiful snowman all those years ago, to surprise his daughter.

Joanie and the Three Bears

The three bears came in on a wet Wednesday afternoon to an empty Delilah's. Joanie, who was sitting on a stool behind the bar, was reading a free sheet wank rag. There wasn't much reading in it – just a collection of garish photographs of young muscle Marys and adverts for everything from cock rings to escorts. The bears saw only the dress and Joanie's blonde wig framing the free sheet. One of the bears chapped on the bar and Joanie looked over the paper at them.

They were quite a trio. The youngest was about thirty with cropped blond hair and blue eyes. He had no facial hair but was a sturdy big bear for all that. He wore a denim jacket, a tartan shirt and jeans. The middle bear was dark, forty-ish, a classic clone with a magnificent moustache and goatee beard. He had a nose ring and a small silver bar through his left eyebrow. Joanie noticed his dark eyes, which were sad and haunted, and his thick, strong arms, bare on the bar. He wore a white tee shirt, black leather waistcoat, and jeans. He was heavier than the younger bear, and paunchy. Last but not least was the oldest bear. He had silvery grey hair, cropped, a moustache as white as fresh snow, and wore a black leather biker jacket with a tee shirt and jeans.

The older bear looked at Joanie, smiled, and turned to his friends 'Now that is one pretty girl,' he declared in an American accent. They laughed.

'How can I skelp you?' asked Joanie, slightly rankled by the bears laughter. They ordered three beers and began chatting to Joanie. The silver haired bear introduced himself.

'I'm Paul,' he said, proffering a hand to Joanie, who shook it.

'I'm visiting from New York. These are my good friends, Andy and Clay, the man with the metal in his face. Andy's from Fife and Clay is from –'

'– Manchester,' interrupted Clay, proudly.

'I've never been to Glasgow before so this is a first for me,' continued the older bear. 'People seem real friendly here.'

'People are and I'm Joanie,' said Joanie, charmed by the bear's easy manner. He listened to Paul intently.

'I'm an engineer,' said the bear. 'My work takes me around the world. I've worked in Canada, Germany and Argentina. I really got the travel bug. I met Andy in New York and Clay – I met Clay through the Internet.'

'We're bears,' said Clay, by way of explanation.

'And I'm Goldilocks,' quipped Joanie.

'We like heavy, hairy guys,' said Andy, in a soft, slow voice.

Joanie didn't really like it when guys got too specific. He didn't like to feel excluded. Joanie himself was a poof for all seasons and had slept with guys that weighed eight stones and guys that weighed eighteen. He wasn't a great one for types, never wanting to narrow his options.

'Size isn't everything,' said Joanie.

The older bear shrugged.

'It's just a preference,' he said, apologetically. He told Joanie they were going to find a seat but asked him if he would come and join them. Joanie said he'd do that. But he stayed at the bar for a while, in the vain hope that more custom would arrive. In between replenishing stock and wiping the bar down a hundred times he stole occasional glances at the bears. They were so masculine, but so queer at the same time. He was intrigued by them, by their different nationalities and the way they interacted with each other. Joanie wondered what the proper name was for a group of bears. He thought it might be a pride, but that was what you called a bunch of lions. Then he thought it might be a set, but wasn't that what you called several foxes? It wasn't like he had never seen a bear, but in Glasgow they tended to go to other watering holes like the Waterloo.

After twenty minutes of prevarication Joanie went nimbly over to see what the bears in the backroom would have.

'Would any of you bears like another beverage?' he enquired.

'Sure,' said Paul. 'Get yourself one too and come and join us.'

Joanie returned with the beers, and a Coke for himself, and sat beside the bears.

'I do hope I'm not intruding,' said Joanie. The bears assured him he wasn't. Joanie asked Paul about his travels. Paul said that he'd once come face to face with a real bear, in Canada, and had escaped through the woods and back to his car. He said he was shaking like a leaf and the steering wheel nearly came off in his hands.

'That's just the sorta impression you bears leave on some of us guys,' joked Joanie. He told them about his childhood memory of a bear that gave him sleepless nights. Joanie asked them if they'd heard of a TV show called *The Singing Ringing Tree*. Clay, the Mancunian, was the only taker.

'D'you remember the bear in that?' asked Joanie. 'I was so scared. It was the eyes. I know it was a man dressed up as a bear. But there was something so scary about the fake fur and then those real eyes, it freaked me out.'

Clay was looking at him across the table, concerned. Joanie looked into his sad, sweet eyes and felt a tingle down his spine.

Paul told some stories of his travels. He said he'd had a fling with a psychiatrist in Argentina. 'This guy was rich. He was also the hairiest guy on the planet. It was like making out with a werewolf.'

Clay made a joke about a full moon.

Joanie heard a tap at the bar and went to serve a businessman in a sharp suit. He had a tongue to match.

'I thought I was in the Marie Celeste,' he snapped. 'Is this dive open or not?'

'I beg your hard-on,' retorted Joanie. 'Now name yer poison'.

'I'll have a white coffee,' barked the punter, like he was telling Joanie to open the till or he'd shoot. Joanie quickly made the coffee and charged the catty customer.

'Fuck you very much,' snarled the creep, shoving his change in his pocket. He wandered to a seat. Joanie was tempted to order the guy out but decided to let it slide.

'Bad day at the orifice?' quipped Joanie, as he shimmied past, back through to the booth and the waiting bears.

'You okay?' asked Andy.

'Did ye hear that?' asked Joanie. 'Some people wurnae brought up, they were dragged up.'

Andy offered to throw the guy out but Joanie assured him he could handle any trouble. Paul then regaled them with a story of a bar-room brawl he'd got caught in the middle of. It was in some saloon in Texas and Paul said it was just like in a movie, tables and chairs flying, guys hitting each other with bottles. Andy and Clay completed some of Paul's sentences, like they'd heard the tale twenty times before.

Of the three, Paul seemed to be the raconteur, spinning yarns of mud-wrestling in Mississippi and fellatio in Frisco. The smash of a coffee cup rudely interrupted them. The four of them turned to see the businessman glaring at them.

'That was the worst coffee I have ever fucking tasted!' he barked. He turned and marched out of the door.

'Temper, temper,' said Joanie. The bears sympathised with him, saying how hard bar work must be.

The bears declined another beer; they had lots to do. They said they were travelling up to the North of Scotland, sightseeing, but planned to be back in Glasgow on Saturday. They were renting a flat and invited Joanie up for dinner. Before Joanie could answer yes or no the address was scribbled on a beer mat and thrust into his hand.

'I'm not sure I'll get Saturday off,' he explained.

'You will,' said Paul, emphatically, at the door of Delilah's. 'And get Sunday off too. We're having a picnic.'

The bears had rented a place slap bang in the middle of Merchant City. It was one of those refurbished tenement buildings with a hi-tech entrance – hi-tech to Joanie at any rate. There was a video intercom system so the occupiers could clock who was calling. Joanie pressed buzzer 4 and waited. Ten seconds later a voice came through the small metal speaker.

'Paul here, who's calling?'

Joanie leaned towards the speaker, pressing a button marked 'Speak'.

'It's Sister Joanie of the Blessed Order of Lewd Vagrants. Will you pray with me, sir?'

'I'm on my knees already, sister,' replied Paul and a sudden buzz at the door signalled Joanie's opportunity.

The small neat flat was filled with a delicious spicy aroma. Paul told Joanie he had made a Mexican bean stew. The three bears looked very smart. Clay and Andy still wore jeans but both wore crisp, fresh plain shirts. Paul wore chinos and a bright yellow shirt. They all wore aftershave. Paul showed Joanie round the wee flat. There were two bedrooms, each with a double bed, which made Joanie wonder who was sleeping with who. The bathroom was really a shower-room and there was a separate WC across the hall. The lounge was a small square, seeming smaller because of the size of the men in it. The guys had rented the place for a week, although they'd been up North for a few days.

They ate the delicious stew with fresh crusty bread and worked their way through a crate of bottled beer. The bears told of their adventures in the Highlands. Their conversation roamed from the beauty of the mountains and glens to the perils of midges. The bears liked fishing and camping.

'You bears are real outdoorsy types,' observed Joanie. The guys agreed. Paul told Joanie about bear picnics he went to in the States. Bears would strip off by the old campfire and give each other backrubs and blow jobs. There were teddy bears, grizzly bears, and he himself was a polar bear on account of his white hair.

The empty beer bottles multiplied around them. They were getting drunker and rowdier. Paul told his story about his encounter with the bear in the Canadian wilds again, only this time he didn't run – he fought the darned creature bear to bear, wrestling through the woods, bouncing off trees until they careered into a river where a passing tugboat plucked Paul to safety. He promised Joanie he'd show him his scars later. The bears told of their trips to leather bars; to dark rooms, where they witnessed everything from fisting to whipping with a cat o' nine tails; camping trips where they'd seen the most beautiful countryside and had felt like the last three men on Earth; and a boat trip with a seafaring S&M bear which involved rum, sodomy, the lash and, finally, a mutiny. Joanie got as drunk as a skunk and fell in love with all of them.

By midnight Clay and Andy were grunting in a bedroom and Joanie was sitting in Paul's lap in the lounge. He closed his eyes and felt the brush of Paul's snowy moustache, tasting beer, bean stew and bear.

'Who's been sleeping in my bed?' said the rumbling voice. Joanie opened his eyes and saw Paul buck naked on the edge of the bed. He was in good shape for a big guy and his face was sweeter than candy. He climbed back into bed and drew Joanie close to him. He looked at Joanie's face and smiled. 'You look just as good as a man,' he said. Joanie's dress and wig lay on the bedroom floor.

'The lady vanishes,' said Joanie.

The bears were very organised. They wanted to pack as much as they could into their vacation. They had scheduled a trip to Loch Lomond and had already bought in provisions for a picnic. Andy drove their hired car first to Joanie's place, where he nipped up and got changed, then onto Loch Lomondside. They threw a blanket on the ground and spread out the provisions: bread, olives, cheeses, grapes, cold meats, mustard, mineral water, wine, beer, flasks of coffee, fruit, nuts and cake.

It was a dry, spring day, but cloudy. The guys decided to ignore the clouds in the hope they'd go away. Eventually they did. The provisions slowly began to vanish from the blanket, the four of them sitting side-on like attentive weans. The bears wore their denim and leather and Joanie wore his Goldilocks wig with a light summer dress, a cardigan draped across his shoulders when he felt cool. They could hear a speedboat zipping back and forth across the loch, and see it too, a small white tooth biting clean through the blue water.

Andy was confined to coffee and water as he was driving, but the other bears had a few beers and Joanie drank red wine out of a paper cup. It wasn't too long before the four of them were belting out a rousing rendition of *Blanket On The Ground*. A large wasp took a fancy to Joanie but the feeling wasn't mutual. He ended up whipping at it with his cardigan sleeve and yelling 'Get tae fuck!

Later, Joanie stood in the cool water up to his knees, his dress hitched up to his thighs. The sky had cleared and more boats had appeared on the loch. From their secluded spot they could see two sailboats, another speedboat, a skier leaning backwards and zooming across the water. Joanie liked the feel of the water on his feet. He turned inland to check the bears. They were rolling around on the blanket, tickling and nibbling and petting each other. They were like pups, thought Joanie. Cubs.

Periodically Joanie would receive a postcard from the bears. One came from Alaska, of Paul in a tour truck with a polar bear standing almost nose to nose with him. Another was a picture of a Norwegian fjord with a note on the back hinting at some serious campfire action. Another card was a picture of Marilyn Monroe, her dress blowing about her thighs. The bears wrote it reminded them of Joanie in the water at Loch Lomond.

'What d'ye call a bunch of bears?' Joanie asked Papa one night in Delilah's.

'A bunch of bears,' said Papa.

'A bunch of bears,' said Joanie.

'It's about time somebody fell in love around here,' said Mama. She was having a coffee with Joanie, discussing Bobbie's forthcoming wedding. It had all happened so fast. Bobbie had been at a party in Shawlands with an old friend and had met a woman called Rae. She was an architect and had gone to private school. She was skinny with a bob of black hair and a funny voice. She reminded Joanie of Olive Oyl but he didn't tell Bobbie that in case he hurt her feelings. It seemed such an unlikely combination. She just didn't seem Bobbie's type. She was too thin and too middle class and too plain for Bobbie. That's what he told Mama.

'There's nothing more surprising in this world than love,' explained Mama, like she was the expert. 'It can creep up on a person before they know it. I've seen this girl and I think she's pretty. They're happy together. Maybe you're just scared of losing her.' Joanie did have mixed feelings. He would never stand in the way of a friend's happiness. But he would miss Bobbie. Something happened when people got hitched. They weren't the same friends anymore. A single person could give you their undivided attention but once they were in a couple they could be downright anti-social. It was like they had been placed under house arrest. Joanie had lost a few pals that way. One old pal had gone from poppers and high heels to pipe and slippers in a matter of months. Another pal had made brave attempts to be sociable but Joanie had hated his partner. He expected Bobbie would go the way of all flesh.

Mama seemed to be full of good advice on the subject. Joanie had wanted to trash Rae but Mama was having none of it. She seemed to be getting her rocks off on this love match and made Joanie feel like a party pooper.

'It'll be wonderful,' she crowed. 'A June wedding in Delilah's.'

Joanie was wishing he hadn't agreed to the event being held in the pub. It meant there was no escaping it. As far as he was concerned Bobbie had simply let desperation get the better of her and had chosen a woman who should really be marrying Popeye. There was no way around it though, Bobbie had set her heart on marrying in Delilah's on a Sunday in June. Not only had she insisted on the venue being Delilah's, she had asked Joanie to be best man, Mama to be maid of honour and Papa to be a page. She had invited her friends and family. Her sister and brother would be attending but her parents had declined.

'We don't mind you being gay,' they had lied to her, 'but why d'ye have tae tell the whole world?'

By day Bobbie was positively bubbly. She was radiant and seemed determined to be happy. By night she seemed to transform herself into a nervous wreck. Joanie fielded a stream of paranoid phone calls from her. Once she had called him at two in the morning and hissed in a crazed whisper that she thought Rae was having an affair.

'There's someone else,' she gasped.

Popeye or Bluto, thought Joanie. Aloud, he reassured her. 'She's having an affair? Of course she is. With you. Now stop bein' yer own worst enemy and get some sleep. Fuck knows I could use some.'

Another night she had called Joanie to say that Rae had left her and had taken all her credit cards. Later she called back to say that Rae had been stuck in a traffic jam and she'd found her credit cards in her purse at the bottom of her bag.

She made a marathon call to Mama in the wee small hours of the morning. 'I'm straight,' Bobbie told her. 'I can't marry a woman. I want a husband. I want children. I'm calling the whole thing off.'

'It's nerves,' Mama had said, soothingly. 'You're going to be a June bride. It's so wonderful.'

'It's you I love,' replied Bobbie. 'Be mine!'

The crazy thing about these calls was that Bobbie never mentioned them when they met at Delilah's. It was as if she was making them in her sleep. Joanie told Mama he was worried about Bobbie's sanity.

'She's like Jekyll and Hyde,' he sighed. 'She's not of sound mind.

You cannae enter intae a marriage if yer not of sound mind.'

'She's in love,' said Mama. 'Love drives you crazy. You only have to look at her to see that. She's blooming.'

Bobbie was blooming. She looked smarter, sexier. She had lost a stone as well as her mind. You had to admit it.

The girl was in love.

Papa joined them at their wee table outside the café. He ordered more coffee for them. 'What does a page do anyway?' he asked.

Joanie said they hold the bride's dress and walk up and down looking cute.

'I can do that,' said Papa. 'But there are two brides.'

'You've got two hands,' replied Joanie. 'Anyway I think these are just honorary roles. Stick to looking cute.'

Bobbie hadn't made any night-time calls to Papa as he was in the habit of disconnecting his phone before he went to bed. 'She's looking good,' said Papa about the bride-to-be.

'What about bride number two?' asked Joanie, wanting Papa to dish some dirt.

'She's solid, dependable. She's bright. Bobbie needs that,' said Papa.

Joanie thought that was maybe what he had against her. He'd expected somebody wild and beautiful and here was someone as plain as the nose on your face. He was losing Bobbie to drab domesticity. He wanted the old Bobbie back, the boozy Bobbie with her tales of finger fucking and fatal attractions. He wanted her on her ownsome at the bar, bitter and blue and bawdy.

'This wedding –,' began Joanie. 'It jist seems so sudden. It's been drawn up like an architect's plan – and with as much passion.'

'Some people are passionate about architecture,' responded Mama. 'Anyway, I hope those girls will be able to build something beautiful together.' It was no good, thought Joanie. He would have to bless this mismatch of a marriage.

It was the day before the wedding and Joanie was at Bobbie's flat in Dennistoun. They were eating a Chinese takeaway at the kitchen table.

'I'm surprised I can eat, I'm that excited,' said Bobbie, sweet and sour sauce on her chin. Joanie wiped at her chin with a tissue, like he was her mammy.

'Bobbie?' he said softly. 'Are ye sure ye want tae do this? Get married?'

'That's whit people do when they fall in love,' she said.

'Straight people,' said Joanie. 'We're queer. We're not allowed tae get married.'

'Don't get sensible with me,' replied Bobbie. 'Rae and I are in love. We want a weddin'. We want our families and friends tae share our joy.'

Joanie shoved a bit of chicken in his mouth to stop himself saying something else. He listened to Bobbie's background music, sweet Carol Laula, the galloping glory that was Horse.

Later, they finished a bottle of white wine in front of the TV. Joanie swore to himself that if Bobbie mentioned Rae again he'd hit her with the empty bottle. All day long it had been Rae this, Rae that.

'Aren't the invitations lovely?' asked Bobbie out of the blue. 'Rae designed them.'

'Wonder Woman eat yer fuckin' heart oot!' snapped Joanie. They looked at each other, alarmed. They both knew the cat was out of the bag. Joanie felt like the murderer unmasked at the end of some crappy old thriller.

'Joanie,' said Bobbie tenderly, 'you're jealous.'

Joanie burst into tears and Bobbie joined him.

The brides stood side by side in their Sunday best. Bobbie wore a cream tailored trouser suit with a jazzy patterned shirt. She looked serene. Rae, her bride, wore a long ivory dress that made her look like a straw, she was so skinny. Gathered around them in the backroom in Delilah's were friends, family, straight and queer, to witness and celebrate their love. Conducting the service was a tiny dyke with the loudest voice in the world. She addressed the congregation with the authority of a Caesar. She told them they were in the presence of two people, two women, Bobbie and Rae, who had pledged to love and honour one another, have and hold, keep each other warm, keep each other from harm.

Joanie looked around at the gathering. Papa was there, immaculate in a charcoal grey suit. Mama was wearing a preposterous hat and seemed to have glued a camera to her right eye. Bobbie's brother and sister were there. Her brother, Lewis, was nearly as handsome as Bobbie. The sister, Fiona, had the biggest hair Joanie had seen since the halcyon days of *Dynasty*. She looked genuinely moved by her sister's wedded bliss. Joanie recognised some of Bobbie's friends, old and new, bunched together. Near the couple, on Rae's side, were a group of ferociously plain people who were apparently her family. Or possibly FBI, mused Joanie. The tiny dyke's voice reached a crescendo and then stopped. Bobbie and Rae turned to each other and tenderly kissed. The place erupted with cheers and applause.

It took a while for Joanie to get near enough Bobbie to congratulate her. Pushing his way through a scrum of dykes the only marker he had to guide him was the huge hair of Fiona. 'Quick! Follow that perm!' he exclaimed. Eventually the friends came face to face. Joanie hugged Bobbie and they rocked in each other's arms. Rae appeared by their side and Joanie saw there was something arresting, something luminous about her. She looked like a lady in an old painting. She had grace, poise. He hugged her too.

After champagne and congratulations the next stop was Kelvingrove Park, where Rae and Bobbie insisted they had their photographs taken. A coach took the key wedding players and selected family and friends there too. It was a bright clear day and the girls posed patiently. They hadn't hired a professional photographer but a friend of Rae's, who had studied architecture with her, was apparently a talented snapper. Mama went through four spools. She got the brides, the brides with their families, the brides with Papa and Joanie, the brides with friends, the brides eating ice cream cones, the brides winching.

As they headed back to the coach Joanie recognised a leather queen with a Chihuahua in his arms coming towards them. He marched past, calling out to Joanie.

'Hi Joanie darling! Fancy meeting you here *during the day.*'

Joanie laughed and ushered the brides onto the bus. He hadn't seen the logic of going to Kelvingrove Park just for photos but apparently it had been Rae's mother's idea. Rae's parents had got their wedding photos taken in the park, her mother saying it was a family tradition. Bobbie saw that as a warm welcome to the family so wanted to honour her wishes.

They arrived back at Delilah's around mid-afternoon. There was a light buffet and champagne ready and waiting for them. Joanie found himself involved in a variety of conversations that left him with an empty glass and a nagging bladder. Several guests, Delilah's regulars, commented on his appearance. Joanie was out of drag (saying he didn't want to upstage the ladies) and wore a light blue suit, white shirt and navy tie. A big homely gal pal of Bobbie's said she hadn't realised how handsome he was. A bitchy queen said 'You must be Joanie's father.' Rae's mother struck up a cryptic conversation with him.

'I hear you dress up as a lady,' was her opening gambit.

'That's true,' said Joanie.

'Have you been realigned?' she continued, bravely.

'Realigned?' asked Joanie.

'Surgically,' she said.

'Naw, pet,' replied Joanie. 'It's aw done with mirrors.'

'Well I think you're all marvellous,' said Rae's mother and then she glided off like a beanpole ballerina into the swarm of guests. Then it was Mama's turn to talk to the best man. She materialised in front of Joanie with two glasses of champagne. Joanie put his empty glass on a table and accepted a glass from Mama, who looked as if she didn't know whether to laugh or cry.

'It's great to celebrate something,' she said. 'To celebrate love. I'm fed up with doom and gloom. There's too many lonely people. You must see it all the time in here.' Joanie nodded. 'People should celebrate,' continued Mama. 'People should jump for joy when they find love. Because it's like finding gold, Joanie. It's like striking oil.' She held out her champagne glass for a toast. 'Here's to love, darling.'

'To love,' said Joanie. They clinked glasses and drank.

'It's what we're here for,' said Mama, with great conviction. Papa appeared beside them. He put an arm around Joanie.

'You two girls havin' a good time?' he asked. They nodded. 'I was speakin' to the bride's family,' said Papa.

'Which one?' asked Mama.

'Rae's. They're sweet. I think they're also quite well-to-do. She's a lecturer and he's a judge.'

'A judge?' exclaimed Joanie. 'And here we are, perverting the course of justice. Well, if he wants to wear his wig, he's come tae the right place.'

They were interrupted by cries of 'best man' and Joanie had to mount the small stage usually reserved for karaoke divas and DJs. Someone handed Joanie a clutch of messages and cards wishing the brides well. Before he read out the messages he made a short speech. Some guests were expecting gags about dildos and muff-diving but Joanie didn't want to do anything too blue. Bobbie had asked for something simple and sincere. Besides if her father-in-something was a judge he didn't want to end up in the jail for breach of the peace.

'Some people think gays and lesbians don't fall in love,' said Joanie. 'Because we're forced tae hide our love. When was the last time you saw two guys walkin' arm-in-arm down Sauchiehall Street? When was the last time you saw two women winching in Argyle Street? Glasgow is full of invisible lovers who can't show their feelings or their love. *They* won't let us. *They* say it's unnatural.'

'Fuckin' breeders!' snarled the tiny dyke with the mighty voice.

'They say we can't get married,' continued Joanie. 'I mean straight people have these big fancy weddings full of pomp and ceremony, mincing about like they just fell off a cake – he's looking like a tailor's dummy and she's like candyfloss, and *they* call *us* camp! Who recognises our joys? Who blesses our unions? We're here today to celebrate the love of two lovely women for each other. Bobbie, my Bobbie dazzler, a very good pal of mine, and Rae, the woman who's come intae her life and swept her off her feet.

Rae, we don't know each other very well but all I want tae say is – any woman who can make Bobbie as happy as you've made her is a fuckin' star in my eyes!'

There was loud cheering and applause and when both had subsided, Joanie began to read out the greetings. There were messages from friends of Rae's from as far afield as Iceland and Rio de Janeiro. Messages for Bobbie tended to be more local in origin, from Possilpark, Pollok, and Partick. A message from Bobbie's parents read simply 'Love Always' and moved her to tears. There were rude and lewd messages and heartfelt and sincere ones. When he had finished reading them Joanie led three cheers for the brides.

Next on the agenda was a coach trip for those going to the evening reception. A marquee had been set up in the grounds of Rae's parents' home and high on the guest list were Joanie, Papa, Mama and a posse of Bobbie's girls. Her huge-haired sister and bonny brother were also going. The rest were Rae's set. Before they could make good their escape there was an impromptu karaoke session which included *Woman* sung by a Japanese transsexual friend of Rae's, who went by the name of Kimonova Here. Then a lady in Lycra who looked like an aerobics coach sang *The Greatest Love of All* in the worst voice of all. Bobbie's brother closed the set with a stunning rendition of *Luck Be A Lady Tonight*.

Classy Caterers had been contracted to provide dinner, which they served in the marquee. Joanie enjoyed the meal and the patter of the guests. After dinner they were entertained for about an hour by an Asian string quartet called The Singh Quartet who played everything from Mozart to Cole Porter.

'I fancy the guy playing the big violin,' whispered Joanie.

'I think that's called a cello,' replied Papa. On closer inspection the cellist turned out to be a chick. Initially guests had sat or stood around listening to the music. Then Rae had persuaded Bobbie to have first dance to *Every Time We Say Goodbye*. The quartet then played *What A Wonderful World* and Papa spun Joanie across the lawn, leading all the way. 'What d'ye call this?' asked Joanie. 'The Shirtlifter's Waltz?'

The guests grew drunker, the quartet was dispatched, and DJ Diva appeared behind her decks, blasting out a selection of disco stompers. People danced in big circles holding hands, formed an impromptu conga chain and finally fell into free fall. Joanie danced himself dizzy, wanked a waiter in the nearby bushes, and finally found himself dancing in Bobbie's arms.

'It's finally happened,' said Bobbie. 'Love. That four letter word that's so much harder to say than shit or fuck or cunt. I love her, Joanie. I love her.'

They held each other close and still as the dancers dallied around them.

A fleet of taxis had been ordered by the father of the bride to take drunken guests home. After they had hugged Bobbie near to death, Papa, Mama and Joanie piled into a cab. Papa fumbled in his wallet and said he wasn't sure he had the money to pay for it. Joanie said he'd work the fare off in the back seat. Mama offered the driver her watch.

'It's paid for,' said the driver cheerily and rattled down the driveway. The journey took twenty-five minutes and the cab had to stop twice so Mama and Joanie could pick Papa up off the floor. Mama ended up with an arm across his chest to keep him in place.

They dropped Mama off first, her leave-taking lasting all of ten minutes and featuring a rendition of *Evergreen*, the Streisand standard, and a myriad of kisses for Papa, Joanie, the taxi driver and a passing policeman. Then the cab moved on to Papa's flat. Papa insisted Joanie come up for a coffee although Joanie suspected he just needed somebody to stick the key in the door.

Joanie made the coffee while Papa lurched around the flat, switching on and off lamps, putting on a CD, and dry retching in the bathroom sink. Eventually they sat down together on the sofa and sipped at their coffee.

'To Bobbie dazzler,' said Joanie.

'To Bobbie dazzler,' said Papa.

Beside Papa's phone were various flyers and menus for fancy restaurants, theatre programmes and personal cards. Joanie was looking for a taxi number. He could hear Papa gargling in the bathroom. Joanie picked up the lemon coloured wedding invitation, which had cordially asked Papa to attend at the wedding of Roberta 'Bobbie' Ross and Rae Duncan. Papa came in, his trousers at his ankles and toothpaste on his lips.

'Where's Mama?' he asked.

'Mama gone home, baby,' said Joanie, softly.

Papa shuffled across the living-room like a wean who had just learned to walk. He stumbled and Joanie stepped forward and caught him in his arms.

He stayed there.

And So They Came to Delilah's

And so they came to Delilah's, bursting out of closets, defying bombs and bigots, leaving day jobs looking for blow jobs, smelling of mothballs and desperation, clutching at condoms and straws in the plague years.

Star-crossed lovers like Ruth and Laura, who were an ill-match; Morag and Carol, who let pussies come between them; Pat and Rick, two halves of the same faggoty self; Greg and Jim, who had a hairy night together; Joanie and Lance, who didn't stand a chance; Harry and Gary, who went up in a poof of smoke; Bernie and Dan, the married man; Caroline and Denise, who were Ellen's degenerates; Rodney and Matt, who were haunted by the people's princess; Maureen and Karen, and two men and a baby; Tam and his transatlantic tricks who swam across an ocean of loneliness; Bobbie and her womyn, who was a bitter lemon; solitary cruisers, brave losers burning with lust and longing, strangers in the night.

They came in peace, they came in a fog of booze and smoke, and they came in each other's arms. Looking for love but unable to love themselves, hiding from their families and exposing themselves to strangers, crying like rivers and screaming like banshees. Drinking to kill the fear and free the fairy in themselves, trying to find Ecstasy in a pill and heaven in a lorry driver's arms, reaching endlessly through the night, the night of a thousand eyes and a million kisses and relentless one night stands they hoped would last forever. Old queens struck by lightning, young queens who wept for Diana and bogarted joints, humming show tunes, riding on a carousel of cock and karaoke, lipstick lesbians and homos in high heels, mourning lost lovers and feckless friends. To Delilah's they came, like the damned to Hell, the saved to Heaven, in terror and triumph, looking for true love and going by false names, only a fuck away from freedom, and in the thick of it all was Joanie. In the throbbing prick of it all was Joanie, like a glorious Madonna watching over her children, their griefs and their gropings, rattling their loose chains at the bar, bitching each other to sweet death, falling in mad love, flying past his funny face like some crazy jailbreak. They were queer on a Saturday night and straight on a Monday morning and they came to Delilah's to dance like dervishes and sing like schoolgirls.

They were Glasgow's invisible lovers, suddenly warm and alive in each other's arms.

Also available from 11:9

A Boy in Summer 1-903238-50-1
R J Price
'Price's imagery is electric.'   *Scotland on Sunday*

Blue Poppies 1-903238-55-2
Jonathan Falla
'You'll be lucky to read a better novel this year.'   *Scotsman*

The Dark Ship 1-903238-57-9
Anne MacLeod
'A fine, mature and moving book.'   *Herald*

Dead Letter House 1-903238-29-3
Drew Campbell
The sour uncertainties of *Pulp Fiction's* spectacular bloodiness, the dreamlike mysteriousness of Kubrick's *Eyes Wide Shut*, the typographical experimentalism of a 40-years-younger Alasdair Gray crash around alongside moral self-questioning and tough optimism ... the pace, energy and drive of the nameless wanderer's nightmare is undeniable.   *Scotsman*

The Gravy Star 1-903238-26-9
Hamish MacDonald
'A moving and often funny portrait ... of the profound relationship between Glasgow and the wild land to its north.'
                              James Robertson, author of *The Fanatic*

Glasgow Kiss 1-903238-26-9
Anthology of new writing from Glasgow
'A remarkably varied and confident batch of tales.'   Edwin Morgan

Hi Bonnybrig 1-903238-16-1
Shug Hanlan
'Imagine Kurt Vonnegut after one too many vodka and Irn Brus and you're halfway there.'   *Sunday Herald*

Life Drawing 1-903238-13-7
Linda Cracknell
'*Life Drawing* brilliantly illuminates the contradictions of its narrator's self image ... Linda Cracknell brings female experience hauntingly to life.'
Scotsman

Occasional Demons 1-903238-12-9
Raymond Soltysek
' ... a bruising collection ... Potent, seductive, darkly amusing tales that leave you exhausted by their very intensity.'
Sunday Herald

Rousseau Moon 1-903238-15-3
David Cameron
'The most interesting and promising debut for many years. [The prose has] a quality of verbal alchemy by which it transmutes the base matter of common experience into something like gold.'
Scotsman

Strange Faith 1-903238-28-5
Graeme Williamson
'Williamson's lucid narrative is philosophically adept and intriguing – a profound insight into changing states of identity and a search for personal freedom.'
Edinburgh Review

The Tin Man 1-903238-11-0
Martin Shannon
'Funny and heartfelt, Shannon's is an uncommonly authentic voice that suggests an engaging new talent.'
Guardian

The Wolfclaw Chronicles 1-903238-10-2
Tom Bryan
'Tom Bryan's pedigree as a poet and all round littérateur shines through in *The Wolfclaw Chronicles* – while reading this his first novel you constantly sense a steady hand on the tiller ... a playful and empassioned novel.'
Scotsman

If you enjoyed this book, here is a selection of other titles from 11:9:

A Boy in Summer	R J Price	£9.99/$15.00
Blue Poppies	Jonathan Falla	£6.99 *
The Dark Ship	Anne MacLeod	£6.99/$15.00
Dead Letter House	Drew Campbell	£7.99/$13.95
Glasgow Kiss (anthology)	new writers	£6.99/$13.95
The Gravy Star	Hamish MacDonald	£9.99/$15.00
Hi Bonnybrig	Shug Hanlan	£9.99/$15.00
Life Drawing	Linda Cracknell	£9.99/$15.00
Occasional Demons	Raymond Soltysek	£9.99/$15.00
Rousseau Moon	David Cameron	£9.99/$15.00
Strange Faith	Graeme Williamson	£9.99/$15.00
The Tin Man	Martin Shannon	£9.99/$15.00
The Wolfclaw Chronicles	Tom Bryan	£9.99/$15.00

11:9 books are available from bookshops or direct from www.nwp.sol.co.uk and www.11-9.co.uk. Alternatively, books can be ordered from the publisher POST FREE (UK ONLY). Just tick the titles you want and fill in the form below. Prices and availability subject to change without notice.

Overseas postal rates:

Postage and packing for overseas orders will be charged at 20% of total cost.

Please enclose a cheque/PO (£ or US$) made payable to Neil Wilson Publishing Ltd. T/A 11:9. Alternatively, payment can be made by credit card (Visa and Mastercard only, in £ Sterling).

Send your order to: Neil Wilson Publishing, 303a, The Pentagon Centre, 36 Washington Street, Glasgow, G3 8AZ. Orders can be sent post free anywhere in the UK as FREEPOST NWP.

E-mail address: info@nwp.sol.co.uk

Name:..

Address ....
....
....

If you would prefer to pay by credit card, please complete:
Please debit my Visa/Mastercard (delete as applicable).
card number:..
Start date: .... Expiry date:...................................
Signature:..

* Not available in USA.